A JARED McKEAN MYSTERY

A TASTE OF
BLOOD AND ASHES

A JARED McKEAN MYSTERY

A TASTE OF
BLOOD AND ASHES

JADEN TERRELL

THE PERMANENT PRESS
Sag Harbor, NY 11963

For information, address:
  The Permanent Press
  4170 Noyac Road
  Sag Harbor, NY 11963
  www.thepermanentpress.com

Library of Congress Cataloging-in-Publication Data

Terrell, Jaden, author.
  A taste of blood and ashes : a Jared McKean mystery / Jaden Terrell.
  Sag Harbor, NY : Permanent Press, [2016]
  Series: Jared McKean mystery
  ISBN 978-1-57962-435-4
     1. Horses—Fiction. 2. Private investigators—Tennessee—
  Nashville—Fiction. 3. Arson investigation—Fiction. 4. Secrets—
  Fiction. 5. Mystery fiction. 6. Suspense fiction.

PS3620.E753 T37 2016
813'.6—dc23   2016022817

Printed in the United States of America

This book is dedicated to
my mother,
Ruthanne Terrell,
who taught me to reach for the stars
and that the most important thing in life is love

A Fire in the Darkness

Monday, 2:16 A.M.

The woman woke to the screams of horses. A surge of adrenaline pulsed through her, and before she was even fully awake, Carlin had swung her legs over the edge of the bed, run her fingers through her blonde spikes, and jammed her bare feet into a pair of scuffed leather boots. The first hint of smoke in her nostrils cut through the fog in her mind.

Oh dear God. The horses.

Tesora.

She snatched her cell phone from the bedside table and two long-tailed cotton shirts from the closet. One, she flung around her neck. The other, she shrugged into, buttoning it as she clattered down the hardwood stairs.

From his first-floor bedroom, her husband's strangled croak froze her for a breath. "Ah-weh! Ah-weh!"

Carlin. Carlin.

She felt a flash of anger, not at him—well, yes, at him too, unreasonable though that was—but mostly at whatever fate had left him broken and frightened, unable even to say her name. Two strides past his door, guilt tugged her back, and she paused long enough to call, "I don't know what's happening yet, Zane. I'll tell you when I know something!"

She hurried through the living room, heart pounding, her mouth filling with the ozone tang of fear. One toe caught on the edge of the Navajo rug they'd gotten on a rare vacation west. She stumbled, recovered, and burst out into the muggy August heat, Zane's anxious caw still echoing in her ears.

The air smelled of smoke. Off to her right, flames leaped into a sooty yellow sky. It was horrible and beautiful, and dread settled deep into her stomach before her mind was able to accept what she was seeing.

The barn was ablaze.

She broke into a full-out run, punching in 911 and rattling off her name and address to the cool voice on the other end of the line.

The crackle of flame became a roar.

The barn looked black against the flames. Fifty yards away in the paddock three mares and two geldings snorted and circled, eyes rolled back to the whites.

Another scream, and she ran toward the burning barn, eyes watering, a blistering heat on her cheeks.

No, no, no, no.

A shower of embers swirled in the entrance. She pulled her shirt up to cover her nose and mouth and started in, then froze, poised on the balls of her feet, as a figure emerged from the maelstrom.

Gerardo. Groom and handyman, but so much more, he'd been her strength since Zane's accident. The sight of him calmed her. His chest was bare, his shirt covering the eyes of a pearl-colored mare, sleeves twisted beneath her chin to create a makeshift halter.

Tesora.

Relief washed through her as the mare, the crown of their breeding program and the love of Carlin's life, danced on the lead.

Gerardo coughed and shoved the mare toward Carlin. "Take her."

She snatched the extra shirt from around her neck and flung it toward him. He caught it one-handed and bolted back into the flames.

She secured Tesora in the paddock with the other rescued horses, then slipped off the makeshift halter and hurried back to trade it for the next horse. Six became seven. Then eight. Nine, ten. Her shirt was drenched, her body slick with sweat.

Where were the sirens?

In the paddock, the horses bumped against each other, blowing and squealing. Gerardo brought a gray mare out of the flames, and then a palomino.

Burns dotted his face and chest. An ember landed on his shoulder, and he slapped it away with a blistered hand. It left a pale pink patch of skin behind.

With an exhausted sigh, he turned back toward the barn, was driven back by heat and flames. A loud crack, and a beam collapsed. The entrance was a wall of flame. He rolled his shoulders, steeling himself, then lowered his head and started inside.

A small cry escaped her as she hooked her fingers into his belt loops and dragged him back. "No more. Enough. You can't."

She snaked one arm around his waist and then the other, felt him strain against her, his muscles knotted into iron.

Then, "*Madre de Dios*," he whispered. The strength seeped out of him, and he sagged against her. Tears and sweat drew pale tracks down his sooted cheeks.

She wanted to comfort him, but her throat was raw. She choked back her own tears, the pointless "why me." Her tongue throbbed where she must have bitten it, and her mouth tasted of blood and ashes.

Gently he turned her toward him and cupped his hands over her ears.

A heartbeat. Then she understood. She slipped her arms through his and pressed her palms flat against his ears. They stood like that until the fire trucks came, hands over each other's ears, while ashes fell like snow around them.

1.

Wednesday, early afternoon

The barn was a blackened skeleton. It had taken the fire department almost forty minutes to arrive, and by then, the building was little more than a smoldering heap of charcoal Pick-up Sticks. The couple who owned it, Carlin and Zane Underwood, were none too happy about that, and less happy that their insurance company refused to pay until the claims adjusters were convinced said couple hadn't torched the barn themselves.

The Underwoods baked in the heat and watched my progress with hostile eyes, she a slim blonde with spiked hair and her arms crossed tightly across her chest, her husband frowning from a heavy electric wheelchair with a high-tech DynaVox communication device attached. Earlier that morning, I'd seen a two-year-old YouTube video of Zane working a colt in a round pen, wowing the crowd with his Hollywood looks and easy grace. Now, with his atrophied muscles, he looked shrunken, dwarfed by the chair. A thin red line creased his jaw where someone had nicked him shaving.

Their groom of eight years, Gerardo Gonzales, stood behind the wheelchair, hands swathed in gauze bandages, a haunted expression on his face. He'd saved twelve horses, lost two. The two weighed heavier than the twelve.

Behind them in the paddock, the horses they'd saved munched hay from a pair of round bales, one at either end of the oval, and beyond that were an outdoor arena and three open pastures bordered by white vinyl fencing. A line of oak and maple trees marked the edge of the property, leaves whispering in the occasional welcome breeze.

Neither our agreement to conduct business on a first-name basis nor the stultifying heat had thawed the Underwoods.

Ignoring their hostility, I stepped over a twisted metal post that had once been a water pump, then nudged a charred beam with my boot and watched it crumble, wishing I knew more about things like flash patterns and points of origin. I was no arson investigator, and the truth was, I knew nothing more about fires than any other private detective, but the insurance company that had hired me didn't care about that. For that they had the fire inspector's report.

I climbed over a mangled metal doorframe to where the tack room should have been. Nothing left but ashes, melted metal latches, a few blackened rhinestones, the shell of a charred refrigerator, and a mishmash of plastic and metal cans melted together and made brittle by the heat. The fire had started here, according to the report. Chemical residue and remnants of the labels identified the contents of the cans as mustard oil, kerosene, lighter fluid, and turpentine, not to mention a few other chemicals used in the unsavory practice of soring horses.

The muscles in my neck tightened as I read the labels. Soring was a way of enhancing a Walking Horse's gait by painting its legs with caustic chemicals or by cutting, abrading, or bruising its feet.

"You kept mustard oil in here?" I said. "Kerosene?"

His nostrils flared. Her chin came up. They knew what I was asking.

The woman, Carlin, narrowed her eyes and said, "We don't sore here. We helped found TASA, for God's sake."

She pronounced it *Tass-ah*, but it stood for the Tennessee Anti-Soring Association.

I held up the report. "Then where did this stuff come from?"

"Isn't that your job?" she said. "To find out where it came from?"

Zane raised an unsteady hand to his DynaVox keyboard. A few moments later, a robotic voice said, "NOT OURS."

"Your trainer's?"

"I'm the trainer," Carlin said. "Until Zane's on his feet again."

From the looks of Zane's medical reports, it seemed unlikely he would ever be back on his feet again. The horse that had attacked him in its stall had cracked his skull and snapped his spine, leaving him paralyzed from the nipples down and with a brain injury that further limited his mobility and rendered his speech nearly incomprehensible.

Carlin said, "We don't sore. And if you don't believe that, you can go to hell."

"It's too soon to believe or disbelieve," I said. "Can I go to purgatory instead?"

She didn't answer for a moment, then took a different tack. "Look, you might be a very nice man. In fact, you probably are. But all we want to know is if you're going to honor our claim."

"That depends," I said.

"On what?"

"On where those chemicals came from."

She blew out an exasperated breath, turned, and straightened Zane's collar. The set of her jaw said she was busying herself with this maternal fussing to keep from jeopardizing their chances of a settlement.

I folded the report and stuffed it into my back pocket, then picked my way back through the rubble, sickened by the occasional scrap of singed leather or a blackened and misshapen snaffle bit. My boot scuffed something small and white, and I told myself it wasn't the bit of bone I knew it was.

I used my toe to cover it with ashes, saw another flash of white among the ash. I'd worked homicides for seven years, and my stomach leaped at the familiar shape. This time, I bent to pick it up.

It was a human mandible. I looked around, found a piece of two-by-four that still looked sturdy enough for the job, and used it to sift through the ashes.

A twisted snaffle bit with the mouthpiece fused, two teeth, and a human skull.

When I got to the rib cage, I set the two-by-four gently aside and said, "Houston, we have a problem."

2.

"What is it?" Carlin said. "What did you find?"

I crossed the ring of parched grass that circled the ruined barn like a moat.

She paled when I told her what I'd found. "A human being? In our barn? But who—" She swayed on her feet, put a hand on Zane's shoulder to steady herself. "The arsonist. It had to be."

I said, "The fire didn't burn long enough or hot enough to render a body down to bone. There would have been muscle left. Cartilage. It would still look like a person, only skinned and charred."

She waved her hands in the air as if to unhear the description. "You're saying there were bones in my barn before the fire started? That's not possible."

"It's possible," I said. "Because they're here."

In the silence that followed, I watched their faces for reactions. Giving them time to think about the meaning of these human bones. Why they were there, whose they might be.

Carlin was pale, Gerardo stoic. Zane's mouth had dropped open, a thin string of drool hanging from his lower lip.

Carlin moved first, bending to wipe the saliva from Zane's mouth with her fingers, then drying her hand on her jeans. He pulled away, a red splotch forming on each cheek, eyes downcast as if he wasn't sure whether to feel grateful or annoyed or ashamed.

"Can we talk inside?" Carlin said. She thumbed sweat from Zane's forehead, wiped it on her pants. "This heat's no good for Zane."

"Of course."

I made the call to 911 as we walked past the paddock, up a driveway made of crushed black stone. Zane's chair churned up gravel dust as he steered between the Underwoods' Dodge RAM and my Chevy Silverado and trundled toward the house, a two-story log cabin with a covered front porch and a long wooden ramp. Zane's chair inched up the ramp, with Carlin taking baby steps behind. I pulled off my boots, which were crusted with ash and soot, and followed in my sock feet. Gerardo took the stairs.

Inside, horse paintings brightened the walls. A sofa and matching chairs made of buttery leather sat on a Navajo rug in a sea of polished wood. Above the stonework fireplace hung a Marlin 336 rifle with a gold plate on the stock. I crossed to the mantel for a closer look: *Zane Underwood, 2013 Tri-State Riflery Champion.*

Carlin jabbed a thumb toward the sitting area. "You might as well have a seat."

"After you."

She perched stiffly at one end of the couch, her husband beside her in his wheelchair. Gerardo leaned against the wall behind the couple, the relaxed posture belied by his rigid spine and the tendons that stood out in his neck. I thought of a pit bull at the end of a chain, controlled but quivering with anticipation.

Carlin said, "It'll take the sheriff a little while to get here. Let's get on with it."

It was obvious who was going to do the talking. Aside from a one-syllable greeting, Gerardo had been silent, and except for noting that the soring chemicals weren't theirs, Zane had kept his own counsel. Only the little green light on the side of his communication device said it was on.

I said, "Okay, let's start with the chemicals. Let's say you're telling the truth about not knowing where they came from."

Carlin flung herself back onto the sofa. "I am telling the truth."

"Who might have planted them there? And why?"

"Take your pick." She pinched the bridge of her nose between her thumb and middle finger. "Someone from the Big Lick crowd. That much should be clear."

The Big Lick is the gait Tennessee Walkers are most famous for. When you see the black silhouette of a Walking Horse with its back legs tucked under and its front legs reaching high, that's the Big Lick. The Tennessee Walking Horse has some beautiful natural gaits. The Big Lick, at least as it's done today, isn't one of them.

There are vets who say you can't get the Big Lick without soring, that the gait is a learned response to pain and that a horse that's never sored will never learn it. Others say you can breed for a high-stepping walk and enhance it with training. That anything a horse *can* do, it can be trained to do. But that kind of training and conditioning takes time and skill, which leads some trainers to take short cuts. Chemical burns, crushed glass, stone bruises. Anything that will cause the horse to snap up its legs. Sored or not, most trainers agreed you needed pads, or stacked shoes, and lightweight ankle chains to get the gait.

I said, "Why would the Big Lick crowd want to burn your barn?"

"Are you kidding me? They've been trying to ruin us ever since we started TASA."

"This antisoring group, this TASA, it's effective enough to make somebody burn your barn down and risk killing your horses just to discredit you?"

"Why should they care about killing horses? They hurt horses every day. To them, horses are just dollar bills on legs. And yes, we're effective enough. Three of the biggest sponsors of the Celebration are backing out this year. Next year there'll probably be more."

The Tennessee Walking Horse National Celebration, held every year in nearby Bedford County, was a few weeks away. The premier event in the Walking Horse world, its success—or lack thereof—was an indicator of the health of the industry. If the Underwoods' antisoring group had cost the Celebration its top sponsors, the fire could have been set by anyone with a stake in the Big Lick performance classes. More likely, though, it was someone they knew. There were several active anti-Big Lick groups, and a disgruntled breeder or trainer would probably move against the one closest to home.

I said, "Who are the major players in the area? The ones most likely to feel threatened?"

She counted them off on her fingers. "Trudy Valentine. Jim and Rhonda Lister. Zane's mother, Eleanor."

At Zane's bleat of protest, she added, "I'm not saying Zane's mother would have burned our barn. Though, honestly—and I'm sorry to have to say this, baby—I wouldn't put it past her. I'm just saying she's part of that crowd."

Zane shook his head and typed, "MOTHER WOULD NOT HAVE BURNED THE BARN. SHE WOULD HAVE BARRED THE DOORS AND BURNED THE HOUSE WITH US INSIDE."

Carlin laid a hand on Zane's forearm. "That's a terrible thing to say. I wish I could say it wasn't true." She let out a long breath and went on. "Then there's Samuel Trehorne. The Trehornes have been breeding, training, and showing since the 1930s. They're like one of those oil dynasties you see on TV, but with horses. They win a lot, which means big breeding fees."

"How much money are we talking about?"

"A top stallion might bring a million if you sold him, but the stud fees can earn you that in a year. Big Lick, of course. That's where the money is. For now."

"For now?"

"It's going south. There's a lot of pressure to get rid of the Big Lick classes altogether, and people like Trehorne are scared to death of it. They think if the Big Lick goes, the whole industry goes, which means pretty much the whole economy in this part of the state collapses."

"Which means their individual economies collapse too."

She gave a thin smile. "Like the Dust Bowl. You wouldn't believe the hate mail I get."

Gerardo said, "All of them, all the Big Lick trainers and breeders and owners, they hate Señora Carlin and Señor Zane. It could be anyone. But Señor Trehorne is the richest and the most ruthless. He has the most to lose."

"Gerardo would know," Carlin said. "He was a groom for Trehorne before he came to work for us."

"These Trehornes," I said. "What are they like?"

With a grim smile, Carlin said, "You're about to find out. Our venerable sheriff is Samuel Trehorne's baby brother."

༄

Sheriff Hap Trehorne was a meaty, balding man in gold-rimmed glasses and a tan sheriff's uniform. His shoulders were broad, his farm-labor muscles just beginning to turn to suet. He stationed himself by the mantel, where he could see all the exits, and fingered his sidearm.

He said to Carlin, "You want to introduce me to your friend?"

"He's not my friend," she said. "He's the insurance investigator. Jared McKean."

"McKean." He gave me a curt nod. "The guy who found the bones. You got ID on you?"

I reached slowly for my wallet and handed it to him. "Driver's license, PI license, carry permit."

"Carry permit." He looked at me through squinted eyes. "You packing?"

"Glock .40 caliber. Waistband."

He seemed to consider this, then handed back my wallet. "That's not going to cause me a problem, is it?"

"No, sir."

"Good." He took my statement, then looked back at Carlin. "So, Carlin . . . Mrs. Underwood. These bones in your barn. Whose were they?"

Carlin picked at a fingernail. "I have no idea."

"Just some stranger?"

"I assume so."

He tried a smile, but it didn't sit comfortably on his face. "Listen, I get it. Crippling medical bills, big unwieldy farm to run, the kind of business the economy hits hard. You're in a financial bind. You get to feeling like you're drowning. So you're not thinking clearly, on account of being desperate and all, and you decide, hey, if something happened to this old barn, the insurance company might pay me enough to get back on my feet. You don't mean anybody to get hurt. Maybe you don't even know there's anybody there. Some transient, you know, who sneaked up into your loft to catch a few z's."

"An accident," she said.

He jabbed a forefinger in her direction. "Exactly. Easy to understand how a thing like that could happen."

"Except it didn't," she said. "Because I didn't set that fire. Because A, it would be wrong, and B, the insurance money wouldn't even come close to getting us back on our feet. Do you know how much a new barn costs? I'll give you a hint. Not as much as six operations and a year of physical therapy."

He leaned back, appraising her over the rims of his glasses.

I said, "Besides, those bones were skeletonized before the fire started. So the bit about transients and her not meaning to hurt anybody . . . you knew better. You were just trying to get her to cop to setting the fire."

He shrugged, unrepentant. That was how the game was played. "Ma'am, is it possible that Mr. Gonzales or your husband, before his accident, might have hidden those bones there?"

Zane made a guttural sound, an unformed protest.

"No," Carlin said. "It isn't possible."

"Let me get this straight," I said. "You think Carlin set the fire for the insurance money, not knowing someone else had hidden human bones in the loft?"

"I think that's one possibility."

I said, "Her whole reputation's built on sound horse politics. It comes out she had soring chemicals in her barn, she's finished. If she'd set the fire, she would have used a different accelerant."

"Maybe that's what she wants us to think," he said. "Or maybe she just wasn't thinking straight. She's under a lot of pressure."

Carlin sank deeper into the sofa, hands curling into fists. "If that's what you think, why haven't you arrested me already?"

"Thinking's not proving," he said. "And I don't like to rush to conclusions. I like to take my time, make sure all my ducks are in a row."

"She didn't do it," I said, though I had no way of knowing that for certain. "And Zane couldn't have."

The sheriff said, "Unless he's faking. I saw a movie once. Guy in a wheelchair would get up at night and commit murders. They figured it out because the bottoms of his shoes were scuffed. You check his shoes?" He grinned, but it looked more like a gas pain.

"His shoes are fine," I said. "I'm pretty sure he isn't faking."

Carlin said, "Seriously, Hap? If you don't have any other theories, maybe you should get out of my house."

"I have other theories," he said. "Maybe nobody set that fire at all. It's just as likely something, maybe a short in an electric wire, sparked those chemicals."

Carlin thumped a fist against the arm of the sofa. "No. Those chemicals weren't there to spark."

"So you say. However it started, I still have to wonder how those bones got there."

"Are you arresting anybody here?" she asked. "Because if you're not, then we're finished."

"Not very hospitable of you," he said. "But no, I'm not arresting anyone today. I happen to know you're signed up for the show tomorrow, so if I need you, I know where you'll be." He looked at me, took a card out of his pocket, and handed it over. "Mr. McKean, you can leave whenever you're finished here. If you think of anything else I need to know, you can call me at this number. The rest of you, hang tight. I'll call some people in to bag these bones, see what we've got."

❦

She closed the door behind him, watched him walk out to his car and drive up to the barn, presumably to call in his forensic team. Or possibly the Tennessee Bureau of Investigation. The TBI had a state-of-the-art forensic lab in Nashville. This was a small county, and the smaller counties, lacking the means and equipment to conduct complex investigations on their own, often called on the TBI for help.

With the sheriff gone, Carlin leaned her forehead against the wood. A shiver began in her shoulders and spread through the rest of her, and she pressed her hands hard against the doorframe to stop their trembling. Gerardo went to her and laid a hand across her back, silent as a shadow. They stood like that until the shivering stopped. Then Carlin turned and rested her back against the door.

I said, "When's the next time all the major players come together?"

She looked at me with tired eyes. "There's a show at Hidden Hollow, just a few miles away. The one Hap was just mentioning. It runs through the weekend. Opening ceremonies start tomorrow." She gave a little laugh. "Unfortunately, it's in this county, so we're still in his jurisdiction."

"Why do you stay?" I said. "There's obviously bad blood between you."

"Zane's grandmother left this land to him before we met. Even without the sentimental value, we could never afford a spread like this someplace else."

Zane lifted a hand and tapped something into his DynaVox. "CARLIN I WOULD LIKE SOME ICE TEA. MAYBE OUR GUEST WOULD TOO."

Her frown made a little line between her brows, a line I'd once heard called an *I want* line. "Is that what we're calling him now? A guest?"

"CARLIN."

She raised her hands in surrender and said, "I'll go make some. Gerardo, could you come and help with the lemons, please?"

Gerardo pushed away from the wall. "Of course, Señora."

Zane watched them go, a shadow of resentment in his eyes. Pretty wife, handsome groom, both hale and whole and off to turn making lemonade into a two-man job. What wasn't there to resent?

He pulled his gaze away from the door and laboriously typed with one finger, "SHE'S SCARED. WE PUT EVERYTHING INTO THIS PLACE. THEN MEDICAL EXPENSES." His bitter gaze swept down his chest and to his withered legs. "AND NOW THIS. I'M USELESS TO HER."

"No—"

"YES." He caught my gaze and held it. A proud man, swallowing that pride to ask a favor of a stranger. "CAN YOU FIND OUT WHO SET THE FIRE?"

"Probably. Eventually."

"SOMEONE IS TARGETING US. TARGETING HER. SHE DID NOT DO THIS. PLEASE. HELP HER."

3.

The tea was sweet and cold, the conversation stilted. I asked a few more questions for form's sake, then finished my drink and took my leave, feeling drained by tension and the weight of their expectations.

On the drive back to the office, I used my new hands-free phone to call my client, Terry Pritchard, an insurance claims officer who gave me work from time to time. He was easy to work for, and he paid well and on time, which put him high on my list of favorite clients. He picked up on the second ring and said, "Good news or bad news?"

"Depends on your perspective. I don't think they did it, if that's what you're asking. He couldn't have, and my sense is she wouldn't."

"What about the groom? This Gonzales?"

"Damn near burned himself up trying to save the horses. I can't see it."

"Damn," he said. "They're covered for arson, which means we gotta pay. You're sure?"

"The only way to be sure is to find out who did it."

"Which means we pay you until you catch the son of a bitch?" He gave a good-natured chuckle. "Way to upsell."

I said, "Once you pay out, whoever did it owes you big money. Maybe you can collect enough to pay my fee."

"I should be so lucky."

"Something else you oughta know," I said.

I filled him in about the bones and the sheriff's theories, and he sighed and said, "No offense, but I hope the wife did it. It would make my job a lot easier. Work fast, McKean."

My office was near Vanderbilt University in a renovated boarding house turned office building. Three floors, each with two office suites facing each other across a narrow hall. The marigolds along the walk were wilting, and the plastic American flags someone had strung along the porch railing were beginning to fade, but it was still a handsome building. When I opened the door, the smell of well-spiced chicken soup rolled out.

I followed it up two flights to my office, where my half-sister, Khanh, sat behind my desk. We looked nothing alike, she small and wiry, with her scarred face and Vietnamese features, me tall and rangy with my father's gray eyes and buck-skin-colored hair, but we were slowly beginning to think of each other as family.

The desk was a massive oak relic from the Old West, given to me by a grateful client whose family failed to see the beauty in the bullet holes and the scorch marks on one side. The first time she'd seen it, Khanh had said, "You need new desk," but I was pretty sure she was learning to love it, along with the wildlife prints on the walls and the *Horse & Rider* magazines on the side table. She looked up when I came in, gave me a wave of her stump. "You solve case?" she asked.

"Not quite."

"You need to solve." She held up a Post-it with a name and number on it, framed by the space left by her missing finger. "I get new case. Skip trace. Easy money."

"You realize I can work more than one case at a time."

She shook her head. "You American, always everything same time. More better focus on one thing."

"Yes, Obi-Wan." I took the Post-it and shooed her out from behind the desk, where a game of Solitaire filled the computer screen. "This is what I pay you for?"

She nodded toward the Post-it. "*This* what you pay me for. But business slow sometime. Smart woman like me, need keep mind busy."

I hadn't wanted a sister, and I hadn't needed a receptionist. I'd hired her because she needed a job, a visa, and a place to stay, and because she was my father's responsibility and he, being dead, was in no position to honor it. But a funny thing had happened. Running a coffee shop in Vietnam turned out to be the perfect training ground for running a private detective business in Tennessee. People often underestimated her because of her thick accent and fractured English, but in the past three months, she'd doubled my business and tripled my income. Even with three more mouths to feed, I was taking home more money than I ever had.

The door to the back room opened, and two more Vietnamese women, one old and one young, converged on me. The young one, Tuyet, was Khanh's nineteen-year-old daughter. I didn't know how old Phen was. Late sixties, early seventies. Her battle with cancer had given her skin an ashen cast. She fluttered to the desk and patted my shoulder. "You having fine day today, yes?" she said. Pat, pat. "I fix you good soup."

"Smells delicious."

She beamed and gestured to Tuyet, who disappeared into the back and returned with a steaming bowl brimming with chicken broth, pho noodles, and an assortment of vegetables, some of which I recognized.

Three months ago, that room had been filled with surveillance equipment and other accoutrements of my trade. Now, the king-sized bed where all three women slept took up most of the room, and in the bathroom where I used to shower on occasion, women's underclothes hung from the rod. The kitchenette was filled with foods and spices I'd never heard of.

If anyone had told me then that three Asian women would be living in the back room of my office, I would have laughed. If they'd said one would be my half-sister and another the woman my father had cheated with during the Vietnam War, I'd have signed commitment papers. But you know what they say: Man plans, and God laughs.

I took a bite of the soup. The infusion of dried chilies and other spices cleared my sinuses and seared the roof of my mouth. "Magnificent."

Phen smiled and patted me again—pat, pat—then watched as I pulled up the background check software and typed in Samuel Trehorne's name. Might as well start at the top of the industry food chain.

Khanh, peering over my shoulder, said, "This case. You can work it from here?"

"Part of it. Then I have to go to a horse show."

"I never go horse show. Sound interesting."

"You know I work alone." I grinned at her. Our private joke.

"I know." She put on her inscrutable face, but her eyes were smiling. "You work alone. I come with you."

4.

Khanh looked over my shoulder while I did the initial background check. According to Google and my special supersecret PI databases, Samuel Trehorne was worth upward of $20 million, which didn't sound all that desperate until you took into account that, a few years ago, that amount had been almost double. Married forty-three years, he and his wife, Rebecca, had a grown son, Samuel Jr., and an eight-year-old daughter, Esmerelda. Trehorne was a deacon in his church and a long-time board member of the Tennessee Walking Horse Performance Association. In the past three years, he'd had seven soring violations. That might have seemed more notable if the other board members hadn't had as many or more.

It took us the better part of an hour and a half to get there. He lived in Hidden Hollow, a small but affluent town a few miles from the Braydon County showground and five miles from the invisible line that separated them from Bedford County. This was convenient, since Bedford County's claim to fame was the annual Celebration in Shelbyville.

The Trehorne mansion was a sprawling stucco monstrosity with Spanish architecture and an ornate wrought iron fence with Trehorne's initials soldered into the gate. A sign beside the gate said, "Trehorne Stables. Visitors Welcome 24/7."

About a hundred yards beyond, the driveway forked, house to the left, stables to the right. I took the right-hand fork and parked in front of a hacienda-style barn that could have housed the whole Spanish riding academy. A Hispanic-looking girl of about eight, in purple jodhpurs and a rhinestoned *Hello Kitty* T-shirt, came out as Khanh and I were heading in. She was a pretty thing, small-boned and brown-skinned, with long black hair and eyes so dark you could hardly see the pupils.

She gave us each a long, slow look and said to Khanh, "What happened to your face?"

Khanh said, "I little bigger than you, I have bad accident."

"It's ugly," the child said without rancor. "You should get it fixed."

Khanh shook her head. If the comment hurt, she didn't show it. "Some things never be fix."

The girl held up her wrist and shook it so the sparkling watchband on it flashed in the light. "This is a Cartier. My mama had it specially made for me, with my name on the back." She flipped it over so we could see: *Esmerelda.* "These are real diamonds. You like it?"

"Very shiny," I said.

She looked at my watch. Scooby Doo, the greatest detective who ever lived. A gift from my son on my last birthday. The look on her face said she didn't know whether to be charmed by Scooby or repulsed by my obvious lack of taste. "Are you here to see my papa?"

I said, "I'm here to see Samuel Trehorne."

With a solemn nod, she pointed toward the house. "That's my papa. He's inside. Do you want me to get him for you?"

"Please."

She skipped away, waving her hand as if directing invisible music and watching her watchband shimmer and flash in the light.

"Poor baby," Khanh said, without a trace of sarcasm.

Eight years old. Maybe I was making too much of a sparkly watchband, but I would have felt better if she'd been out catching tadpoles.

Or if she hadn't been so quick to call Khanh ugly.

"Poor baby," I agreed, and wondered how a rural white couple in their sixties had ended up with an eight-year-old Hispanic child.

I held the door for Khanh, then followed her into the stable. Florescent lights illuminated the place, while industrial fans set into vaulted ceilings pushed cool air down wide aisles swept clean of hay and debris. I moved along an aisle and saw a black stallion in a large box stall with sliding doors below and metal bars above. He had a window, shuttered against the elements, and an electric fan, which he stood in front of as if to drink in the coolness. The stall was clean, the water bucket full, a hay net tacked to the back wall.

A metal plate beneath the stall said *Rogue's Honor*.

He was tall, but the stacked shoes made him taller still. When he saw me, he pricked his ears forward and poked his nose through the bars. I gave it a stroke, and when he seemed to like that, I reached through and rubbed the broad place between his eyes, where a single whorl of hair marked him, if the old cowhands could be believed, as an uncomplicated, honest soul.

Khanh stepped in close behind me and touched his nose with a tentative finger.

A booming voice behind us made us both jump. "He's a beauty, ain't he?"

"He is." I took my hand out from between the bars and turned to face a jowly man with a ruddy complexion. His beige suit, expensive by the cut of it, had sweat patches under the arms, and his belt was fastened tight beneath a watermelon belly. He was a little balder and a little paunchier than his brother, and looking at him was like looking at Sheriff Hap's future.

"Gonna take first prize at the show this weekend," he said. "If the USDA assholes don't boot him."

There was a longstanding animosity between the Big Lick proponents and the United States Department of Agriculture, which had been charged with enforcing the antisoring laws. The brittleness in Trehorne's voice left no doubt which side he was on. He mopped his face and forehead with a handkerchief and held out the other hand for a moist shake.

I grasped his hand and said, "Why would they boot him?"

"They gun for all the top horses. Can't admit you can get a good gait without soring. Bunch of dickwits." He pumped my hand like he might draw water from it. "Samuel Trehorne."

"Jared McKean," I said, extricating my hand and surreptitiously wiping my palm on my jeans. "This is Khanh. And this—" with a nod toward the stallion, "—is a good-looking animal."

"You in the market?" His tone said he doubted it but didn't want to miss an opportunity.

"Thinking on it. I got a little money saved up, thought this might be a good investment. Stud fees, you know? I heard they can be high for a blue-ribbon Walker."

"Yep." He hitched up his pants and grinned. "You know anything about horses?"

"A bit."

"Walkers in particular?"

"Not as much. Mostly quarter horses. Say I wanted this guy here. What would he run me?"

A good cutting-horse stallion could bring almost half a million dollars, a winning Thoroughbred much more.

"Well now, this fella, I'm not sure I'd want to let him go. His granddaddy was one of the greatest Walking Horses that ever lived. He's a shoo-in to win the show this weekend, maybe even this year's Celebration, if the USDA doesn't throw a wrench into the works. Then I'm thinking to retire him and let the stud fees roll in."

"You got one that is for sale?"

"Sure. I just happen to have another real nice stallion for one eighty-five."

"Thousand?" I said. Khanh's eyes widened. "For that I could buy a house."

He laughed. "But not a very nice one. Want to see him, or are you just kickin' tires?"

One didn't preclude the other, but I said, "I want to see him."

He led us down the aisle, past more stalls, each with a horse with a gleaming coat and stacked shoes, and stopped in front of a stallion so white he looked like he'd been spun from starlight.

Trehorne said, "This is Galahad. He's a good stud. Only thing is, he don't step out quite the way he ought to. Don't get me wrong, he's won his share of ribbons, but he's not the athlete Rogue is. That's why I'm letting him go so cheap."

"Cheap?" Khanh squeaked.

He chuckled. "Little Lady, cheap is relative." He looked at me. "Is she the one I need to convince, or do you wear the pants in this relationship?"

"I wear the pants," I said. "But one eighty-five . . . I need to think on that. Run some numbers with my accountant.

And I probably want to look around, make some comparisons. This show you mentioned . . ."

"The Hidden Hollow Walking Horse Classic, just a few miles down the road."

"Maybe I'll go there and look around."

"You do that, boy. You'll see a lot of fine horse flesh. And then you'll come running to me."

"I heard Zane and Carlin Underwood have some top-notch animals."

"Zane's mother sells good stock, but if you want to make a profit in this business, steer clear of Carlin Underwood. The money's in the Big Lick, and she only shows flat shod."

"I prefer flat shod," I said. No stacked shoes, no chains.

He snorted. "A flat-shod stallion might bring $15,000, not much in the way of stud fees either. The audience just ain't there. Course if she has her way, there won't be any audience at all."

He'd referenced Carlin twice, no mention of Zane. It seemed he'd already dismissed Zane as a force to be reckoned with. I said, "I'm not all that comfortable with the Big Lick. The soring thing—"

His ruddy face turned redder. "We don't do that anymore. Few bad apples, here and there. You check the stats. We have horses showing twenty, twenty-five years. They couldn't do that if we weren't taking damn good care of them."

"But you have violations. You, personally."

"Hell, son. Everyone's got violations. Those USDA judges? You think they can't be bought? I've seen those fellas poke and prod a horse's legs until it's just plain sick of being squeezed and pulls away. Then they say he's sore." He mopped his head again. "You see any soring going on here? Hell, I love these horses like they were my own kin."

"They look well cared for. But I don't like the stacked shoes."

"That's cause you're a quarter horse man. A Walking Horse ain't built the same. Anyway, the pads and chains don't hurt 'em none. Hotshots over to the University of Auburn did a study that proves it."

"If you say so."

"I got to hand it to Zane and Carlin, though. They breed good stock. If you had the time and the know-how, you could take one of their stallions, train him in the Big Lick, maybe win a couple titles. Drive up the stud fee that way. That's how I got Rogue there." He nodded down the aisle toward the black stallion's stall. "Got him for a song from Carlin Underwood this time last year."

"I'm surprised she sold him to you, knowing you'd show him in Big Lick classes."

"Nobody else would have him." His grin broadened, and he gave his face a final swipe with his handkerchief. "That's the horse that almost killed her husband."

5.

I was quiet on the way back to the office. Khanh held her peace until we'd made it to the interstate, then poked the bobblehead Batman on my dashboard and said, "You angry?"

Batman nodded. I said, "I don't know. A little."

"Angry why?"

"I'll let you know when I figure it out."

There was a lot I didn't like about the Walking Horse show world. I didn't like the stacks and chains. I didn't like the long-shanked bits the riders used. I didn't like the fact that the horses were stalled most of the day during the long show season, and in some cases, year-round.

Trehorne was right about the Auburn study. I'd read it myself when I rescued Crockett, my own Walking Horse, but it didn't take into account the vicious things some trainers did to enhance the effects of the pads and chains. A six-ounce chain placed just above the hoof on a healthy pastern might be no more annoying than a diamond watchband on a little girl's wrist. That same chain on a pastern already irritated by caustic chemicals was a different story. A two-inch pad, or stacked shoe, alone might be harmless, but that same shoe could conceal objects—like broken glass or half a golf ball—that cut or put painful pressure on the soft tissues on the bottom of the foot.

The problem was nobody knew for sure how common soring was. It was everybody or hardly anybody, depending on which experts you asked. So while I knew I was pissed, I didn't know enough to know how pissed I ought to be.

I pushed it from my mind and turned my thoughts to Rogue's Honor. He'd seemed calm when I'd approached him. Friendly even. Not aggressive in the least. So why had he attacked Zane Underwood?

It was true that some horses, especially stallions, were more territorial inside their stalls, but Rogue hadn't sent out any such signals, not so much as a flattened ear. Had there been a mare nearby the day of the attack? That seemed like a rookie mistake, one someone as experienced as Zane would not have made.

Khanh said, "You think that man set fire to the Underwood barn?"

"I didn't like him much. That doesn't make him an arsonist."

"He good ol' boy." She grinned, proud of herself for knowing the term. "Everybody like."

"Not everyone. How about you? Did you like him?"

She wrinkled her nose, smile fading. "Not me. He too much politician."

We drove the rest of the way in silence. As I opened the passenger door and lifted her down from the Silverado, I said, "If you still want to see the show, I'll pick you up at seven. Bring a bag. We'll stay at the showground."

"Four day?" At my nod, she smiled and said, "See you at seven. I make coffee."

I watched until she'd closed and locked the door behind her. Then I drove home to the Victorian-style farmhouse I shared with my friend and landlord, Jay Renfield. Jay and his lover, Eric, were on a three-week vacation in Italy, and I was glad of it. Jay and I had known each other since kindergarten, and our friendship had survived his uncloseting, his AIDS diagnosis, and the uncertainties and dangers of my job. It had put him at risk more than once, and short of moving out and cutting him out of my life completely, a cure he deemed worse than the disease, I was damned if I knew how to keep it from happening again. But for the next few weeks, it was something I didn't have to worry about.

By the time I got out of the truck, both horses had their heads over the pasture fence. I paused to give them each a scratch. Tex, the palomino quarter horse I'd had since I was a boy, had just celebrated his thirty-seventh birthday. Crockett was a black Tennessee Walker, rescued from a trainer who'd sored him. He was a trail horse now, and I liked the walk God gave him well enough.

I pointed toward the barn and said, "Suppertime."

Unlike Samuel Trehorne's stable, mine had only four stalls, two of them occupied. Each had a gate that opened out into the aisle and a door in back that led into a paddock. These, in turn, connected to the pasture. Unless one of the horses had to be confined because of injury or illness, the back doors and the paddock gates stayed open so the boys could come and go as they pleased.

By the time I got inside, both horses were in Tex's stall. I gave Crockett a gentle push and said, "Go to your own room, go on." He looked at me for a moment, as if to make sure I meant it, then flicked his tail and sauntered out the back and around to his own stall. Tex whickered and nuzzled my hand.

"Get some rest tonight," I told them after they'd been fed, brushed, and watered. "Tomorrow's a big day."

∽

Luca, the papillon pup we'd inherited from Jay's ex met me at the front door, bouncing like a popcorn kernel in hot oil. I rubbed his ears and grabbed a cold beer from the kitchen, then let him out and watched him putter in the garden. I kept half an eye out for hawks, since at six pounds, Luca was about the size of a rabbit.

I sipped my beer and drank in the scent of lavender while the dog did his business and the sky turned red, then plum, then purple-blue. The shadows lengthened, and the part of my awareness tuned to danger turned from hawks to owls. The little dog came to lie on the step beside me, a warm spot against my thigh. I took one last swallow, then pulled out my phone and dialed my son's number.

Paulie's mother and I had given him the phone, along with a Scooby watch of his own, for his ninth birthday. It was hard to say which made him prouder.

He picked up, and his gravelly voice, typical of children with Down syndrome, said, "Daddy!"

"Hey, sport. How'd you know it was me?"

"Said *Daddy* in the window."

Pride tugged my lips into a smile. He'd recognized my name in the caller ID function. "Good job, buddy. How's school?"

"Good. I can read *Clifford the Dog*." He rattled off a few lines from one of his favorite books, then said, "You come get me this weekend?"

"Not this time. It's your mom's week. You remember where she and D.W. are taking you?"

"Sky High!"

With its ten trampoline floors and trampoline walls, the indoor park on Harding was Paul's new favorite hot spot. "You got it, sport. Bounce a few times for me, okay?"

He chattered for a while about the trampolines, school, and his baby sister's latest exploits—putting blocks in a bucket and crawling up steps. Then we said good-bye, and the pup and I went back inside for supper.

I gave the dog a high-dollar, grain-free kibble, then grilled myself a rib eye and roasted a hobo packet of garlic cloves, new potatoes, carrots, squash, and corn on the cob. I ate in front of my computer, reserving a camping spot at the Hidden Hollow showground and working my way through the red tape required to take Crockett and Tex along.

The stalls at the showground were all spoken for, but for a hefty fee the show organizers would let me set up a portable corral at the campsite. When I'd finally tracked down the necessary links and filled out the additional forms, I settled in to learn everything I could about what Carlin Underwood had called the Big Lick crowd.

"HELP HER," Zane had said. His need—and his wife's—had given me a sense of urgency, exacerbated by the bones of a victim unidentified and unavenged.

But there was something more personal to it than even that. Someone had set fire to a barn full of live horses. One way or another, there was going to be a reckoning.

6.

Early the next morning, I hitched the horse trailer to the Silverado and loaded Tex and Crockett into it. It was a sweet little gooseneck, with room for both horses in the back, a compartment for feed and tack, and connectors for the portable corral. The living quarters were cramped but functional, with a closet, kitchenette, shower and toilet, and a short ladder leading up to the small loft with a double bed.

I stashed Luca in a soft-sided crate in the storage area behind the front seat of the Silverado, along with a tote bag of dog food and chew toys and as much camping and surveillance equipment as I could squeeze in. A faded quilt covered the metal box that held my rifle, a shotgun, and a few boxes of ammunition.

At the small of my back, slightly offset and tucked into a holster inside the waistband of my jeans, the Glock was a familiar weight. A little Beretta Tomcat rested against my left ankle.

I dropped off the pup and the tote with a sweet, elderly woman who carried a Smith & Wesson revolver tucked into the waistband of her skirt. She gave me a dry kiss on the cheek, wished me luck with the case, and promptly forgot me in her haste to scoop up my dog and spoil him rotten. Since the arsonist obviously had no compunction about hurting horses, I would have liked to leave Tex and Crockett behind too, but with Jay in Italy, there was no one to take care of them.

I stopped at McDonald's to fortify myself with a cup of black coffee and pulled the rig up to the sidewalk in front of the office at three minutes after seven. Khanh waited on the front stoop, the strap of an oversize duffel slung over one shoulder, a stainless steel thermos in one hand and another clasped between her stump and her chest.

She scanned the rig with a scrutinizing eye. "Big trailer."

"Modest," I said. "On a relative scale."

"Only modest, maybe you let me drive."

"On the can-you-drive-the-truck scale, it's big. It's very big."

Khanh pretended to pout, but I knew it was a sham. She was a small woman, and it was a big truck. She had to climb up or be boosted into it, but once there, she was just tall enough to reach the pedals and see over the dashboard. Maneuvering a loaded trailer raised the difficulty quotient exponentially. Ignoring the theatrics, I stashed the duffel in the trailer and boosted her into the passenger seat.

"Buckle up," I said.

"You always say buckle up," she said. "You think I forget?"

"I know you do. Only it's not forgetting. It's willful disregard."

"Fancy talk." She buckled up and handed me a thermos filled with Vietnamese coffee. Made from strong coffee and condensed milk, the *ca phe sua da* was more dessert than beverage, but since Khanh made it for me almost every morning, I'd acquired a taste for it.

Khanh took a sip and said, "How we going to learn who start barn fire?"

"Talk to people. See who has a motive, who doesn't have an alibi." That was simplifying things, but not by much.

"Alibi?" She wrinkled her nose. "Everybody lie."

"There is that. But if being a detective was easy, everybody would be doing it."

"I watch you three month. Think you have some different plan."

"Enlighten me."

"Talk to everybody. Stir pot. See who try to kill you."

"Well," I said, because I couldn't deny it, "it's worked for me so far."

⌒

West End traffic was already heavy, and I-440 all but a parking lot. I brought Khanh up to speed on the case while we inched along. Then we hit I-24, going against the stream, and things opened up. I kept it under the speed limit, careful not to unbalance the horses in back, but we made it to Murfreesboro in less than an hour and stopped to stock the fridge.

All the staples. Eggs, milk, cheese. Beer. Potatoes for hash browns, flour for biscuits, sausage for gravy. Rack of ribs, bacon, a couple of steaks, some chicken breasts . . .

With my vegetarian housemate an ocean away and the prospect of grilling over an open flame on the horizon, my inner carnivore was asserting itself.

"We need vegetable," Khanh said, holding up a head of broccoli and a root that looked like it had come from the rear end of a goat.

"I don't even want to know what that is."

"You not needing to know. Just need to eat. Make you strong for when people try kill you."

"Usually when people try to kill me, there are firearms involved. Maybe I should eat something that'll make me fast."

"You need something make you lucky," she said. "But this not help you there."

⁇

Once past the college town, traffic grew sparse. I took the ramp toward Bell Buckle, home of the RC and Moon Pie Festival. Then the road narrowed and the landscape changed from fast-food restaurants to small neat houses to farmland. We turned off the main road and wound our way past half a dozen small towns marked only by a tighter clustering of shotgun houses and the city-limits signs.

The sign for Hidden Hollow had Old English lettering and a barren tree motif echoed by a handful of businesses on the square. In front of the stone courthouse, a boy in a Titans baseball cap straddled a Civil War-era cannon, licking a Popsicle shaped like a rocket.

Khanh gave the Popsicle a longing look and fanned herself until I dialed up the air conditioner.

We passed an old-fashioned diner, two antique shops, a hair salon, a grocery store, and then a series of tack shops and horse-themed gift shops interspersed among the houses and mom-and-pop stores like mushrooms dotting a field. No hotels, just a log-cabin steakhouse, a cowboy bar with a neon sign that said *Jake's Place*, and a stream of bed-and-breakfasts, each with a sign extolling its claim to fame—*Momma's Special Homemade Pecan Pie, Fluffiest Biscuits You'll Ever Taste, Custom Quilts and World's Best Redeye Gravy.*

The turnoff to the showground was marked by a strand of plastic flags and a series of handmade signs. We followed the red Sharpie arrows until a security guard in a Day-Glo lime-green vest waved us through the gate. A few yards farther on, the road pitchforked—campground to the left, stables to the right, a state-of-the-art indoor arena in the center. Concentric

rows of freestanding vendor booths spread from the front of
the arena like peasant huts surrounding a medieval castle. It
would have been more efficient to put the stables next to the
campground, but that would have spoiled the effect.

A teenager in another Day-Glo vest waved us toward the
camping area, where trailers, trucks, and campers converged
into a metal and canvas village. Some sites were already
decked out with awnings, grills, and folding director's chairs,
and many had portable corrals like the one I had in the back
of the Silverado. Some of the awnings were stamped with
the names of the owners' stables: Rosewind, Willow Creek,
Copper Springs.

A Day-Glo girl with braces on her teeth pointed us toward
site fifteen, and we pulled in between a rig twice the size of
mine and a bubble-shaped aluminum camper that looked like
something out of *Lost in Space*. A Dodge D-Series pickup sat
beside the bubble, the trailer connector unhooked. The scal-
loped hood and pocketed taillights marked the pickup as a
model from the early seventies.

When I opened my door, a rush of heat rolled in. By
the time I'd helped Khanh out of the truck, my armpits
were moist, and sweat trickled down the back of my neck.
I unhitched the trailer and set up the portable corral while
Khanh set up the campsite, pausing every few minutes to fan
herself with her hand. As I unloaded the horses and loosed
them in the corral, the man in the silver *Lost in Space* camper
sauntered over and watched with blinking, bloodshot eyes the
color of cola in sunlight. Contacts, I guessed, and probably
new, from the telltale gouges on the bridge of his nose.

He was a young guy, maybe twenty-three, with ginger
hair, pale freckled skin, and oversized ears that looked like
they belonged on the cover of *Mad* magazine. His jeans
were crisp, his snakeskin boots shiny, the silver band on his

wide-brimmed cowboy hat polished to a sheen. The buttons on his denim shirt were mother-of-pearl. In his breast pocket were a small steno tablet and a pen.

He watched me dump two bales in the corral, one at each end and another in the middle, so Tex could guard two while Crockett ate at the third. When I'd filled their water buckets, the red-haired man put his hands in his pockets and said, "You're not showing these."

"No, I'm good, but not good enough to pass off a quarter horse as a Walker."

"That would be a challenge." He gave me a friendly grin. "You might slide the black one in though."

"Couldn't get him past the inspectors." Crockett had visible scars on both pasterns.

He nodded. "The scar rule is pretty nebulous, but I don't think even a blind judge could pass this one through. Whoever fixed him didn't do a very good job."

"I wouldn't call it fixing," I said. Fixing was a euphemism for soring.

He smiled as if I'd passed some kind of test. "I won't disagree with you on that. I assume it wasn't you?"

"You assume right." I nodded toward his truck. "Nice ride. What year is it?"

"Seventy-two. It was my grandfather's."

"You keep it running yourself?"

His grin was half-proud, half-embarrassed. "YouTube tutorials. You'd be amazed at the things you can find on the Internet."

I introduced myself and Khanh, and he said, "I'm Eli Barringer, reporter for the *Sextant*. Call me Eli."

"The *Nashville Sextant*? Or is this something local?" We hadn't had a competitor for the *Tennessean* in a lot of years, not since the *Banner* went under, but the *Sextant* was trying its best, a small dog with its eye on a big bone. I'd have had higher hopes for it if the name didn't evoke snickers from a third of the population and puritanical outrage from another third. The third who understood the name probably got its news elsewhere.

"*Nashville Sextant*," he said. "Sports reporter. Human interest. You name it, I'll write about it. Most of the other guys only want hard news."

"You got something against hard news?"

"Oh, it's not that I don't want it. But look at me." He circled a hand around his boyish face. "I'm low man on the totem pole."

"The new guy, huh?"

"So new the ink on my diploma's still wet. But I'm okay with that. You never know where hard news might turn up."

"The soring controversy."

He winked and fired his index fingers at me like a pair of revolvers. "Got it in one. You get this kind of power, money, and tradition all in one place, and then somebody threatens it? It's a powder keg. Had an arson a few nights ago, and odds are good they'll never find who did it."

"How'd you know it was arson?"

"I may be young, but I have sources." He rocked back on his heels and squinted into the distance. "Besides, an Underwood's barn burns down, you've got to figure someone had a hand in it. These people have been killing each other over soring for the past forty years."

I lifted an eyebrow.

Khanh said, "Forty year long time. Nobody stop them?"

A quick lift of his shoulders dismissed her question as naive. "Most of them are accidents and suicides, according to the story books. Excuse me, I mean the medical examiner's reports."

I said, "Forty years of accidents and suicides? That's a hell of a conspiracy."

"Look at the names on those medical reports. Then look at the names of the investigating officers, and tell me there's not one." A burst of trumpet music came from the arena, followed by a discordant jumble of sax and cello and the trill of a clarinet. The musicians, warming up. Just-Call-Me-Eli touched his fingertips to the brim of his hat. "I gotta run. Sounds like the show's about to start, and I want to be there for the fireworks."

7.

There were no fireworks, at least not then, except perhaps in a metaphorical sense. It was too early in the day. While Eli Barringer, cub reporter, wandered off in search of social pyrotechnics, Khanh and I finished setting up camp.

"We go seeing horse show now?" Khanh asked. "Or go stir pot?"

"Could be both," I said. "Let's head that way and see what happens."

The campground smelled of pine trees, hay, and diesel fuel. As we neared the vendor booths, those scents were lost beneath the sweet-and-savory carnival smell of burgers and funnel cakes. Khanh cooed over jewelry, leather goods, airbrushed T-shirts, handcrafted toys, and plastic souvenirs made in China. I paused to admire a tooled leather saddle with silver inlay. Too fancy for me, but a fine-looking saddle nonetheless.

We made our way to the arena and bought a pair of fourday tickets and two pocket program books. I handed one of each to Khanh and flipped through my book, looking for the names Carlin had given me. According to the schedule, Jim Lister was about to show a horse called Troubadour in a flatshod class.

I showed the page to Khanh.

"This say flat," she said. "Mrs. Carlin say Mr. Lister a Big Lick man."

"That's right. I didn't expect this. But you know what they say."

Her lips quirked upward in a smile. "Man who plant wind, harvest storm?"

"Adapt or die. I guess Mr. Lister is adapting."

It was cooler inside, but not by much. An industrial fan at each end moved lukewarm air through the building, while below, six horses cantered around an oval-shaped arena. Their riders, four men and two women, wore old-fashioned suits with derbies. The men rode with an odd, hunched-over posture some called the "gangster gait." It looked crabbed and awkward to me, but maybe that was my own bias.

In the center of the arena was a white wooden structure with a sound system, a microphone for the announcer, and a row of chairs for the judges to sit on between classes. Three tiers of theater seats stretched up around three sides of the oval. The fourth side had a gate below, where the horses entered, and restrooms and a concession booth above, where a trio of teenage girls in short shorts and cowboy boots clustered around the condiment aisle, sipping on giant colas and piling jalapeños onto a mountain of nachos.

The section closest to the announcer's stand consisted of individual boxes, each with a row of cushioned chairs and a small table, presumably for refreshments. A sign on the back of each box said *Reserved, V.I.P.*

It was midday on a weekday, and most of the seats were empty. A gate steward stood near the entrance to the arena, the participants for the next class lined up to one side to allow

room for the current class to exit the ring. Jim Lister, looking a few years older than he did on his driver's license, was
fifth in line, riding a good-looking black horse with two white
socks and a white star. The horse was better looking than the
man, who had basset hound eyes and a face like a wrinkled
bed sheet.

His wife, Rhonda—wife number three, according to the
background check—stood with her forearms on the railing.
She looked better in real life than in her DMV photo, which
had looked pretty damn good. Just shy of thirty, she was forty
years Lister's junior, with intelligent blue eyes, a flawless complexion, and hair of that pale clear gold that rarely occurs
naturally in anyone over thirteen. She wore it well, though,
along with the tight jeans and the powder pink shirt knotted
under her breasts.

The ring on her left hand was the size of a quail egg,
a ring of sapphires around a diamond so large it should have
come with its own curse. Her necklace and earrings matched it.

Khanh rolled her eyes. "Uh oh. This one very dangerous."

"She doesn't look dangerous," I said.

"Never know. Just as easy for woman start fire as man."

"I'll keep that in mind."

"Glad you using mind. See how you look at her, think
maybe other parts get in way."

"I'm gonna go talk to her. I'll try to keep control of all
my parts."

She settled onto the bench. "I stay here. Not want to
cramp you style."

I stood up as the judges started handing out the ribbons.
A chestnut with a white blaze took first, followed by a couple
of blacks and a bay. The class filed out, those with the top ribbons smiling broadly, the rest looking either stalwart or glum.
The steward waved in Lister's group. I rolled up my program

booklet and tucked it into my back pocket, then walked down to stand by Rhonda Lister and crossed my forearms on the rail beside hers.

She glanced up, gave me an appraising look and a smile. "Tourist?"

"Just a guy from the quarter horse side of the tracks. Decided I'd come on up and see what all the fuss was about."

"And have you?"

"Not yet."

In the ring, the announcer called for a flat walk, and the riders fell into a relaxed, counterclockwise circle around the ring. The horses' heads nodded in time to the four-beat gait, each foot striking the ground at separate times, rear feet overstriding to the forward edge of the track left by the front feet. The head-nod and overstride are unique to the breed.

A champagne horse flung up his head and shied, nearly unseating his rider, a young man who looked barely old enough to shave. Rhonda Lister shook her head and nodded toward the ring. "That boy's overhorsed. You got somebody showing out here, or are you just checking things out?"

"Just checking things out. You?"

"That one's mine," she said. "Number 33."

"He your trainer or your father?"

"My husband."

"I wouldn't have guessed that."

She cocked her head. "This is the part where you're too polite to call me a gold digger."

"This is the part where I say he's a lucky guy."

A smile tugged at her lips. "Smooth talker. Are you thinking of getting into the business?"

The announcer called out, "Reverse, flat walk," and the riders turned their mounts in the opposite direction. The champagne horse danced sideways before his owner managed to turn him. The horse lurched forward a few steps and finally fell back into the rhythm of the walk.

"He's hopeless," Rhonda said. "The rider, not the horse."

"Well, he's young," I said. "Maybe he'll learn."

She lifted the hair off the back of her neck and smiled as the fans blew across her damp skin.

"Canter," the announcer said, and Lister, nearest the wall, nudged his horse into a perfect rocking-chair canter. A guy in a blue suit and matching derby passed Lister on the left, his bay's haunches brushing the shoulder of Lister's black. With no place to go, Lister tightened slightly on the rein, and for a moment, the black seemed suspended in air. It was an illusion, a brief hesitation no longer than a breath, but when it was over, the black fell back and was clear of the bay. Lister moved it toward the outside and away from the man in blue.

"Your husband's good," I said. "The black didn't even blink when the other horse bumped him. But why the gangster slouch?"

"Frees up the horse's front end, lets them lift their legs higher."

"Looks funny though."

"Depends what you're used to. But Jim doesn't care how it looks. He says it's not about him. It's about getting the most out of the horse."

"He's in the Big Lick classes too, isn't he?"

"They save those for later in the evening so more people can come. Those are the most popular classes."

"Still?"

She rolled her eyes. "Oh, God. You drank the Kool-Aid, didn't you?"

"I see what I see. What's wrong with this gait? It looks just fine, if you ask me."

"But no one's asking you." She gave her head a rueful shake. "And we were getting along so well, too. Look, the problem is, this is media fodder. Everybody wants to gnash their teeth and wail about the poor abused horses. But we've done everything they've asked of us and more. Thirty years ago, sure, this industry was a cesspool, but they've cleaned up their act."

"They? Or we?"

She gave an embarrassed laugh. "Okay, you caught me. I'm not exactly an insider. I'd never even been on a horse before I met Jim."

"And now?"

"They're beautiful animals, amazing athletes. But I'd just as soon drive a Ferrari."

We talked about cars for a few minutes. Her dad had been a Busch league stock car driver, and she'd learned to change the oil in a car before she was seven. Back then she was proud of the grease beneath her fingernails.

"We had a 1963 Mustang convertible we were restoring," she said. "My mom used to complain that the only time she saw me was when she had to wrestle me into a dress for church."

There was a note of sorrow beneath the nostalgia in her voice. I said, "What happened to him?"

She lowered her gaze, rubbing her fingertips lightly on the rail. "Story for another time. You wanted to know why Jim was showing flat shod."

"Just curious. I didn't mean to pry."

"The Big Lick is coming back. For the first time in years, there's been an uptick in the number of horses sold and the prices they went for. And then the Texas Supreme Court found the scar rule unconstitutional. Since no one knows how to interpret it, there's no way to administer it fairly. Finally, someone's admitting there's a flaw in the system. So we're turning a corner."

"But Jim's showing flat shod anyway."

"The anti-Big Lick groups, they're really vocal, and they have a lot of political clout. So he's covering his bases. Laying a foundation so no matter what happens, which way the chips fall, he'll land on his feet. That's what he does."

The announcer said, "Walk on!" and the riders dropped their mounts into the running walk. The head nod and over-stride became more pronounced, a flat walk on overdrive. Lister's horse, Troubadore, blew past the rest of the field with a long, ground-covering stride that must have clocked near twenty miles an hour, rear feet overstepping the front track by more than a foot. It was an impressive walk.

I said, "Your husband's going to win it, isn't he?"

She nodded, a proud smile lighting her face. "I think he's going to take it all this time. Maybe even the Celebration in Shelbyville in a few weeks."

"I hear Samuel Trehorne has a good shot at it."

She shook her head. "Trehorne's got a good horse, and Junior—Sam Junior, his son—can ride the hell out of anything with four legs. But Rogue's the only one he has that's good enough, and . . . well, I can't see the judges giving the top honors to a horse that almost killed a man. Plus there's been some controversy about him."

"What kind of controversy?"

The announcer called for the contestants to line up in front of the judges' stand. Lister eased his stallion into place while the champagne horse skittered sideways and finally came to a halt at the end of the row.

Rhonda said, "A few shows back, the USDA inspectors disqualified Rogue, said there was scarring on his legs. Tre-horne contested it, sent Rogue to the University of Auburn vet school for a second opinion. They said there was no scar. And Rogue passed the next three inspections, all with industry inspectors. But Trehorne won't enter him today, because the USDA is here, and they'll have to violate him."

"But if there's no scar—"

"They can't say there's no scar. He can't be scarred one week and not the next, so they'll fail him for sure. If they don't, it will be like admitting their last inspector didn't know what the hell he was doing. That's the problem with the scar rule. Nobody can agree on what it means."

"How can they not agree? There's a scar or there's not."

"You said you were a horseman. You know how it is. If your horse bumps his leg on the trailer, is he scarred? Is a scratch hidden by the hair a scar? How about a bump or a row of bumps you can't see but you can feel? How can you tell that from a little row of insect bites? Shoot, one inspector said a scar two-skin-cells thick was still a scar." She gave a humorless laugh. "Some of these guys will call it a scar even if you'd need an electron microscope to see it."

"So Trehorne won't show."

"Not today. But the USDA judges hardly ever come two days in a row—there's no budget for it. They may even be gone by tonight. Then it'll just be the industry judges, and he'll be fine."

In the ring, Jim Lister took his victory lap, the blue ribbon hanging from one side of Troubadore's bridle, then headed for the gate. The others filed in behind him, the rider of the champagne bringing up the rear. As he passed the judges, he gave them an embarrassed grin.

I glanced back at Rhonda. "Does it scare you? I mean, there was that arson a few nights ago."

"Are you sure it was arson?" She looked me in the eye, her gaze clear and impossibly guileless. "You know what they say: Sometimes a fire is just a fire."

"Cigar. Sometimes a cigar is just a cigar."

"Does it matter? They both burn." She touched the back of my hand with her fingertips, a gesture that might have been a promise or a good-bye. Then she pushed herself away from the railing as the steward opened the gate for the class to exit. "Sooner or later, everything burns."

8.

I went back up and plopped into the seat beside Khanh.

"Very dangerous," she said again. "That woman no good for you."

"Don't worry. I couldn't afford her if I wanted to."

I pulled the program book out of my back pocket and ran my finger down the schedule. "None of our players are on until later this afternoon. Let's go check out the rest of the place."

"Okay by me, Boss Man. I thinking a horse show gonna be interesting, but no, it all the same. Nothing but go round and round and round."

"You can't be bored already," I said. "We just got here."

She shrugged. "No problem. Probably, thing get exciting soon."

I wasn't sure I should have brought her. She was bright and brave, and I enjoyed her company, but someone had been desperate or angry enough to set fire to a barn full of live animals. How big a stretch from that to harming one of us?

But if something happened to me, I wanted management of Maverick Investigations to go to Khanh. Since she didn't have her PI license, she'd have to hire someone who did, and to do that wisely, she needed to understand how it all worked. Besides, the showground and campground were crowded, and an overt attack here was a risk I didn't think they'd take.

Not yet, anyway.

I was thinking about these things while part of my brain scanned the grounds for suspicious characters and the part that understood we were having a conversation put words in my mouth. I thought I was pulling it off until Khanh poked me in the side.

I snapped into the present. "What?"

She pointed to a booth where Zane Underwood hunched in his electric chair watching his wife, his groom, and a pair of volunteers set up the TASA booth. Carlin worked quickly and efficiently, folding T-shirts that read "Walk on—Naturally" into perfect squares, while Gerardo arranged TASA buttons and ball caps on the table, his movements awkwardly protective of his bandaged hands. The volunteers were busy organizing pamphlets, flyers, tote bags, and a stack of coffee-table books about the history of soring. A quick look at their name badges told me the plump woman with the mane of brown frizz was Maggie James, the wiry blonde Sue Blankenship. Sue had a body that said she'd put in plenty of hours at the gym and a leathery complexion that said she'd spent years slathered in baby oil, basting herself in the sun.

Maggie stuck out her hand for a quick handshake. With the other she pointed to her name tag. "Maggie James."

"Jared McKean. This is my sister, Khanh."

Maggie looked us both over. "Well, y'all don't favor much, but there's all kinds of kin. Adopted, step, or half?"

"Half. Need a hand?"

Maggie flashed me a smile that brightened her plain features. "Helping hands are always welcome."

Khanh pointed to Maggie's feet. "Love you boots!"

They were shiny calf-high leather, tinted with purple and indigo and painted like a pair of Ukrainian Easter eggs. Maggie spun to give us a better view and said, "Thank you! They were way too expensive, but I saw them and it was love at first sight. Some people think they're a bit much, but every time I look at them, they make me smile." As if to prove her point, she grinned again. "Awful nice of y'all to lend us a hand."

A muscle in Gerardo's jaw twitched, but he didn't look up. "We have everything under control."

Carlin gave him a sidelong glance, then said to me, "I didn't expect to see you here."

I gave her what I hoped was a winsome grin. "I'm full of surprises."

"You want to help? Fine. You can carry the coolers from the trailer." She dropped the shirt she was working on and went to fetch a dolly propped against the back wall of the booth. "Gerardo, why don't you show him where they are?"

"As you wish, Señora." He nudged a cap into alignment on the table, gaze lowering a beat too late to hide the resentment in his eyes.

"I help here," Khanh said. While she went to help arrange the tote bags, I took the dolly and followed Gerardo back to the campground. He moved with an easy grace, glancing around with that attentiveness to surroundings that said he was, or had once been, a man who lived with the constant threat of bullets from the darkness. Soldier, cop, assassin, witness protection . . . there was a long list of possibilities, all of which made me hope his loyalty to the Underwoods was as steadfast as it seemed.

The Underwoods were in site three, a few rows to the right of our trailer and several rows farther in. They had a Featherlite Country Estate trailer, Villa style. Fifty-three feet of luxury, thirty-three of which were devoted to living quarters.

They'd probably gotten it before Zane's accident. The outside sported a custom paint job with their logo and a pearl-colored horse against a sky blue background.

Tesora, I remembered, their prize mare.

We didn't go inside, so I didn't get to see the upscale interior advertised on the Featherlite website. Instead Gerardo opened a storage compartment at the bottom edge of the trailer. Three coolers shared the space with a box of extension cords and six bales of hay.

I started for the nearest cooler, but he got there first and swung it out of the compartment and onto the dolly, wincing as his hands closed over the handles.

"Jesus Christ, Gerardo." I slid the second out and the third on top of it, slung them both onto the dolly at the same time, wondering how I'd ended up in a pissing contest with a man who had second-degree burns on both hands.

We grappled briefly over the dolly, then broke apart and stared each other down, panting. Each of us had a hand on one handle. There was a fire in his eyes I didn't understand.

I held up my other hand as if in surrender. "What the hell are you trying to prove? And who are you trying to prove it to?"

He glared at me across the coolers. "Why are you here?"

"Because you're a pigheaded ass who doesn't need to be carrying coolers full of whatever the hell they're full of across hell's half-acre."

"Not here." He jabbed a finger at the ground, then made an expansive gesture that encompassed the whole of the showground, and possibly the universe, "Here."

"Investigating the arson. I'd think you'd want that."

"You want Señora Carlin to think you care what happens to her. But you work for them, the insurance company. Your interests are their interests, not hers."

I rocked back on my heels. "Did she set the fire?"

His fist tightened on the handle of the dolly. "Another day, another time, I might have killed you for suggesting that."

"Another day, another time, you might have tried."

He murmured an expletive in Spanish, then drew in an angry breath. "She did not set the fire."

"Then my interests are her interests. Gerardo, I'm not the enemy here."

"So you say," he said, but he took his hand off the dolly.

The weight of the coolers over the uneven ground made the trek back to the booth an Olympic event. By the time we got there, sweat dripped into my eyes and plastered my denim shirt to my back. A restless crowd had gathered around the TASA booth, where Carlin Underwood faced off with three men wearing the same kind of old-fashioned suits and derbies I'd seen in the ring.

Eli stood at the fringes of the crowd, scribbling in a yellow steno tablet. Zane had been relegated to the outskirts, circling the mob in search of a way through, expression darkening each time the shifting crowd closed a gap in front of him. He backed off, a hostile glint in his eyes that said he was thinking of effective ramming speeds.

The guy at the front of the crowd had the thick neck and broad shoulders of a linebacker. He was big but not fat, his chest straining the buttons of his jacket. He looked strong, which he probably was, and he looked ponderous, which I knew better than to take for granted. Sometimes these big guys were surprisingly fast, like charging rhinos. I recognized him from my search the night before. Samuel Trehorne's son, the man Rhonda Lister had called Junior.

He and Carlin had squared off across the display counter, leaning toward each other as if to spew their anger onto Carlin's neatly folded shirts.

Junior's companions were smaller, more like a pair of running backs, raw-boned farm boys who looked out of place in their long jackets and short-brimmed hats. One was fair-haired and thick-jawed, with a nose that looked like it had been broken more than once, the other dark, with thin lips and a smudge of a mustache.

As I pulled the dolly toward the entry gate at the side of the booth, the one with the smudge moved to block me. Beside me, Gerardo sucked in a sharp breath. I paused to set the dolly upright, freeing my hands in case somebody needed to be punched.

Smudge held his ground but took a step back, palms up as if to assure me fisticuffs weren't on his agenda.

Junior jabbed a finger at Carlin. "You aren't welcome here. Nobody but your animal rights kooks is buying what you're selling. Hell, even your own judges can't agree on what's sore and what's not."

"They're not my judges," she shot back. "Most of them are in the Big Lick's pocket, bought and paid for."

He plowed on as if she hadn't spoken, the smoldering anger in his eyes tinged by fear. The fear made the anger more dangerous. "You're like one of those cargo cults that think we're still at war with Japan. Nobody sores anymore, nobody but a few jackoffs on the fringes, but you keep on fighting, even when there's nobody left to fight. Pretty soon they'll disqualify a horse if some asshole judge can *imagine* a scar. When's it ever going to be enough for you?"

She gave him a tight smile. "It'll be enough for me when people like you stop hurting horses."

Junior looked at Eli. "You know everything in those brochures is a lie, right?"

Eli cocked his head. "Lies, damned lies, and statistics. Plenty of those on both sides."

"Idiot." Junior laid his palms flat on the display table and leaned in toward Carlin, close and menacing. "You go on and on about the Big Lick, but you and I both know you can sore a flat-shod horse same as a stacked one."

"Maybe, but it's harder to hide." She waved a hand at him as if shooing away a fly. "Now, much as I enjoy your company, Junior, if you're not going to buy a T-shirt, maybe you could move along."

The murmur of the crowd became an angry buzz.

A sudden movement at the corner of my eye drew my attention, and I turned back toward the dolly just as Smudge braced an oversized boot on the top cooler and pushed. The cooler slid to one side, toppled, and landed with a thunk. A tumble of ice, canned soft drinks, and bottled water poured out, sparkling in the sunlight. Ice melt and condensation darkened the dust.

Smudge giggled, looking toward Junior for approval. "Oops."

Gerardo made a sound low in his throat. I pulled him back by the shirt. "It's just water and soda. Not worth it, buddy."

He shook me off but held his peace. Maybe my victory with the dolly had set a precedent. He bent to right the cooler and retrieve the scattered drinks, and after a moment, I followed suit, watching the argument unfold in my peripheral vision. Khanh came to help. Reaching for a wayward Sprite, her fingers brushed Gerardo's, and she yanked them away as if she'd been burned. He seemed not to notice, his attention riveted on the altercation in front of the booth.

Junior spat in the dirt by his feet and said to Carlin, "You want to be such a do-gooder, why don't you go someplace and champion some orphans? But no, you won't be happy until you kill this breed and put twenty thousand people out of work."

"People like you?" Carlin said. "I'll take it."

His hand shot up, drew back as if to strike. I dropped the soda I was holding and pushed past Smudge to intercept Junior, Gerardo on my heels.

Junior paused, fist trembling in the space between them. There was something in his eyes, half anger, half uncertainty, like a dog that doesn't know whether to flee or bite.

From the wheelchair, Zane made a gurgling sound. His head lolled, and his eyes rolled back to the whites. Then he slumped to one side, twitching like a thousand volts were coursing through him.

9.

The argument forgotten, Carlin rushed to Zane's side. Junior backed away as if Zane's brain injury might be contagious, while the rest of the crowd, uncertain whether to hover or drift away, milled uneasily at a distance like livestock in a slaughter pen. Off to one side, Eli scribbled in his steno pad, not looking at the page, gaze fixed on the drama surrounding Zane's seizure.

Carlin swung the DynaVox to one side and tugged at the Velcro strap around her husband's chest. "Help me get him on the ground."

I yanked open the strap across his lap, pretending not to notice the stench of urine and the dark stain at his crotch. Together Carlin and I eased him out of the chair and onto his side in the dust.

"Get something between his teeth," someone said. "A wallet or a belt."

"No," Carlin said. "Just wait."

While I knelt beside Zane, one knee pushed against his back to hold him on his side, one hand cupped over his shoulder, Gerardo poked Junior hard in the center of the chest. They faced each other off, fists clenched, gazes locked.

Heat rippled off the asphalt and rose like steam around them. Gerardo was the smaller man, but Junior blinked first, holding up his hands and taking a step backward, out of Gerardo's space.

For a moment, Gerardo stood his ground. One heartbeat. Two. Then he drew in a breath and spat on the ground. Swore softly in Spanish and turned his back on Junior, a gesture so full of contempt I wondered if he was baiting the bigger man. If he was, Junior didn't take the bait. A quick nod signaled his men, who drifted away into the crowd, Smudge still grinning at his victory over the cooler. Then Junior went to stand by Eli, watching with smoldering eyes as Gerardo plucked a folded TASA shirt off the stack on the counter and slid it beneath Zane's cheek.

We watched Zane shake for less than three minutes. It seemed like thirty. I looked across at Carlin and said quietly, "Who were those asshats with Junior?"

She spared me a distracted glance but seemed grateful for the conversation. "We call them the Walking Horse Mafia."

Officially, there was no such thing as a Walking Horse Mafia. They were just a bunch of bullies with too much old money, influence, and testosterone. But I remembered what Eli had said about killings and wondered if the title might be more than a joke.

"When you say Mafia," I said, "are you talking about actual organized crime? Graft and blackmail and murder?"

She gave a surprised little laugh and said, "Not unless by blackmail you mean the do-what-we-want-or-we-make-your-life-hell type. This is rural Tennessee, for Pete's sake. Not exactly Godfather country."

I said, "You'd be surprised what sprouts up when there's big money on the table. No threats about concrete overshoes and sleeping with the fishes? You told me you got death threats."

"Hundreds. Mostly e-mails, all from strangers pissed off about my interference in their abuse of horses. *I hope you get raped a thousand times and die a slow and painful death,* or *if I ever see you in person, bitch, I'll ram my hunting rifle up your female parts and pull the trigger.* Crazy ugly stuff."

"They said female parts?"

Her cheeks went pink. "Well, no, not in quite those words. But you get the gist."

"And none of these are from Junior?"

"Junior isn't that imaginative, thank God. He's more like, everybody hates you, you're going to be ruined, you'll be sorry when you've destroyed this whole breed, there's a special place in hell for people like you. That sort of thing."

Somehow I didn't think the Underwoods were the ones driving a stake through the industry's heart. "You think he'd hurt you?"

She frowned. "I'm not afraid of him, if that's what you're asking."

"Maybe you should be."

Zane moaned and blinked. The seed of a smile froze on his face as he looked past Carlin to where Junior in his derby and Eli in his Stetson stood silhouetted by the sun.

"Oh-weh? Oh-weh?" Zane blinked. Frowned. He squeezed his eyes shut, every muscle in his face tightening. "Owennnnnnnn."

Carlin stroked his forehead. "He isn't here, baby. He moved on around this time last year. Right after . . ."

She didn't finish. She didn't have to. Around this time last year, Zane had stepped into a stall with a friendly young stallion and never walked again. As if to dislodge the memory, she gave her head a small shake and said, "Can you help me get him back to the trailer? The seizures wear him out. He's going to need to rest."

And a change of clothes, but neither of us said so.

"Of course," I said.

"Señora." Gerardo's voice was brittle. "You don't need this man. I can help you with Señor Zane."

She laid her hand on his forearm. "I know you can. But you're still hurt. And I need you to take care of things here. No one else would even know where to start."

He looked at me with sullen eyes. "As you say, Señora."

A thread of drool trickled from the corner of Zane's mouth. Carlin slipped the shirt from beneath his head and used it to wipe his lips. Then we lifted him into the chair and strapped him in.

When she'd swung the DynaVox into place, he reached unsteadily for the screen. As her fingers touched the chair's control lever, he typed, "I CAN."

"Baby—"

"I CAN."

She sighed and raised her hands. "Fine."

The chair made its ponderous way across the showground, Carlin on one side, tight-lipped and anxious, me on the other. Occasionally it veered in one direction or the other, and Zane would nudge the lever to correct its trajectory. The constant corrections made our path slow and serpentine, as if we were dodging bullets in slow motion.

"Who's Owen?" I said.

Carlin kept her gaze straight ahead. "Just some stable hand."

The chair came to a stop. "NO," said Zane, via his machine.

"Some stable hand," she repeated. "He worked for Zane's family. Zane's known him since he—Zane, not Owen—was a kid. He and Owen used to go out for a few beers at least once during every show they both went to. Just catching up. Zane's family disowned him when he married me. I think it meant a lot to him that Owen never cut the ties."

"WHERE IS OWEN?"

"He left, baby."

"I'M NOT A BABY."

"Okay, okay, ba-" She stopped, blinked hard. "Okay, Zane. He left after your accident. I don't know where he is."

His eyes welled, and I thought of all he had lost and all he had yet to lose. "I WANT TO HAVE A BEER WITH MY FRIEND," he typed.

She gave a little hitching breath, but when she spoke, her voice was steady. "He's probably just getting his head together somewhere. Coming to grips with what happened. I'm sure we'll hear from him soon."

I said, "He didn't say good-bye? Didn't come to see Zane in the hospital?"

"No, he just took off."

"Seems odd after they'd been friends for so long."

"Not that odd. He and Zane had been drinking the night it happened. I think he felt guilty, like if Zane hadn't been drunk he wouldn't have—"

"NO." The robotic voice sounded like it always had, but my mind heard a strident tone. "NO NO NO NO NO."

"You don't know," she said. "You might not have been thinking straight. You might have been distracted. You might have just been slower than usual."

"NO."

"You don't remember!"

"I HAD A FEW BEERS WITH OWEN I WAS NOT DRUNK."

"You remember that?" she said. "Since when?"

"JUST NOW WHEN I SAW HIM AND JUNIOR IN THE SUN."

"That wasn't him," I said. "The guy you just saw beside Junior was a reporter. Eli Barringer. What else do you remember?"

"NOTHING." His chin trembled. He pushed the lever, and the chair hummed forward and resumed its slow serpentine.

Their trailer had been adapted with a double-wide door and a wheelchair lift. She rode up on the lift with him, and I took the steps into a living area with hardwood floors, maple cabinets, a breakfast nook with leather love seats, and a hospital bed where the sofa would normally be, across from the flat screen TV and the electric fireplace. Swanky digs. You could have fit two of my trailer in theirs, but the hospital bed and the oxygen tank beside it were reminders that swank could be an empty pleasure.

Carlin saw me looking at the heavy silver tank and said, "The seizures deplete the oxygen levels in his blood. Sometimes if the seizure goes on a long time and he's really groggy afterward, the oxygen helps." She pushed the DynaVox aside and knelt to take off Zane's shoes. With an angry moan, he shoved her away.

"Zane—" She rocked back on her heels and squeezed her eyes shut. When she opened them and spoke again, she'd erased the note of annoyance from her voice. "Honey, I need to get you cleaned up."

His chest hitched, and he looked away, his hand moving to cover his crotch. I tried not to see the humiliation in his eyes as I helped his wife lift him out of the chair and into bed.

She forced a smile. "I can take it from here. Plenty of practice."

I stepped outside while she undressed him and tucked him into bed. As I closed the door, I heard his muffled sob.

Carlin came out twenty minutes later. She blinked in the bright August sunlight. "I get why he's so angry. Really, I do. But . . ." She made a helpless gesture.

"But it's wearing," I said.

She nodded. "I get so tired sometimes. Sometimes I think, if I could just talk to Zane about all this . . . But the one person I'd want to talk to most about it is the one I can't talk about it with."

"Why can't you talk to him about it?"

"Are you serious? He's going through enough. He doesn't need to listen to me whine. And . . ." She looked down, picked at a fingernail. "It's like he's two different people. The old Zane, and . . . someone else."

"The head injury. It happens."

"That's what the doctors say. That makes it easier to understand, but not much better to live with." She ran her fingers through her short spikes. "Thank God it's not worse than it is. They said he might get verbally abusive or violent. Or suicidal. I don't know. Maybe he is. Suicidal, I mean. If he was, he'd never let me know it. I try to take precautions, but . . ." She spread her fingers, an I-don't-know gesture.

Head injuries were tricky that way. I'd once worked a case where, after a brain injury at a construction site, a guy who hadn't thrown a punch since kindergarten bludgeoned his wife to death with a hammer. That kind of extreme shift was rare, but there was almost always some degree of change.

Sometimes it was hard to distinguish changes caused by brain injury from the normal grieving process. Zane had lost more than mobility and the power of speech. He'd lost his sense of self. The words he'd once used to define himself—athletic, agile, charming—no longer applied, and while he'd one day find his way to a new self, it could be a long time coming.

Carlin hugged herself and changed the subject. "You going to tell your company to honor our claim?"

"I'm working on that."

She tilted her head back, looked up at the cobalt sky. "Without that insurance, we go under. I don't know if I can handle that."

"You can," I said, "but I don't think you'll have to."

She reached out, touched the back of my hand with her fingertips. "Thank you."

"One more thing."

"Why do I get the feeling there's always one more thing?"

"Gerardo. What's his story?"

"Gerardo isn't part of this," she said. "And his story isn't mine to tell."

Her tone said the subject was closed. Maybe she'd tell me in time, but that time was not today. "He's got a past," I said. "It might be relevant."

"Everybody has a past."

She took a step toward me and slipped her arms around my waist. There was nothing sexual about it. She needed comfort, the warmth of another body, a heartbeat against her ear. I held her for a long time.

Then she pulled away and straightened her shoulders. Gave me a peck on the chin. "I have a class in about twenty minutes. Better go get ready."

"No rest for the weary," I said.

She gave me a watery smile. "You can say that again."

By the time I got back, Maggie James was emptying a fresh bag of ice into the spilled cooler, while Khanh sorted pamphlets and Sue handed out promotional buttons: *Walk On—Naturally, Don't be a Sore-Head, I'm for Sound Winners and Sore Losers.*

No sign of Gerardo.

"Everybody okay?" I said.

Maggie chirped, "Oh, we're fine. I've known Junior all his life. He growls a lot, but he's just a big old bear."

"He young bear," Khanh said. "And he very afraid. That when a bear most dangerous."

10.

With the booth in good hands, I looked at the schedule and said to Khanh, "There's a trail class in fifteen minutes. Trudy Valentine and Carlin are both in it."

"What is trail class?"

"You'll see."

Maggie said, "Oh, you'll love it. It's my favorite class. I hope Carlin makes it in time. She just called to let us know how Zane is and get Gerardo to have Tesora ready for her at the gate. Poor girl. And poor, poor Zane. My heart just goes out to those two. But she told me how Zane suddenly remembered having drinks with Owen Bodeen. Wasn't that exciting?"

Her chatter made me smile. "It was."

"You going to watch her ride?"

"If you guys think you'll be okay here by yourselves."

"Oh, we'll be fine." She made a shooing motion with her hands. "You two go on and enjoy the show."

We settled onto the bleachers as a bronze-skinned man rode a tractor in to rake the track. While the riders lined up outside the ring, two pairs of ring workers carried out the obstacles for the trail class. It was a complicated course, with a bridge, a gate, a mailbox, three barrels, a series of orange traffic cones, and ground poles placed in a variety of configurations: parallel rows, a box, an L-shaped corridor, and a spoked shape, like a starburst or wagon wheel.

Khanh perked up. "Finally. This look interesting."

I nodded. It was my kind of class, the horses in western tack and simple snaffle bits.

With the course set up, the workers left the arena. The steward opened the gate for the first rider, watched him pass through, and closed it behind him just as Carlin, flushed and breathless, rode up and took her place in front of Trudy Valentine. They were at the end of the lineup, a lucky draw, since it meant they could watch the other riders and strategize accordingly.

Gerardo went to stand beside the railing, arms resting on the bar where Rhonda Lister had stood.

There were six riders in front of Carlin. None rode clean. The first lost his grip on the gate and had to take three passes at it. The second horse panicked at the sight of the mailbox and later balked at the bridge. The third knocked a ground pole out of place in the "L" and another in the spokes. The fourth horse, a black-and-white spotted gelding, bumped several poles lightly but gave an otherwise fine performance, while the fifth made notable errors at almost every obstacle— a displaced ground pole, a missed cone, an overturned barrel, an awkward turn. The sixth did the box before the barrels and was disqualified for taking an obstacle out of order.

"This hard?" asked Khanh. "Look hard."

"I used to do this with Tex," I said. "Takes work."

The sixth rider left the ring, shoulders rounded in a dejected slump. Carlin rode in wearing a white hat with a gold band and a white vest trimmed in gold. Her ice-blue shirt and chaps, both edged in pale blue rhinestones, matched Tesora's saddle blanket. The pearl horse gleamed in the light.

"Oh," Khanh said, a wistful note in her voice. "So beautiful."

I'd never asked Khanh how much her scars bothered her. For the most part, she seemed to have made peace with the accident that had taken her arm and left the right half of her face like a melted candle, but there must have been times when another woman's flawless cheek reminded her of what she'd lost. She'd been a beautiful child, with good bone structure and well-proportioned features. The unmarred side of her face was beautiful still, but I didn't say so. She would have found no comfort in it.

In the ring, Carlin lined the mare up parallel to the gate, bent to unlatch it, then swung it open. Keeping her hand on the top rail, she rode through and turned the horse to face the gate. She nudged the mare a few steps forward so she could close and latch the gate behind them, then turned to the next obstacle, a series of parallel ground poles. She guided the mare cleanly across them and then turned the horse to straddle a lone pole placed at a ninety-degree angle. She took her time. Front feet on one side of the pole, rear feet on the other. A deep breath and a subtle pressure of her right calf, and Tesora side passed slowly but cleanly along the length of the pole.

I stole a glance at Gerardo. He was watching Carlin intently, brow furrowed in concentration, nodding as she paused at the mailbox. Tesora stood on a loose rein while Carlin opened the box, removed the envelope inside, and waved it at the judge. He gave her a curt nod. Too curt, I thought, but maybe I was reading too much into it.

After placing the envelope back in the box, Carlin flipped up the flag and gave the mare an affectionate scratch on the withers. Then on to the barrels. She backed the mare through in a serpentine pattern and turned her again to weave through the cones. Trudy Valentine watched with narrowed eyes.

Tesora stepped into the square. The mare did a 360-degree turn to the left, then another complete turn to the right. One hoof thumped against a pole, which jumped a fraction of an inch. Carlin grimaced and urged the mare out of the box and into a canter toward the starburst. She cantered over the spokes in both directions, then pulled the mare into a halt.

Almost home free. She lined the mare's backside up against the entrance to the "L" and backed through. One to go.

Carlin turned Tesora toward the bridge. The little mare paused, lowering her nose to smell the planks. Then, at a squeeze of Carlin's legs, she walked across. There were a few boos and a smattering of applause as Carlin left the ring.

Trudy Valentine swept past her without a glance. Trudy rode a mouse-gray gelding named Sultan, who wore a black saddle trimmed with silver and a Navajo blanket with lots of red. Trudy wore black jeans and show chaps fringed with silver conchos, a blood-red shirt with a lot of bling, and a black suede cowboy hat with a red rhinestone band. When the light hit her, she flashed like a mirror ball.

Her horse was tall and she fit him well, lean and lanky, with an olive complexion and dark hair pulled into a silvery net. Strong features, maybe Greek, maybe Italian. Something Mediterranean.

Sultan was sleek and sure-footed, with an eagerness that said he knew his job and liked it. They breezed cleanly through the gate and the round poles, then came to the mailbox. He stood still as stone while Trudy pulled out the envelope, showed it to the judge, and replaced it with a flourish. The other riders had raised the flag themselves, but Trudy gave the judge a mischievous grin and turned Sultan toward the mailbox.

"Up," she said, dropping the reins. With a self-satisfied whicker, the gelding nudged the flag up with his nose.

While the crowd, sparse as it was, hooted and cheered, Sultan tossed his head and whinnied, clearly pleased with his own performance. Trudy gave his neck a quick pat. They finished the course without a misstep.

I glanced at Carlin, who stroked Tesora's neck, a frozen smile on her face. The judge announced the winners—first place to Trudy, second to the guy on the spotted horse, and third to the rider who had knocked down two poles. Carlin, with her nearly flawless performance, came in dead last. The steward swung the gate open for the winners to pick up their ribbons and make their victory laps.

With a forced smile, Carlin leaned in and said something to Trudy. Trudy didn't answer, just pushed Sultan into a running walk and went to pick up her blue ribbon.

Afterward, while Carlin and Gerardo trudged back toward the campground, I followed Trudy and Sultan into the staging area, a large indoor enclosure with a dirt floor. Trudy swung out of the saddle and landed on bent knees, her boots sending up a cloud of dust. She was detaching the blue ribbon from Sultan's bridle when I stepped up beside her and extended my hand for a shake.

"Great ride," I said. "That bit with the mailbox . . ." I kissed the tips of my fingers and made a kissing sound. "Bravissimo."

"Seriously?" She had a torch-song voice, rich and warm and throaty. "Bravissimo? Who says that?" But she looked pleased. She gave me an appraising look, then turned her attention to Khanh. "I've never seen you two around."

There were several hundred people in attendance, and at the larger shows, there could be thousands, but I didn't ask her how she could have expected to remember everyone who ever came to a show. I might have been forgettable, but Khanh was not.

I said, "Someone told me you might be able to help me find a good starter horse."

"They told you right. You looking to show, or trail ride, or what?"

"I'd like to show. I like the Big Lick, but I've heard you can't win if you don't sore."

She rolled her eyes. "Fifteen years ago, maybe."

"It worries me though. There was that undercover film on YouTube. A top trainer, cooking chemicals into horses' legs, pressure shoeing . . . If he had to do all that to win, what's everybody else doing?"

"Soring is a shortcut," she said. "A way to make an inferior horse do something it was never made to do. I don't deal in inferior horses. Ergo, no need to sore."

Ergo. You had to like a woman who could drop that into a casual conversation.

I said, "You show in the Big Lick classes, right?"

"I do, and I come out in the ribbons more often than I don't, but that's not all I do. Take Sultan here . . ." She gave the gray horse a pat. "He's not a Big Lick horse—doesn't have the movement—but he's the best damn versatility horse I ever rode." She gave him an affectionate rub behind the ears. "Trail, pleasure, he even jumps a little."

"You train him yourself?"

"Since he was a foal."

"And your others?"

"Mostly I just buy proven winners. Good show horses, good breeding stock. I start with the best, so I can breed the best." It sounded like a marketing slogan, but she seemed sincere.

"Then you don't know if they're sored or not."

"Don't know, don't care." She gave a self-conscious laugh. "That sounds awful. What I mean is, I check them for scars. My vet checks them. I don't buy anything that doesn't look clean. I don't know how they learned the Big Lick. All I know is, once they come to me, they live like royalty." I opened my mouth to answer, closed it as she plowed on. "And before you get on your high horse, let me point out that it would be pretty hypocritical, coming from a man in leather boots."

I cocked an eyebrow. "Defensive much?"

"I know the look," she said. "You're a crusader. But if your delicate sensibilities can't handle the Big Lick, show flat shod. Nobody's twisting your arm."

"No, I guess not."

"Who's this mystery person who steered you my way, anyway?"

"Carlin Underwood."

She snorted. "That explains the delicate sensibilities. It would be a cold day in hell before you heard a good word about me from Carlin Underwood."

"Bad blood between you?"

She tilted her head and gave me a long look, as if to determine how close to the Underwoods I might be. She shifted her gaze to a roped-off area at the back of the building, where three men in jeans and work shirts were conducting inspections for a long line of sullen-looking riders. We watched as an inspector with a *Magnum, PI* mustache shook his head and wrote something on a clipboard. Then Trudy heaved a sigh and said, "She's a wrecking ball."

I lifted an eyebrow.

"You asked about Carlin, so I guess you know about Zane. She got inside his head. Turned him against . . . everyone. Against his friends, against his parents. It broke their hearts. He didn't even come to his father's funeral, and you can bet little Miss Carlin had a hand in that."

"A lot of people seem to share your opinion of her. You heard about the barn fire?"

"Everybody's heard about that." She gave a bitter laugh. "Carlin will do anything to get attention."

"You think she set the fire?"

"Anybody who thinks otherwise is either stupid or naive. Zane's medical expenses must be out the roof. He was all that held their business together. God, that man could charm the pants off an Eskimo in a snowstorm. If that fire was set, I guarantee you Carlin set it. How do you know her, anyway?"

"I'm looking into the fire. Who might have started it."

"A cop?" Her eyes flashed. "So you lied to me."

"No, I'm looking into the fire, *and* I'm looking into buying a horse."

"But mostly the fire."

"That's what pays the rent. But I'm private, not a cop."

"That makes it better." The curl of her lips said it didn't. "Carlin told you I set it?"

"She gave me a list. It was a long list, and you were on it. But you could be right about how it went down."

"You'd say that whether you thought so or not."

From the set of her jaw, I could tell she'd made up her mind, and since she was right, I changed the subject. "How did Zane's father die?"

She stroked Sultan's muzzle, still angry but reeling it in. "Cancer. Pancreatic. It was awful, watching him just shrink away. Like he was being eaten up from the inside." She ran her palm down Sultan's neck. "I guess that's how it is with Zane now."

"That was a hell of a tragedy."

"It was stupid. Zane was one of the best horsemen I ever met, and he broke the first rule of working with horses."

Khanh piped in, "What first rule?"

Trudy gave her an amused smile. "Keep three quarters of an inch between yourself and the horse's hooves."

Khanh frowned, piecing it together.

I said, "It means don't get kicked."

"Well," Trudy said, "Zane broke it pretty spectacularly, don't you think? The Zane I knew would never have been so careless. But then again . . ." She laid her palm against the wide flat part of Sultan's face and rubbed. "He hasn't been the Zane I knew for a long time."

11.

As Trudy led Sultan away, Khanh said, "Sound like she hate Carlin Underwood. You think maybe she set fire?"

"Could be. Like you said, a woman could have done it."

"Could be anybody." A thoughtful look crossed her face. "Could be everybody."

"*Murder on the Orient Express?* I guess we can't rule it out."

"I not familiar *Murder on the Orient Express.*"

"It's a mystery by Agatha Christie. The victim was such a despicable piece of work that everybody on the train wanted to kill him—and they did. They were all in on it together."

"Carlin Underwood have many enemy," Khanh said. "Make everything more hard. You think Miss Valentine right about Mrs. Underwood set fire?"

"No. That's pretty much the only thing I'm sure of."

"I pretty sure too. So what we do now?"

"I think I'll take a look around the barns."

"You not need me, I go help at TASA booth."

Smart cookie, my sister. Maybe she could earn Gerardo's trust, find out a little more about his work for the Underwoods and his previous employment with Trehorne.

Or maybe she was just a good person, and I had a suspicious mind. Or maybe . . . I thought of her fingers brushing Gerardo's, her blush as she snatched her hand back.

"Tell Gerardo hi for me," I said, and grinned.

For a moment, she seemed at a loss for words. Then, with exaggerated dignity, she said, "He too young for me. Too handsome too," and fled.

∽

There were twenty barns in the stable area. Nothing picturesque about them, just rectangular block buildings, each with a covered sitting area and a tack room at one end, and two rows of five stalls each, built back to back with the stall gates facing outward. I wandered up and down the aisles, getting a feel for the players and a sense of the layout. Occasionally a horse would poke its head out of its stall and get a rub or a scratch for its trouble.

Each participating owner/trainer had been assigned a barn, and from the signs and banners, all twenty were occupied. Some had horses in all ten stalls, while others had only one or two. Some of the sitting areas were austere—a couple of chairs and a stack of pamphlets on an end table. Others were elaborate, with fountains, potted plants, and videos of their top horses.

Trehorne had a luxurious setup, with a red carpet, a stand of potted plants, and a wide-screen television showing videos of Rogue's Honor and a few of his other horses. Red velvet cushions softened the lines of a wrought iron bench and matching chairs. The stalls were empty. Waiting for the USDA judges to leave, I guessed.

On the next aisle, a chestnut mare with a blaze stood with her head pulled hard to one side, bridle attached to her girth with a hand's breadth of play in the rein. I'd seen this done at Arabian and quarter horse shows, and I hadn't liked it any better then. Some trainers think it's a clever way to teach a horse to give to the bit. They say that, by turning its head to relieve the pain of the bit on its mouth, the horse becomes more supple and effectively trains itself to give to pressure.

Some trainers are idiots.

But this was not my business. I had no idea whether the horse had been there five minutes or fifty. She was uncomfortable but not in mortal danger. There was no blood at the corners of her mouth. And maybe her owner was on his way back at that very moment to untie her. Still, the blood pulsed in my temples, and the muscles in my neck grew tight.

Trudy would have called it hypocritical, but it left a sour taste in my mouth.

I found a steward, who promised to look into it. Not as satisfying as thumping the owner with a stick, but not as likely to get me thrown into jail, or at least out of the showground.

A few rows down from the little red mare, I came to a barn with a faux marble fountain in front and a blue and silver banner I remembered from my research the night before. Silverwood Springs. Before Dalton's death, it had belonged to the senior Underwoods. Now I supposed it belonged only to Eleanor.

A woman in black jeans and a white lace blouse sat in a stainless steel chair with a pale blue cushion, a Diet Pepsi in one hand and an unfiltered cigarette in the other. She was leathered and lean as a strip of jerky, and the lines on her face weren't smile lines. Still, you could see the beauty she must have been once. Her features were regal, her hair dark and full with a touch of gray at the temples. A wayward strand curled across her forehead. Even if I hadn't seen her picture on the Silverwood Springs website, I would have known her for Zane's mother. That curl would have given it away.

I walked over to the chair nearest her and said, "Mind if I join you?"

"Not at all." She waved away her cigarette smoke, gave me an instinctive smile. "How can I help you?"

The sitting area was decorated with potted silver-leaf plants and miniature blue roses. Above us was a ceiling fan, between us a small white table, where a stack of glossy flyers lauding Silverwood's champions fluttered beneath a blown-glass paperweight.

I introduced myself and gave the same story as before, that she'd been recommended as someone who could help me find a show-quality Big Lick horse.

She arched a brow. "Recommended by whom?"

"Samuel Trehorne, for one."

"Samuel is a good friend, but I wonder why he's recommending my horses when he's got some perfectly good ones of his own to sell."

"I asked for a list. Told him I wanted to make some comparisons. He seemed pretty confident I'd be back."

She chuckled. "A lack of confidence has never been one of Samuel's faults. But you said 'Samuel Trehorne, for one.' Who else?"

"Your daughter-in-law. She said you were a breeder of some influence in the Big Lick crowd."

A chill came into her eyes, and the metaphorical temperature lowered a few degrees. "Carlin finds the Big Lick classes on a par with sacrificing infants to Ba'al. If she thought you were planning to show Big Lick horses, she'd have shown you the door, not offered you a list of recommendations."

"You don't like her much."

"She thinks she's going to get rid of the Big Lick and save the pretty horses. Not the slightest concern that she's destroying an entire industry. It's stupidity. Like burning down your house to get rid of a few spiders in the attic."

"And she convinced your son she was right."

"I had one child, Mr. McKean. She took him from me. Then she turned him against me. Then she got him . . ." She took a long drag from the cigarette. "You've obviously met Carlin. Did you see my son?"

"I spoke with both of them."

"Before he met that woman, my son would not have put himself in a position to be trampled to death in a stall. He knew how to control an animal. But she put those ideas in his head. Made him soft. And it got him killed."

"Zane isn't dead, Mrs. Underwood."

"You said you'd seen him."

"I did."

She took another long drag, then dropped the cigarette onto the concrete and ground it out with her heel. "Zane was an athlete. A consummate horseman. And now he can't even take himself to the bathroom. In every way that matters, he isn't even a man anymore. If he isn't dead, he might as well be."

"Harsh words."

"I loved my son," she said, but her eyes were flint. "I changed his diapers and wiped his nose, and I'd do it again if he'd come home and forget that blonde bitch and her foolishness. You think I'm harsh? Maybe I am, but I didn't abandon my son. He abandoned me."

12.

She was a hard woman, uneasy with forgiveness, and while I couldn't rule her out, I also couldn't rule her in. She had an alibi for the time of the fire, a charity event in the next county, at Shelbyville's Calsonic arena, but that didn't mean anything. Like the others, she could have hired someone to light the match. I listened to a few bitter memories, then excused myself and made another circuit of the stables.

It was a major faux pas to interfere with another person's horse. All the same, when I passed by the third time and the little mare was still pulled tightly to the left, I slipped into the stall and latched the door behind me. She was a pretty horse with a kind eye, and when I came in, she didn't startle or even move away. She just looked resigned.

She was in a long-shanked bit that must have put a lot of pressure on the bars of her mouth, and if I'd had the owner there, I'd probably have punched him in the teeth. Instead I loosened the reins, slipped the bridle off her head, and hung it on the door of the stall. I slid my palm up under her mane, found the muscles of her neck hard and bunched.

I was rubbing the knots out when a voice behind me barked, "What the hell do you think you're doing to my horse?"

The mare flinched, and I spun to see a guy in gray slacks and a matching jacket standing in the doorway, clenching and unclenching his fists. About my age, midthirties, maybe, a little under six feet and the kind of muscular that came, not from a gym, but from long hours of hauling hay and working horses. A black Harley Davidson bandana stamped with skulls circled his head. It looked out of place with the suit.

I said, "I reckon you forgot you had her all bound up like this."

"It's called training, you dickweed. Not that it's any of your business."

"If you think this is going to teach her anything but that her neck hurts, maybe you should try strapping your nose to your knees, see how you feel in a couple of hours."

He snorted. "Hell. You're one of those PETA nut jobs, aren't you?"

"Not even close."

"Whatever you are, get the hell away from my horse."

I gave her neck a final stroke. "As soon as I have your word you won't tie her back up as soon as I leave."

"How about you have my word I'll shove that saddle up your ass?"

His voice had risen, and a crowd was beginning to gather, some looking curious, others resentful.

There was a pressure in my body, a bubble of rage pushing against the inside of my skin.

Let's do this.

I stepped out of the stall and reached behind me to shoot the latch home. He did a little boxer's dance on the balls of his feet. I rolled the tension out of my shoulders.

There was a charge in the air, a current of violence flowing between us as if we were connected by cables. It seemed to pulse for a long moment, while he shook out his arms and did his little dance. Then he launched forward, leading with a fist the size of a rugby ball.

I jigged to the side, and the fist shot past. Time slowed, and I noticed, with the clarity that often comes with violence, that his knuckles were red and swollen, sprouting with thin black hairs. Momentum carried him stumbling past me. As he passed, I clapped a hand onto his shoulder, turned him toward me, and swept his feet out from under him. He hit the ground hard, sending up a cloud of dust, and the air whuffed out of him.

He kicked out blindly, missing me by a yard, and scrabbled to rise.

A flash of red at the corner of my eye warned me. I spun and shot out a back kick that caught a second attacker in the gut. He was a lanky man in jeans and a plaid shirt. No one I recognized. He dropped, retching, to his knees, and an ax kick to the shoulder blades finished him.

I stepped away, glanced around at the crowd. The curious had edged back, effectively turning the semicircle into a corral. Three of the resentful—a chubby guy with a wispy black comb-over, and the two men I'd seen with Junior earlier—had peeled off from the group. The blond man and the guy with the comb-over darted toward me, while Smudge hung back.

The blond one came in fast with a flurry of punches that made my ears ring. One glanced off the bone beneath my eye. Another caught me in the temple, a sudden slicing pain as his ring split the skin, and I put him down with an elbow to the jaw.

I shot out a low side kick at comb-over guy, felt a fierce satisfaction as the knee gave way with a snap. He bellowed and toppled onto his side in the dirt, clutching at his knee.

Where was Smudge?

No time. The mare's owner had found his feet and charged, swinging wildly, blinded by rage and humiliation. The rage gave his punches power. A roundhouse punch clipped my ear, followed by a couple of rabbit punches that sent jolts of misery from my kidneys to my knees.

Enough.

I clapped a hand to either side of his head, yanked down with my hands and up with my knee. Knee met forehead with a satisfying crack, and he fell backward, eyes glazed, blood gushing from a broken nose.

As I turned to look for Smudge, a metallic blur whooshed past. Pain exploded in my side. I dropped, setting off another explosion in my ribs, and rolled away half a second before the shovel clanged down where my head had been.

I came to my feet, my breath ragged and shallow. Little knives shot through my side with every breath.

Smudge grinned, baring straight yellow teeth beneath his mustache. "Gotcha," he said, and drew back the shovel for another blow.

It's only pain, I told myself.

He swung the shovel, and I ducked beneath—*it's only pain*—and slammed the top of my head into his chin. His head snapped back. His eyes rolled. Then his knees buckled, and he fell straight back into the dirt.

I looked around again.

Spectators buzzed with anger and confusion. The crowd had swollen since the fight started, and I glimpsed Rhonda Lister's blonde hair near the back.

Eli Barringer, with a reporter's nose for trouble, had found his way over and was snapping photos with a Nikon camera that probably cost more than a thousand bucks.

Smudge lay on his back, moaning. A thin red line trickled from the corner of his mouth. The blond man blinked hard and pushed himself to his knees, then toppled backward and sat down hard on his rump. Comb-over man cradled his injured knee, eyes wild, tears streaming.

The mare's owner lay motionless in the dust. Blood streamed from his nose and gurgled in his throat. Ignoring the stabbing pain in my side, I grabbed him by the armpits and propped him against the stall door.

Let him bleed. At least he wouldn't drown.

Rhonda pushed her way through the crowd and brushed a thumb lightly beneath my eye. It throbbed at her touch, but there was a pleasant tingle where her skin met mine.

A line of wetness trickled from my temple. I touched a finger to the place the bull's ring had skimmed, and when I pulled it away, my fingertip was red.

"Better get that looked at," Rhonda said. "I'll take you to see Doc."

13.

The clinic squatted between the vendor booths and the arena, a small white building with a red plus sign on the door and a pair of wicker chairs on the concrete stoop. Rhonda pointed at the chairs and said, "Sit. I'll go get Doc."

"I'm fine," I said.

"Humor me." She pointed again. "Please?"

It was the *please* that did it, imbued with just the right touch of helplessness—*I know I can't make you, but I'd feel so much better if you did*. She'd somehow managed a blend of sweetness, sincerity, and manipulation that worked even though we both knew exactly what she was doing. With a dutiful nod, I sank into one of the chairs. A dull ache pulsed through my side.

I ran my fingers over the place where the shovel had hit, pressed gently, and gasped at the sudden sharp pain. Not broken, though, I thought. I'd had broken ribs, and this was a different kind of pain. Less like being stabbed in the side with an ice pick and more like a quick rap with a mallet.

After a while, the ambulance kicked on its siren. I sat in the wicker chair and sweated, listening to the siren fade and trying to breathe normally. It hurt less than it had in the beginning, which I thought was a good sign. My temple had stopped bleeding and begun to itch.

Eventually the door to the arena swung open, and Rhonda came out, followed by a tall man with a familiar mustache and a thatch of dark hair, silvering at the temples. I recognized him as one of the inspectors I'd seen in the staging area. As they approached, I pushed myself out of the chair and extended a hand for him to shake. I realized with surprise that my knuckles were scraped raw. Probably raked in the dirt when I dodged the shovel. The rush of adrenaline had blurred the memory.

Rhonda must have filled him in on what had happened, because as he shook my hand, he gave me a long look and said, "Didn't anybody teach you not to interfere with another man's horses?"

"They tried. I guess it didn't take."

He pulled out a set of keys and unlocked the door. There was a plastic Bugs Bunny on the key chain. He caught me looking at it and said, "A gift from my grandson. Sorry to take so long. I had four other patients to see to. Broken nose, broken knee, probably a couple of concussions. But you'd know all about that. Had to send them over to the county hospital. It's the closest emergency room."

"Am I supposed to apologize?" I said.

"Only if you feel like it." He stepped inside, and I gestured for Rhonda to go ahead of me, then followed them both in. She propped herself against the far wall where she'd be out of the way.

Our host gestured to the stainless steel examining table. "Climb on up there, Mr. . . ."

"McKean. Jared McKean."

"Mr. McKean. Dave Willoughby here. Most folks just call me Doc."

"If we're being informal, most folks just call me Jared. You're an MD? I thought the inspectors were veterinarians."

"We are, but I was an EMT. Then I served as a medic in Iraq and decided I'd rather patch up animals than people. Applied to vet school the day I left the service."

"Sorry to break your streak."

"Hasn't been much of a streak," he said. "Some damn fool is always trying to take some other damn fool's head off."

He pulled on a pair of white latex gloves and took a gauze pad and some peroxide from the first-aid kit. "This is going to sting."

It did. I winced as he flushed the wound at my temple with peroxide, wiped it clean with a gauze pad, and pressed another against the wound, which was seeping again. "Here. Hold this. Firm pressure, not too hard. Just enough to stop the bleeding."

He shone a light into each eye and rattled off a series of questions—*Nausea? Dizziness? Blurry vision?* When I'd answered them all to his satisfaction, he said, "You were lucky. No concussion."

"It wasn't much of a punch. If his ring hadn't grazed me—"

"Lucky punch, huh? They're all lucky punches. Nobody ever gets hit by the other kind." He gave a humorless chuckle, checked the cut again, and replaced the gauze with a butterfly bandage. "That eye's blacking up pretty good too. You'll want to ice it. Another lucky punch, I guess. Take off your shirt."

I peeled it off slowly and laid it to one side, folding it so the drying blood on the shoulder and collar didn't smear on the table. Rhonda said, "You'll want to soak that. Cold water. Heat'll set it."

I told her I knew, and she and Doc exchanged amused glances. She said, "I bet you do."

Doc pressed his fingers to the same spot I'd explored earlier. I was ready this time, but a sharp breath still whistled through my teeth.

"On a scale of one to ten," he said, "how bad does that hurt?"

I thought about it. "Six, maybe seven. Bad, but could be a lot worse. Feels better now than it did."

He pulled a stethoscope out of a drawer and listened to my chest, then listened again with the scope pressed just beneath each shoulder blade. If he noticed the pistol inside my waistband, he didn't mention it. Instead he said, "I don't think anything's broken. Bad bruise, probably. Come morning you're going to wish you'd stayed out of that stall."

"If you say so."

He gave an exasperated huff. "You think you accomplished something? You didn't. All you did was put yourself on their radar." He took two frozen gel packs from the mini freezer and handed them to me. "One for the side, one for the eye. Thirty minutes on, thirty minutes off. You got Tylenol?"

"In my truck."

"Take some. And I'm going to write you a prescription."

"Can you do that?"

He grinned. "Why don't you let me worry about that?"

I looked at Rhonda. "Who was the guy with the horse and the Harley bandana?"

"Mace Ewing."

"Big Lick man?"

She nodded.

"Got a temper on him," I said. "Is he likely to burn down my barn?"

Doc raised an eyebrow. "Why would he do that?"

"Somebody burned Zane and Carlin Underwood's. And I just met a reporter who said people have been killing each other over this stuff for the past forty years."

"People have been killing each other since Cain and Abel," Doc said. "Nothing new about that."

Rhonda said, "Speaking of Zane, I heard he got back some memories today. That's good, right? He's getting better?"

News spread fast.

"I wouldn't read too much into it," Doc said. "Head injury like that, there's only so much better it can get. His whole life long, it could play tricks with his memories." He scribbled something on a prescription tablet and handed it to me. "Here you go. Just might save your life."

Rhonda craned her neck to see what it said: *A wise man keeps to his own business.* I held it up so she could read it, then handed it back to Doc and said, "Sound advice, Doctor, but I'm afraid I can't follow it."

Doc rolled his eyes. Shook his head again. "I figured."

Rhonda smiled. "Hard-headed. I like that in a man."

14.

I stopped by the volunteer booth for Khanh. Maggie James and Sue Blankenship stood behind the counter, Sue tallying the money in the cash box, Maggie straightening the merchandise.

"Your sister's not here," Maggie said brightly. "She heard about the fight and went back to the campsite to wait for you."

I frowned. "How'd she hear about the fight?"

Maggie laughed. "Oh, honey. News spreads like wildfire around here. Usually it's just some old guy with sunstroke or a heart attack. As soon as she heard some cowboy accused Mace Ewing of horse abuse and went all Steven Seagal on him, she knew it was you."

Maggie went on. "Once they told her you were okay, she said you'd end up at the campsite sooner or later and went back to wait for you." She gave me an appraising look. "You'll want to soak that shirt. Cold, not hot."

"I will," I said. "Thanks."

Sue closed the cash box, picked up a cardboard fan on a stick, and waved it in front of her face. "She said you sure knew how to stir a pot."

⌀

I found Khanh in the trailer with the AC blasting, tapping away at the laptop. She looked up when I came in. Thinned her lips in disapproval. "Only here one day, already you fight?"

I shrugged. "I was doing all right until one of them hit me with a shovel."

"You okay?"

"Couple of bruised ribs. Everything else looks worse than it is." I got a clean shirt out of the closet and left the bloody one to soak in the sink. Cold water. "What're you working on?"

"I looking up Mace Ewing." She turned the laptop toward me. Ewing's website. The home page photo showed him working a spotted horse in a round pen. I leaned in to click a tab labeled Horsemanship Articles, then scrolled through a mix of solid training tips and outdated techniques, a weird blend of force-based training, behavior modification, and natural horsemanship.

I said, "He's spouting the rhetoric, but he doesn't understand the concepts. Either that or he's just trying to cover up that he's a jackass."

"You think he set fire?"

"I think he could have. He's got a bully mentality and a hot head."

She shot a pointed look in my direction. "Lot of that going around."

"I'm not a bully." I stopped. Thought about it. "Am I?"

"No." She smiled, pointing to the butterfly bandage at my temple. "But you have hot head sometime."

❧

It took a long time to feed and water the horses. My ribs sent out little jolts of pain as I put out water buckets and flakes of hay, then gave Crockett a scoop of grain and Tex a mash of timothy pellets, senior feed, and high-fat competition pellets. As I was filling the last water bucket, Eli Barringer strolled over, carrying three bottled beers. He lifted them in greeting when he realized I'd noticed him.

Crockett poked his nose under the nozzle to suck up the fresh water, then shook his head, spraying himself and me with shimmering droplets.

"That was brave, standing up to the assholes," Eli said, blinking his bloodshot eyes. "But you're tilting at windmills."

"I've always been told I had a quixotic personality."

He cocked his head and gave me an appraising look, like he was surprised I got the reference. In answer to his unspoken question, I said, "Classic Comics."

"Right." He grinned. "I brought you a brew. One for your sister too, but I guess she's inside."

I rubbed Crockett between the ears and turned off the stream. "Thanks. There's an extra chair in the tack area, if you want to pull it out."

While he rummaged for the chair, I rolled up the hose and turned it off at the source, then tapped on the trailer door and told Khanh we had company.

She peeked out and took the proffered beer, gave Eli a thank-you nod, and disappeared inside. The smell of onions told me she was chopping vegetables, but maybe she was just giving us some space.

Or maybe she needed some space of her own.

Eli unfolded the chair and set it beside the fire pit, then dropped into it and uncapped his beer. "I'm writing up a little something on the fight. Thought maybe you could tell me your side of things before I talk to the other guys."

I couldn't see a downside. He was writing about it either way. I ran it down for him, then said, "What did you mean when you said people had been killing each other for forty years?"

He grimaced. "More than that, probably. But you won't find them listed that way in the official reports. I did some digging, came up with thirteen that looked suspicious. They all went down as accidental deaths or suicides." He ticked them off on his fingers. "Sylvia Whitehead, age fifty-four, big antisoring activist, helped push through the legislation that made soring illegal back in 1970, then spent the next five years going after trainers who sored. In '75, she drank herself stupid and drowned in her bathtub. They say she just slipped under, too far gone even to wake up when the water went into her lungs. But her daughter said there were bruises on her shoulders, like someone held her down."

"That's in the medical report?"

"No, but Trehornes run this county. There hasn't been a sheriff or a coroner here since the 1930s who hasn't been related to them, one way or the other. They've got the media sewed up too. Only one newspaper in the whole county, and guess who owns it."

"A Trehorne?"

"A Barryman, but he's Eleanor Underwood's brother. Which is the next closest thing to a Trehorne. They've got an incestuous little group going on down here."

"Okay, go on."

"Daniel Bitmore, forty-two. Went undercover a year ago for an animal rights agency and got some stellar video of a top trainer soring horses. Died in a hunting accident a few weeks later, shot by a buddy of his, who just happened to be a cousin-by-marriage to the Trehornes. You know the guy, actually. Mace Ewing." He waited a moment for that to sink in, then said, "Some of those Trehornes, it so happens, used the services of said top trainer."

"Nobody thought that was suspicious?"

"His wife screamed bloody murder. But who ever listens to the spouse?"

"Not the Trehornes, I assume."

"She tried to bring a civil suit, but she couldn't find a lawyer who would touch it. The sheriff and his cronies made her look like a fruitcake. Neighbors would harass her, and when she'd call it in, they'd write it up like she was just some crank, or maybe drinking heavy. They destroyed her credibility."

"*Was* she drinking heavily?"

He lifted a shoulder. "She'd take a snort every now and then. Doesn't mean she doesn't know what she's talking about."

"Where is she now?"

"Moved to California. As far away as she could get, she said. She was afraid they'd get to her too, if she stayed around. Then there was Tommy Cole. Thomas, but everyone called him Tommy. He even signed his newspaper articles that way. Wrote a series of articles back in the sixties and seventies blasting the practice of soring. Lot of folks think they were a big reason why the Horse Protection Act passed in the first place."

"Which ran him afoul of the Big Lick bigwigs."

"Then he exposed some of the trainers and owners who were soring." He ran down a list of names. I recognized some of them. Jim Lister. Samuel Trehorne. Dalton Underwood. And David Willoughby—Doc.

I felt a pang of disappointment. I'd liked Doc, and it bothered me to think he'd sored horses. He'd been young then, brought up in a culture that saw soring as commonplace and even necessary, but it made his decision to become an industry inspector less clean. Seeking redemption, or protecting his cronies?

I pulled my attention back to Eli's story.

In the summer of 1975, they'd found Tommy Cole lying face down in a creek ten miles from home, pants unzipped and a half-empty bottle of whiskey in one hand. "The papers said it looked like he'd stopped to pee, passed out half in and half out of the water, and drowned." Eli's cheeks pinked with indignation.

"That's two drownings so far. What makes you think this one was foul play?"

"For one thing, there was no reason for him to be out there. When he left home, he told his wife he was going out to meet a source. She always thought he'd gone out to meet Sam Trehorne and his pals—Doc Willoughby and Dalt Underwood. Maybe some others, but those three for sure would have been there. They were thick as thieves back then."

They'd have been young in those days. Late teens, early twenties. I said, "The police investigated?"

"Yes, and this was Davidson County, almost to Nashville. Well out of the Trehornes' turf. The cops should have been able to make a case, but Trehorne and his cronies all alibied each other, and Doc's wife swore they were all in her living room, drinking wine and playing poker. Jim Lister and his wife were there too. Wife number one. This was just before he went to Texas and traded her in for a younger model."

"One of these things is not like the others. Lister was quite a bit older, wasn't he?"

"In his late thirties. But he was kind of a mentor to them, I guess. Old family ties and all that. Then a woman came forward and said Tommy'd been with her and that he'd had a lot to drink, and well, that was that. Accidental drowning."

"You got some reason to believe she was lying?"

His cola-colored eyes flashed, the effect somewhat diminished by the redness in them. "He wasn't that kind of guy. Nobody who knew him thought so. Sure he'd drink a few beers, maybe a couple of shots. But so drunk he couldn't stand up to take a piss? No way."

"You seem pretty sure of that."

He gave me a cool look and said, "You get a feel for these things. He wasn't a cheater, and he wasn't a drunk. Believe me, he wasn't the type."

He was young and idealistic, and he had plenty of time to learn that you could never tell who was and wasn't the type. Sometimes you didn't even know those things about yourself. I could have told him, but I didn't have the heart to disillusion him. He'd find out soon enough.

15.

Eli gave me ten more names, with case numbers and dates spanning the past forty years. I tapped them into the notepad function of my cell phone, and when I'd finished, he tipped his empty beer bottle in my direction and sauntered back to his own camper. Khanh came out and handed me a frozen gel pack.

"You sit down," she said. "I make the fire."

It was too hot for a fire, but it would be hard to grill the ribs without one.

"I'm fine," I said. "I can build the fire."

Her forehead furrowed. "You think I not knowing how make fire?"

Of course she knew how to build a fire. She'd been cooking over an open flame since she was a girl. I took another sip of beer and said, "Fine. You make the fire. I'll just sit here and be useless."

"You cook later," she said. "Then I sit here, be useless."

⁂

I was sitting in my director's chair, a beer in one hand and the gel pack on my side, when Hap strolled into camp, his sheriff's

106

badge gleaming in the firelight. He hooked his thumbs into his gun belt and looked at me, then at Khanh, who knelt beside the fire pit, feeding twigs to the flames. She studiously avoided his gaze, and after a while, he turned his attention back to me, hitched up his pants, and said, "Mace Ewing says you assaulted him."

"Mace Ewing is mistaken."

"He has half a dozen witnesses, and three of them say you assaulted them too. They all mistaken?"

"Mistaken, or liars."

"Bold talk."

"Bold but true."

His small eyes glittered. "You know what I think, son? I think you have a chip on your shoulder, and when Mace figured to knock it off, you went ballistic."

"I didn't go ballistic. I was in complete control."

"If that's what you call control," he said, "I don't want to see what happens when you lose it."

"Ewing threw the first punch," I said. "I was just defending myself." I didn't mention that raw energy I'd felt pulsing beneath my skin as I'd stepped out of the stall. Mace had thrown the first punch, but I was just as culpable. I'd wanted him to hit me. "If you want a more objective witness, Rhonda Lister was there. Why don't you ask her what happened?"

"She going to tell me anything other than Mace caught you messing with his mare?"

"Depends on how you define messing with her."

"He found you in the stall with her."

"I grant you that."

"A reasonable man might have thought you were trying to steal his horse."

"A reasonable man would have thanked me."

"How'd you figure that?"

"She got her bridle caught on her girth. Funny how she managed it, what with having no opposable thumbs, but somehow she got herself all tied up. I was just trying to give him a hand. Figured he wouldn't want her hurting herself."

"Mace has been training horses since he was in high school. I reckon he knows what he's doing."

I shrugged, thought of the articles on Mace's website. He knew a little about horse training, maybe a lot. But as the pundit said, it's not what you don't know that gets you. It's what you don't know you don't know. There was a lot Mace didn't know. I said, "I guess we'll just have to disagree on that."

The sheriff narrowed his eyes and nodded toward the corral, where Crockett and Tex were munching on orchard grass. Okay, so Crockett was munching and Tex was mostly gumming, but they were both attacking the hay with relish. "Those your horses?"

I said they were.

"Imagine you came home and found a stranger in your barn, undoing all your training, how'd you feel?"

"Depends. Did I go off and forget I tied my horse's nose to his tail?"

"You got a smart mouth, son. Could be somebody's gonna shut it for you one of these days."

"Somebody's welcome to try."

He barked a laugh. "You talk big. So you took down a bunch of shit kickers. That don't make you Chuck Norris."

"Doesn't make me Mary Poppins either."

He hitched up his pants again. As threatening gestures went, I'd seen better. "Seems you got a habit of putting your nose in where it doesn't belong," he said.

"Doc told me that would get me into trouble."

"Doc's a wise man. You should listen to him." He gave me a grim smile. "But somehow I don't think you will."

"I'd be out of a job if I did." I wanted to ask him why the fire trucks had taken so long to get to Carlin's barn, how his investigators had missed the bones among the ashes, why they'd done such a cursory investigation. But attacking him wasn't likely to get me any answers, so instead I said, "Look, I'm sorry about Mace and those other guys. But like I said, I didn't throw the first punch."

"You instigated it when you went into his horse's stall. And, no offense, son, but I saw those guys when you got through with them. They looked like they'd been run through a wood chipper."

"Maybe that makes me Chuck Norris after all."

"What that makes you is a dangerous man. Which means I'm going to have to ask you to leave the showground."

I gave him a long look.

He held my gaze for a count of three, then looked away. "Here's the truth of the matter. I don't care who started that fight. You're the stranger here, and you're the one who went through four guys—guys I've known since they were knee-high to grasshoppers—like they were butter. Even if they were a bunch of shit kickers, I'd just as soon you were out of my jurisdiction, and I'd rather you didn't wait for morning. Got it?"

I sighed and shifted the gel pack, which was beginning to turn to slush. *Thirty minutes on, thirty minutes off.* Time to put it back in the freezer. "Got it."

16.

The sheriff was a big man, and he left a big silence when he left.

"Well," I said. "That's that."

Khanh poked another twig into the flames. "You case just get more harder?"

"Maybe. It was convenient, having all our suspects in one place. But that's okay. We have some options." Not the least of which involved a theatrical mustache, a pair of reading glasses, and a bottle of temporary hair coloring.

She rocked back on her heels and wiped her hand on her thigh. "We going home now?"

"No. You made that nice fire. We might as well put it to use."

Her lips quirked, a hint of a smile. "I go get you ribs."

The ribs came out tender and juicy, with a secret sauce that was just enough spicy and just enough smoky and just enough sweet. We roasted corn in the shucks and Khanh's vegetables—sprinkled with sea salt and drizzled with olive oil—in aluminum foil packets and followed it all with wedges of ice-cold watermelon. If it wasn't the best meal of my life, it was pretty damn close.

It was well after dark by the time I'd iced my side again and loaded Tex and Crockett into the trailer. The air had cooled, and an occasional light breeze ruffled my hair and dried the sweat on my face. It smelled of pine and wood smoke and horses.

I was taking down the corral and trying to ignore the pain in my side when Samuel Trehorne sauntered out of the shadows, looking like a paunchier but less disgruntled version of his brother. Khanh, kicking sand over the embers, looked up, her lips thinning into a disapproving line.

Trehorne said, "That was quite a stunt you pulled back there."

"What stunt was that?" I said.

"Outmanned and on their turf? I don't know if you're brave, impulsive, or just plain stupid."

"I feel compelled to point out that I won."

He laughed. "So you did. Though not without cost." He nodded toward my blackening eye.

"Point taken."

"Nonetheless, you handled yourself well." He gave me a greasy smile. "Word is, you're pretty tight with Carlin Underwood."

I said, "I don't know that I'd call it tight. I helped her move a couple of coolers and get her husband back to the trailer after his seizure."

"Where he regained his memory, or at least some small part of it. Very touching, yadda, yadda, yadda." I wasn't surprised he knew. Maggie had been so quick to tell me about it, it was probably all over the grounds by now. He gave a dismissive wave and said, "Anyway, my point is, you're a stranger around here, and you helped her. I'd say right now you're the closest thing to an ally that girl has."

"If that's true, then that girl's got a problem." But it wasn't true. She had Zane and Gerardo, Sue Blankenship, and Maggie James. Maybe in Trehorne's world, they didn't count.

Trehorne tugged his belt up over his paunch, a gesture reminiscent of his brother's. "I hope she's got a problem, son. And I hope it's going to be you." I felt my eyes narrow, and he hurried to add, "Now don't get all bent out of shape. I'm not asking you to hurt her."

"What are you asking?"

"Carlin Underwood is a thorn in my side. She won't stop until she's brought down my whole family, and I need to know what she's up to. What's her strategy? Who is she talking to? I'm prepared to pay well for the information."

Again, no mention of Zane. Maybe, like Zane's mother, he'd written Zane off as a man as good as dead.

I said, "What exactly is it you're looking to learn? Seems to me like they've been pretty open about what they mean to do."

"What they mean to do is bankrupt us all, and there's no lie they won't tell to get it done. Don't be on the wrong side of that, son." He reached into his pocket and pulled out a check with the pay-to-the-order-of line blank. I couldn't have bought Trehorne's silver stallion with it, but I could have taken a couple of vacations to Italy.

I said, "You know what I do?"

"Private detective. I Googled you last night. Plus, Trudy was most anxious to share the news."

An incestuous little group, Eli had called them. If his suspicions were right, they had secrets on top of secrets. That could breed distrust, but it would also make them quick to

tip each other off. I wondered if Trehorne knew about the
bones we'd found, suspected he did.

I said, "Then you know I already have a job."

"I know you have a colorful history. Not exactly a stickler
for protocol, are you, Mr. McKean? What's a little double dip-
ping to a man who makes his own rules?"

Khanh sent a fierce kick into the fire pit.

I held his gaze. "You shouldn't believe everything you read
on the Internet."

"What about the name of your business? Maverick Investigations? Should I believe that?" He waved the check, as if
drying the ink. "You a maverick, Mr. McKean?"

I imagined him forty years younger, holding Tom Cole's
head beneath the water, and felt a sudden revulsion. Had he
acted alone, then persuaded the others to cover for him, or
had they all been present? Or was this forty-year-old conspiracy just a figment of Eli's imagination—the hopeful fantasies
of a young reporter hoping for the story of a lifetime?

"Technically," he said, "there's no reason you shouldn't be
able to do both jobs. Reporting Carlin's actions to me should
in no way interfere with finding out who set fire to her barn."

"Unless you set it, in which case that would be a serious
conflict of interest."

He grinned. "Oh, I don't think so. Of course you'd have
to cash the check before you sent me to prison. But I didn't
set the fire, so you have nothing to worry about."

He was probably telling the truth, as far as that went. If
he'd had a hand in setting the fire, he'd done it with a pen
and a check. Or he'd called in a favor, or asked one. Either
way, I doubted he'd been the one to throw the match.

"Of course," he said, "there's a very good chance she set
it herself, which would be the best outcome of all, from my
perspective."

I said, "Even if I wanted to help you—" He started to interrupt, and I held up a hand. "Not saying I do, but even if I wanted to, it wouldn't do you any good. Your brother just banned me from the showground."

He gave a dismissive snort. "My brother can sometimes be shortsighted. I can take care of that. Are you in?"

I thought about it, but not for long. When the wind turns in your direction, you unfurl the sails.

I hooked the corral back into place and, ignoring Khanh's disapproving look, said, "I'm in."

Trehorne had been out of earshot for about three seconds when Khanh punched me in the shoulder, sending a shock of pain through my ribs. "We detective, not spy."

I made a show of rubbing my shoulder, then put the check in my wallet and said, "Don't worry. We're not cashing it."

She frowned, pursing her mouth in a confused moue. "I not understand. We work for Mr. Trehorne or no?"

"No, it's just a way in." There was nothing illegal about what I was doing, but it was still dancing at the edge of a conflict of interest. Trehorne was going into it with his eyes open. I'd call Terry later and fill him in so everything would be aboveboard. In my line of work, a conflict of interest isn't necessarily a deal breaker, but everyone involved has to know the score.

"Good," Khanh said. "Minute there, I think you lose you marbles." She circled her index finger around her ear and gave me a proud grin at mastering another idiom.

"Live and learn, Grasshopper," I said.

She frowned. "Yesterday, you call me Obi-Wan. Today I Grasshopper?"

"You have to keep up," I said. "It's my turn to be Obi-Wan."

∽

We sat by the fire and batted ideas around for a while. Then she went inside to wash dishes. "Going for a walk," I said as the door closed behind her. "Maybe I'll check on Zane."

I felt restless and out of sorts. I was no closer to knowing who had set the fire at the Underwoods' barn or who the unnamed bones belonged to, and I was tired. Tired of Samuel Trehorne, tired of Gerardo's suspicion, frustrated that I could do nothing about Zane's loss or Carlin's desperation. It was too early in the game to be feeling this way, but I felt it nonetheless.

Back at the arena, the Big Lick classes were starting, but I didn't want to watch. I'd had enough of them and of the Trehornes. I walked through the prep area where two vets I didn't know were doing the inspections. Doc, I assumed, had gone on break. Jim Lister, holding the reins of a big black stallion, stood in line while the inspector manipulated the lower legs of a copper-colored mare with a flaxen mane. I passed them without speaking and went down to the stalls as daylight faded and the sky turned the color of blueberries. The lights came on with a hum, turning the shadows crisp and dark.

There was no sign of Mace, so I stopped to give his mare a clandestine scratch, then made my way over to Trehorne's block of stalls. Junior was saddling Rogue, while a groom brushed the tangles out of the stallion's mane. The USDA judges must have left after all. Rogue looked off into the distance, still as a statue. The playful animal I'd seen at Trehorne's stables was gone, and in his place was a horse with a single focus—the job at hand.

There was no overt abuse, nothing beyond the usual stacks and chains, and while Junior showed no obvious affection for the horse, he also showed no cruelty. All the same, something about the scene unsettled me. Junior glanced in my direction once, then heaved his bulk into the saddle. It creaked beneath his weight. With a growing sense of unease, I watched him ride off. Then I moved on.

At the Underwoods' barn, a video ran in the empty lobby—Carlin on Tesora, some kind of New Age music in the background. A framed poster with the TASA tenets on it shared wall space with pictures of Carlin and Zane on a variety of high-stepping, flat-shod horses, each more beautiful than the last. Tesora was the crown.

There were no pictures of Rogue.

I started around the corner to the stalls and heard a man's voice from behind the stable. "Señora, you are making a fool of yourself."

I eased to the corner and peered around it, staying in the shadows, pressed against the stalls.

Gerardo stood with his back three-quarters toward me. His bandaged hands gripped Carlin's upper arms, and his back was rigid with anger, or perhaps pain.

Carlin lifted her chin. "I don't know what you're talking about."

"I saw you today. You and the detective. This afternoon."

"Oh, for God's sake, Gerardo. He's just—"

He gave her a small shake, shoulders trembling with barely controlled rage. "I saw you in his arms!"

She put a hand on each of his forearms, pushed out of his grasp. "I was tired and sad and frightened. I needed a friend."

"You have friends," he said softly. "You wanted a man."

The accusation hung between them. His lips were an angry line, his empty hands curled into fists. My muscles tensed, ready to move if he struck her, or if it looked like he might.

Her voice broke. "Gerardo—"

"He carries a few boxes, helps you lift your husband from the ground. Your husband, Señora!" He held up his hands, and the bandages glowed in the lamplight. "Would he do this for you?"

Her small hands clenched. "What is it that's bothering you? That I was in a man's arms, or that they weren't yours?" She reached for his belt, tugged him toward her by the loops. "Is this what you want?" With her other hand, she yanked open her blouse. Buttons flew, and the blouse gaped to reveal small perfect breasts in a white lace bra. A sob burst from her throat, harsh and aching. "Is this what you want? Is it?"

His shoulder muscles bunched, and for a moment, I thought he might strike her. Maybe he thought so too. Then he sucked in a ragged breath and said, "You know what I want."

Gently, he closed his hands over hers and laid her palms flat against his chest. He pulled the edges of her blouse together, tilted her face upward, and kissed her lightly on the eyelids.

"You know what I want, *mi amor*," he repeated, as she came into his arms. "And we both know why I can never have it."

∽

I left them standing in the darkness and walked back to the campground with heavy feet. Things had just gotten complicated.

The night smelled of sugar and grease with an undertone of sawdust and pine. As I neared the camping area, I could see the glow of an occasional campfire, smell burning wood and the singed-fat aroma of grilling steaks.

I passed a trailer where five people sat around a camp-fire in director's chairs, sipping beers and laughing as an old man in a straw hat regaled them with a story about collecting semen from a bull. The light of a television flickered from a nearby camper. Most of the others were dark and quiet, their owners still at the arena or maybe at the cowboy bar in town.

The light was on in Eli's camper, the Dodge parked catty-corner on the far side. There were things I might have asked him, but I didn't care for company. Instead I found myself walking in concentric circles, or as near as I could manage, from the outside edges of the camping area toward the center. I wasn't sure what I was looking for, but moving felt better than not moving, and I wanted to feel like I was doing something.

I felt bad for Zane, and maybe that, more than anything, was what drew me toward the Underwoods' Featherlite. I slowed as I came near it. It was dark inside, the door half open, swinging gently in the breeze.

The hair on my arms prickled.

From inside came two quick thumps and a muffled cry, then a metallic clang and an explosive hiss.

I drew the Glock from my waistband and broke into a run.

17.

I burst through the door of the trailer into shadow. The figure bent over Zane's hospital bed snapped upright, lifting his weight from the pillow pressed against Zane's face. Zane sucked for breath, scrabbled at the pillow with clawed hands. A sliver of light spilled through the doorway and onto the man in black. Even in the dimness, I could see the dark ski mask, both hands on the pillow, no visible weapon.

The hiss was coming from the overturned oxygen canister. Maybe the regulator had snapped off when it fell. Maybe it had been punctured somehow in the struggle. Even if I could have shot an unarmed man in the dark and with Zane in danger of being hit with a through-and-through or a ricochet, there was no way to know how damaged the container was or how much oxygen was already in the air. The charred cockpit of Apollo 1 flashed through my mind, and suddenly the thought of muzzle flash in an enclosed room filling with oxygen was enough to make me slide the Glock back into its place just to the left of my spine. As it settled into position, the man in black flung himself at me.

Time slowed.

I sidestepped, sending a lance of pain through my bruised ribs. He lashed out with an elbow, caught me in the shoulder.

Grunted as I rabbit punched him in the kidneys. A punch to his solar plexus whooshed the breath from his diaphragm. Then, gasping for air, he lowered his head and rammed it into my injured side.

Pain exploded through my torso, as if every bone in my rib cage had shattered, as if all the nerves on my left side had ruptured and been set on fire. The man's weight carried me backward through the open door. Momentum took us past the step and into open air. I hit the ground hard, flat on my back, half a second before his weight crashed onto my chest. His head bounced off my chin. For a moment, I was deaf and blind, nothing but a pulsing black hole of pain. My vision cleared, and I felt his weight lighten as he rolled away and stumbled to his feet.

His footsteps faded as I lay there listening to my heart pound, unable to move. Gradually my arms and legs began to tingle. Another few minutes, and I pushed myself over and onto my knees and vomited. The spasm sent another wave of pain and nausea through me.

Two inches, I thought. If the Glock had been at the center of my back and not two inches to the left, it would have snapped my spine.

I ground my teeth against another small explosion in my ribs and pushed to my feet, then limped back to the trailer on wobbling legs and paused at the steps. I couldn't do it.

My palm found the controls for the lift, and I rode it up, afraid of what I might find. Above the whirr of the lift, I heard Zane's whistling breaths, and a flood of relief rushed through me. He was lying on his back on the bed, breathing hard and fast, the pillow half across his face. A broken nail clung to the cloth.

I pushed the pillow aside. "You okay?"

He shook his head, eyes wild.

"Okay, buddy. Try to slow it down. Breathe two counts in, two counts out. Slow and easy. Now try three." I pulled out my cell and punched in Carlin's number. She answered on the third ring.

"Carlin? I'm at your trailer. Zane's okay. I think he's okay. But I need you to bring Doc."

She was gone before I finished. I put the phone back in my pocket and sat on the bed next to Zane, counting long breaths in and long breaths out until the whistling stopped and his breathing evened out. By the time the cavalry arrived, I was pretty sure we were both going to live, and pretty sure that, for the next few days, we were both going to wish we hadn't.

✍

"He looks okay to me," Doc said, after taking Zane's pulse and shining a light into his eyes. "But you might want to get him over to the hospital to make sure."

Zane shook his head, shot a meaningful look toward his DynaVox.

There were five of us crammed into the trailer—Doc, Carlin, Gerardo, Zane, and me. I'd propped myself against the far wall where no one was likely to bump into my injured ribs. Gerardo sat on the leather sofa, his head in his hands, while Doc sat on the edge of Zane's bed and Carlin hovered beside him, dressed in her show pants and a faded flannel shirt she must have had at the barn.

She handed the DynaVox to Zane, and he typed, "NO HOSPITAL."

Doc shook his head. "You need to get checked out by a real doctor."

"YOU'RE A REAL DOCTOR."

"I'm a vet with an EMT license."

"I TRUST YOU," Zane said.

Doc's eyes misted, and he laid a callused hand on Zane's shoulder. "I know, Zane, and you've no idea how that honors me. But I don't have the right equipment here to make sure nothing's going wrong inside. Seriously, you ought to get checked out."

Carlin closed her hand over his. "Please, baby. You know all the things that could go wrong. Just let them take a look."

Zane's eyes squeezed shut. "FINE," he typed. "DO WHAT YOU WANT."

Carlin ran her fingers over the veins in the back of his hand. "I get why someone set that fire," she said. "They ruin us, discredit me. But why would anybody want to hurt Zane?"

As if she were in the room with us, I heard Eleanor's smoker's voice. *If he isn't dead, he might as well be.* I hadn't fought Zane's mother in that trailer, but that meant nothing. She had money and influence, which meant other people did her dirty work. Would she really try to kill her own son? It was anybody's guess.

"I've given up trying to understand people," Doc said. "That's why I work on animals. Do you need me to call an ambulance?"

"NO AMBULANCE," Zane said.

Gerardo shifted on the couch. His face was ashen beneath his tan, and the skin beneath his eyes looked bruised. "I will drive to the hospital."

"What about you?" Carlin said to me. "You look like fifty miles of bad road."

"Gee, thanks." I flicked my tongue across a split in my lower lip. Tried on a smile.

A hint of mischief lit her eyes. "I mean that in the nicest possible way."

Doc said, "She's right though. You should get those ribs looked at."

"I'm fine," I said.

"Uh huh," she said. "We'll drive you."

"I hate to bring this up," Doc said, "but we need to call the sheriff."

Zane wagged his head from side to side until the wayward curl fell across his forehead.

Carlin snorted. "What would be the point? He'll make a lot of noises like he's going to do something, and then he won't."

"Maybe. Probably. But I still have to tell him." Doc sighed and ran his big hands through his hair. "He's not a bad man, Carlin."

Her narrowed eyes said what she thought of that, but she let it go, as if she knew there was no point in arguing.

"Seriously," Doc said. "Somebody tried to kill Zane tonight. There needs to be a watch set on his room."

Carlin snorted. "I wouldn't trust Hap or his men to guard my outhouse."

I said, "I know a guy."

"He's good?" she asked.

"He's very good. But he's not cheap."

She looked at Zane, his broken nails, his grayed complexion. For a moment, I could see her waver, weighing the economics against the danger. Then she said, "I don't care how much it costs. Call him."

I went outside to make the call, and as I stepped off the lift and glanced around, I saw a small dark lump beside the back wheel of the trailer.

I eased myself down to pick it up, held it up by the edges with two fingers.

A black bandana with skulls on it, still damp with sweat. On the inner surface, someone had scrawled his initials in Sharpie. M.E. The last time I'd seen that bandana, Mace Ewing had been wearing it.

18.

My friend's name was Billy Mean. He'd been Special Forces in Vietnam and now ran a shelter and rehab center for homeless veterans. He was old enough to be my father, but I'd still rather have him at my back than a dozen younger men.

"Be there in an hour," he said, after I'd filled him in and given him directions and an address for his GPS. "As long as these directions don't lead me to the butt end of nowhere."

I grinned, though he couldn't see it. "When you get to the butt end of nowhere, you're halfway there."

In actuality, Braydon County hospital was a straight shot from I-24, half an hour off the interstate on a highway that widened and narrowed from two lanes to four and then back again. The hospital was a block off the main road. Remarkably, there was no wait at the emergency room.

We filled out paperwork. Then Zane and I were whisked to separate examining rooms, while Doc and Gerardo waited in the check-in area and Carlin trailed in her husband's wake.

X-rays showed hairline fractures in two of my ribs. I'd been lucky with the shovel, but breaking the assailant's fall and the head-butt to the midsection must have been too much to take. The doctor, a no-nonsense woman with tortoise-shell glasses and salt-and-pepper hair, showed me the films and said, "There's not much we can do about a break like this. Back in the day, I would have taped you up, which would have made you feel a little better, but as it turns out, could restrict your breathing and lead to pneumonia. I'd recommend staying out of fistfights for the foreseeable future. Another hard hit to the rib cage could snap the bone and puncture a lung."

I looked at her name badge. Dr. Anne Genaro.

"I'll do my best," I said. "But then, I didn't plan on this one."

She tapped her pen on the edge of her clipboard. "You're going to want to take shallow breaths. Try to resist the temptation. Breathing normally is going to hurt, but you should do it as much as you can. And be sure to breathe deeply or cough at least once an hour."

"Why do I think that's going to hurt like hell?"

"Probably because it will." She peered at me over her glasses. "I'll write you a prescription for the pain. You can take an over-the-counter anti-inflammatory if you prefer, but you might as well have the other if you need it."

She scrawled something on a prescription pad and handed it to me. I glanced at it. No sage advice about minding my own business, just an illegible scrawl I presumed would mean something to a pharmacist well versed in code breaking. I thanked her and put it in my shirt pocket.

She said, "Should I be asking what the other guy looks like?"

"Probably a lot better, since he was on top."

"TMI," she said, and laughed. The laugh made her seem more human.

My cheeks warmed. "I mean, I broke his fall."

"I know what you mean," she said. "Next time, let him break his own fall."

"Next time, I'll just shoot him."

She snapped her pen into place on her clipboard. "Don't tell me that. I don't have time to testify at your trial. Or worse, at mine."

"You're not culpable," I said. "Just say you didn't report it because you thought I was out of my mind with pain."

"You are out of your mind with pain. But how about you just don't shoot anybody? That way neither one of us is culpable."

"I couldn't if I wanted to," I said. "Since I'm not sure who the son of a bitch is."

She pushed her glasses up and gave my back a gentle pat. "All kidding aside, they told me what you did for Mr. Underwood. I wish I could give you a medal, but maybe you could settle for a lollipop."

By the time a nurse in *Cat in the Hat* scrubs wheeled me back to the waiting room, Carlin and Gerardo were gone and Doc was pacing like a caged lynx. Window to door to coffee machine and back again. He paused in his trajectory when the nurse tipped me out at the doorway.

He said, "Is that a Tootsie Pop?"

"I was a very good boy. How's Zane?"

"They're moving him to a regular room for observation. We're supposed to join them there. Room 318. What did they say about your ribs?"

"Cracked in two places, but as long as I don't get hit again, I should be okay."

He laughed without mirth. "What are the odds of that? You scared this guy off, but there's no way he's not going to try again."

"He wasn't trying for me," I pointed out. "Seems like if we can keep someone on Zane and Carlin, we can put a kink in his plans."

"You don't know what he's capable of."

"No, I don't. Do you?"

He hesitated. Then he spread his big hands. "I know he tried to suffocate a crippled man. I'm guessing he's not the type to lose sleep over collateral damage."

The elevator opened on a tiled corridor, a window at one end, an open T at the other. Room 318 was three doors down and across the hall. Carlin leaned against the wall outside Zane's room. Her head was bowed, her fists clenched. She looked up when she heard us coming. "Sheriff's in there with him, said he needed to take his statement right now, without me. And him so wrung out he can hardly hold his head up. I'm so mad now I could spit."

I didn't answer, just put my fingertips against the door and pushed. The sheriff, standing beside Zane's bed with his arms crossed, looked up with a scowl. "I'll get to you soon enough."

"If we were going to taint each other's statements, we'd have done it by now."

"I know that. I just want to hear what happened while it's still fresh on your minds." His frown deepened. "Not that I owe you an explanation."

"No, you don't. I just popped in to make sure you didn't have a pillow over his face."

He looked at me through narrowed eyes. "And why would I do a thing like that?"

"Family business. Your brother has a few thousand reasons. Maybe a few million."

"You overestimate Zane Underwood's importance."

"He's a small cog in the cosmos," I acknowledged. "But people hardly ever try to kill you if they don't think you're important."

From the bed, a tinny voice said, "SILVER LINING. FIRST TIME IN A YEAR I FEEL IMPORTANT."

The sheriff shifted his weight, looked at his feet. "I reckon I'm done here, Zane. You sleep tight." He looked at me. "Okay, McKean, let's take a walk."

I would have made a smart-ass comment about not being that kind of guy, but I didn't feel up to it. I held the door so he could pass. My plan to fall into step beside him was foiled by a protest from my battered ribs. I sucked in a sharp breath through my teeth and dropped back. I might have tried to push through the pain, but there was no upside to stressing my body any further tonight. He could damn well trudge along with me.

He gave Carlin a stiff nod as we passed her, gave another to Gerardo as he stepped out of the elevator with three cups of coffee in his hands. No sign of Doc. I supposed that, having delivered me to Zane's room, the lucky bastard had headed back to catch a few hours of sleep before sunrise.

"Good thing you went by Zane's trailer when you did," the sheriff said, as we plodded through a warren of antiseptic corridors. He'd lowered his voice, but it sounded loud in the nighttime quiet, a quiet underscored by the soft hum of machinery and the occasional beep of a monitor. "What were you doing there anyway?"

"I don't know exactly. I wasn't getting anywhere with the investigation. Too many suspects, which isn't much easier than not enough."

"So you . . . what, went there to hash out possibilities? With Zane?"

"His body's broken, not his mind."

His shoulders slumped. "Point taken."

"But I didn't go there to see Zane. Not specifically. I just needed to do something. I walked a grid, and I ended up there. And the door was standing open."

We passed a sitting area, two cushioned chairs and a matching love seat, but neither of us suggested stopping there.

"Where were Carlin and Gerardo?"

"The arena, I presume. Or maybe at the stables."

He said, "Run through it with me."

I did, leaving out the argument I'd witnessed between Carlin and Gerardo, and when I'd finished, he said, "You never saw this guy's face? Never heard him speak?"

"No."

"Big guy, little guy?"

"He felt big when he landed on my chest, but I'd say average overall."

"Not a big guy."

"No, and I get where you're going with that. It wasn't Junior, but that doesn't mean he or his father didn't pay to have it done. I found this on the ground outside the trailer. You might be able to get some DNA from it."

I pulled the bandana from my pocket and handed it to him. To his credit, he didn't bust my chops for picking it up. He must have known as well as I did that, if I'd left it there, it would have been long gone before he or his crew arrived to work the scene.

I said, "Mace Ewing's tight with Junior, isn't he? At least, he runs with the same thugs."

His eyelids twitched. "You already made up your mind Junior's behind all this?"

"No. Have you already made up your mind he isn't?"

He paused, midstride, back stiffening. "This is the second time tonight you've implied I'm a dirty cop."

"You made it pretty clear you look after your own."

"The people of this county are my own. And you're damn right I look after them."

"Does that include Dan Bitmore and Sylvia Whitehead?"

His voice was chilly. "You've been talking to Eli Barringer."

"He says both of them were antisoring activists."

"Last time I heard, that didn't make you immortal."

"He says there were bruises on Sylvia Whitehead's shoulders."

"He says a lot of things. He's so damn hot to prove his dear old granddaddy was murdered—"

"Wait a minute. His grandfather?"

"Didn't tell you that part, did he?" His grin was vicious. "Tommy Cole was Barringer's grandpa. The kid never even met Cole, but to hear him tell it, his grandfather was the next best thing to Jesus. Did everything but walk on water."

"You disagree?"

"I was fifteen when he died. I didn't know him much, except to know he was a threat to us. But he was just a man, and men have feet of clay."

"Eli thinks Doc and your brother killed him and then alibied each other."

"Don't forget Dalt Underwood and Jim Lister. Takes more than two for a good conspiracy. But let me tell you something, Mr. Private Dick." He poked me in the chest with his index finger, and a wave of pain surged through my body.

I gasped through gritted teeth.

He poked me again and said, "My brother didn't murder Tommy Cole. And when they pulled Sylvia Whitehead from that bathtub, her shoulders were as white as buttermilk."

19.

He stopped at the elevator just as Eleanor Underwood and Trudy Valentine stepped out of it. Billy Mean came out behind them, and the two women exchanged anxious glances. I guessed sharing an elevator with him was one thing, being followed out of it another. The sheriff didn't seem surprised to see the women, but he hadn't been prepared for Billy.

Billy was a big man but not a tall one, an inch or two below my six feet. His beard and mustache were clean but not trimmed, and in his camo pants and a Shrine of the Silver Monkey T-shirt, he looked like a fugitive from *Duck Dynasty*. A web of thin scars etched his face, neck, and hands, where he'd once been shoved face-first into broken glass.

"Billy," I said.

The women, looking relieved that he wasn't some random stranger, stepped aside to let him pass.

"You look like shit," Billy said. His big paw hovered over my shoulder as if it had started to give me a pat and then thought better of it.

I said, "You look like a lifeboat to a drowning man."

The sheriff lifted his eyebrows and said to me, "You know this guy?"

I laughed. "He's practically my father."

"I'm too young and too good lookin' to be your father," Billy said. "But I appreciate the sentiment."

"I hate to bail out on old home week," the sheriff said, "but that's exactly what I'm gonna do. Try not to get yourself killed tonight, Mr. McKean." With this reassuring advice, he tipped an imaginary hat toward the women. "Ladies."

When the elevator doors had closed behind him, Trudy glanced at her companion. Trudy was a strong woman, but there was no doubting who was alpha in their friendship. Eleanor didn't look alpha now though. She looked lost.

After a moment, Trudy looked at me and said, "How is he?"

"Better than somebody planned for him to be. But he's pretty wrung out. They're keeping him overnight for observation."

A sad, strangled sound burst from her throat. It cut through Eleanor's fog and snapped her head around. "Oh, for God's sake, girl, don't make a fool of yourself."

Trudy's cheeks flushed. "I'm sorry. I just—"

"You *just* might want to focus on your young man and let go of this torch you're carrying for my son. Fat lot of good he'd be to you now, even if he wanted you."

Trudy shot her a look that could have scorched earth. "Just because I care what happens to him doesn't mean I'm carrying a torch."

I said, "This young man she's talking about . . ."

"Is none of your business," Trudy said.

"Is Mace Ewing." Eleanor smiled, but there was no kindness in it. I sensed this argument had been going on between them for years and that their relationship was something both more and less than friendship. Something familial, with all the warts and baggage that went along with that.

Trudy glared at me. "What are you? Sodium pentothol? You just say the word and people spill their guts to you?"

Billy bobbed his head affably. "That he does. It's sort of his super power."

"One of many," I said. "Hold tight, all of you. I'll go get Carlin."

Zane's room was dim when I pushed open the door. Carlin slumped in the chair beside Zane's bed. Gerardo stood behind her, a cup of coffee in one hand, the other resting on Carlin's shoulder. Her palm rested on the back of his hand. A sweet tableau. When she saw me at the door, she moved her hand away.

"My buddy's here to guard the room," I said. "But he's not alone."

"That's good, right? He brought somebody to trade off shifts with?" I gave my head a small shake, and she put her head in her hands and said, "Oh no."

By the time she came out, she was composed.

Eleanor looked at Carlin's frayed shirt and smirked. Carlin gave her a frozen smile and said, "He's sleeping now. You can't go in."

"I'm his mother," Eleanor said.

Carlin laughed. "First sign I've seen of that."

The words hung in the air and charged it. For a moment, no one breathed. Then Eleanor's hand shot out.

The slap echoed in the corridor.

Carlin put a hand to the reddened palm print on her cheek. Softly, she said, "I'll let that go, for Zane's sake."

As if invoked by the sound of his name, Zane's voice called from inside, "Ah-weh! Ah-weh!"

A brief hesitation, then Carlin slipped inside. Her muffled voice spoke, low and brittle, answered by Zane's mechanical proxy. After a while, she came out, red-eyed, and said, "He wants to see you both. Eleanor, you first. Ten minutes. If you're not out by then, I'm coming in after you."

Billy looked at me. I shrugged. "I don't think she'll smother him herself. Not with all these witnesses."

Eleanor's spine stiffened. With a brittle glance over her shoulder, she shoved the door open and stalked inside. Gerardo, on his way out, stepped out of her path, and she plowed through the space where he'd been as if his deference were assured, or as if, had he stayed where he was, she could have walked right through him.

"Piece of work," Billy said.

Carlin rubbed her temples. "You have no idea."

While we waited, I made introductions. Billy stationed himself by Zane's door, and Carlin sent Gerardo in search of a vending machine. "Please?" she wheedled, and the look in his eyes said he was as susceptible to that word, in that tone of voice, as I had proven to be. "I'm dying for something chocolate."

I looked at Trudy. "Mind if we go talk?"

"I want to be here when Eleanor comes out."

"It won't take long. We can go to the end of the hall so you can keep an eye on the door."

She hesitated, then said, "You saved his life tonight. I guess that's worth a conversation. But make it quick."

She matched her pace to mine without comment. Neither of us spoke until we were out of Carlin's earshot. Then I said, "Tell me about Mace."

She cocked her head. "About Mace, or about me and Mace."

"Both. Either."

"You can't think he did this." She nodded toward Zane's door.

"He could have. I didn't see him beforehand, and whoever did it was smaller than Junior." And then there was the bandana.

"Mace is a big guy," she said.

"I'd put him on the larger end of average," I said. "I wouldn't say he's at the top of the list, but size doesn't rule him out."

"You don't know him."

"I know he has cronies. One of them hit me with a shovel."

"Cronies. You're making him out to be some kind of super villain. He's not like that."

"So humor me. Tell me what he *is* like."

"There isn't much to tell. I like him. He likes me. He's into horses, and he doesn't sore." She gave a small, humorless laugh. "He also doesn't win, but then, I guess you can't have everything."

"No surprise there, since he doesn't know jack about training."

"He knows jack," she said, "just not much more than jack. But that I can help him with."

"Do you know where he was when Zane was attacked?"

"It would be convenient if I could say he was with me," she said. "But he wasn't. Probably in his trailer, probably drinking. He does that a lot since Dan died."

Dan Bitmore, the man Mace had shot. "What a catch."

She lifted her chin. "So he's going through a rough patch. So what? He's not an angel, but he's not a killer either. You want to know about that arson at Zane's place, you might start looking closer to home."

"You still think Carlin set it?"

"Maybe not. Your new girlfriend has a reasonable theory about the soring chemicals, that Carlin had nothing to gain and everything to lose by using them, so now I think maybe fifty/fifty."

"My new girlfriend?"

"Word spreads fast, and no one has to be a mind reader to see her making goo-goo eyes at you." She batted her lashes as if to make a point.

"Nothing's going on with me and Rhonda. She just walked me to the clinic, for God's sake."

She ignored that. "Rhonda likes her men, and history would indicate that you're her type. But you know what she likes even more than men?"

"No, what?"

Her lips twitched with amusement, a smile without good-will. "You seem like a smart guy. I thought you would have figured it out by now. The girl likes fire."

20.

The door to Zane's room opened, and Eleanor came out. Her back was rigid, her jaw tight. She walked like something hurt inside.

"You're up," I said to Trudy.

She took a deep breath. Said, "It isn't true, you know."

"What isn't true?"

"What Eleanor said. About me carrying a torch for Zane. He did what he did, and he chose who he chose, and I'm not fool enough to think things have changed just because he's in that chair and she's humping the help."

"She's not humping the help." The heat in my voice caught me by surprise. She wasn't saying anything I hadn't suspected—how Carlin had asked Gerardo for help with the lemonade, the look of resignation in Zane's eyes, the tableau by Zane's hospital bed. But I'd heard them at the stables, and whatever was between them, I didn't think they'd acted on it yet.

"Little Miss Perfect," Trudy said, spinning away from me. And over her shoulder, "Maybe she's not as perfect as you think."

Little Miss Perfect had propped herself against the wall across from Billy. She yawned and slapped at her cheeks with her palms as Trudy pushed into Zane's room. Her eyelids drooped, the adrenaline that had carried her this far running low.

Eleanor walked stiffly to the window at the other end of the hall, fumbled with a cigarette, then looked around as if realizing where she was and put it back into the pack. I went to stand beside her and said, "What did he say to you?"

"Nothing relevant."

"It's hard to say what is and isn't relevant."

"He told me he loved me," she said, "but that I was dead to him until I learned to love his wife."

"And what did you say?"

"I told him it would be a cold day in hell." She turned back to the window, lips trembling, staring silently into blackness.

∽

I went to stand by Billy for a while, making small talk, then finally gave in and peeked inside Zane's room. Trudy perched at the edge of the bedside chair, her hand over Zane's. The look on her face said her feelings for him were more complicated than she wanted me to believe.

Voyeurism was a part of my profession. Still, something turned me from their private moment, and I stepped back, pulling the door closed quietly.

"Childhood sweethearts," Carlin said without emotion. "They were engaged when I met Zane. Does that make me a home wrecker?"

"You've been married for eight years. It might be time to let that particular piece of baggage go."

"Hard to do," she said, "when people keep throwing it back at me." She scrubbed at her face with her hands. "Oh, God. I hope he's going to be okay."

Gerardo came back with the chocolate, spoke quietly with Carlin, then walked over to me and jerked his head toward the elevators. "You have no vehicle here. I will take you to fill your prescription and drive you back to your camp."

I thought suddenly of Khanh, and a sense of shame washed over me. Not because I hadn't called to tell her where I was, but because, in the excitement of the attack and its aftermath, I'd forgotten her completely.

⁀∽

She was waiting for me when I got back to the trailer. She sat on the little pull-out step, knees tucked up, her good arm wrapped around them like a little girl at story time. Her eyes looked tired and hurt and angry.

"I'm sorry," I said. "I should have called you. I have no excuse."

She rested her chin on her knees. It should have made her look relaxed, but it didn't. She said, "I hear somebody try to kill Mr. Underwood."

The Big Lick crowd had a hell of a grapevine. And why not? Doc had told the sheriff, and the sheriff had told God knows who. There was no way to keep a lid on a thing like that.

I said, "Someone tried. It didn't work."

"Because you catch."

"I didn't catch. He got away."

She rocked a little on the step. "I have something to say."

"Okay."

"I come here, you, me, not like each other much. You help me find my daughter. Bring mother here, buy medicine, give us place to live."

I knew all this, and wondered where she was going with it. "You give me work, say you big PI, need help in office." "So?"

"So? I go to work, think you, me, good team. You say you work alone, big joke. Everybody laugh. But now I think maybe not so big joke." She pushed herself off the step and came to cup my chin in her hand. Ran her thumb lightly across the bruise beneath my eye. "I wait here long time, worry about you. Maybe someone kill you. Hurt you bad. And I not know because you work alone."

"Khanh—"

"I know you not really need me. Only say you do so I feel . . . useful. Give you reason to give us everything."

"That's not true. I mean, it was at first. But now . . ." I smiled, thinking of the chatter from the back room of the office, of the spicy Vietnamese meals Phen made for me, Khanh's coffee so thick and sweet. They'd helped me heal and banished at least a few of my ghosts. But I didn't tell her any of that. It wasn't what she wanted to hear. Instead, I said, "Khanh, you're the best thing that ever happened to Maverick Investigations. You think I'd have tripled my income without you?"

I don't know what she saw in my eyes, but she stared into them for a long time, then gave me a small smile and said, "Okay, boss man. Next time, you call."

She turned and went inside, back straight, shoulders square, a small one-armed woman with a fierce spirit.

I wondered again if it had been a mistake to bring her along. I wondered if I could protect her from whoever had tried to kill Zane and who, after tonight, might have my sister and me in his sights.

21.

There was one bed in our living quarters. I gave it to Khanh. Then, steeling myself against the pain in my ribs, I put the horses back in the corral, pulled my sleeping bag and air mattress out from behind the seat of my truck, and slid them into the bed of the pickup. While the battery-powered compressor filled up the mattress, I mulled over what Eli had said about the murders.

Thirteen suspicious deaths over a period of forty years. All people who, like Carlin Underwood, had taken on the Big Lick community. If Eli was right, someone, or several some-ones, had been both patient and clever.

And lucky.

A twig snapped, and as I turned to look, a figure came out of the darkness. Moonlight gleamed off mother-of-pearl buttons and a tumble of blonde curls. I recognized the curve of her hip, the swell of her breasts.

Rhonda Lister.

She laid her forearms on the side of the truck bed and said, "I came by to see how you were. That was a nasty hit with the shovel."

"I'm good. Thanks for getting the doc for me."

"No problem. Just call me a Good Samaritan." She went around and put her palms on the open tailgate, boosted herself up. "Let me help you with that."

There wasn't much left to do, but she crawled across the truck bed and knelt beside me, reaching for the sleeping bag. While I unhooked the compressor, she unzipped the sleeping bag and spread it across the mattress, then gave it a gentle bounce. Her hair smelled of some lemony shampoo.

"This is nice," she said. "But don't you have a sleeper in the trailer?"

"My sister's using it."

"It's a good night for sleeping under the stars anyway." She smoothed the sleeping bag with her palm. "I don't suppose you'd like a little company."

"I don't draw too many lines," I said. "But I do have a few, and one of them is, I don't sleep with married women."

She made a small, disappointed sound. "I could tell this afternoon. You have that look."

"What look is that?"

"I don't know. Something chivalrous. I think that's what I liked about you. Only . . . Jim's out drinking with the boys. He won't be back for hours. Could we just, you know, maybe just lie here and talk?"

"Your husband might have a problem with that."

"He won't. Discretion is important to him, but he gives me a certain amount of freedom."

I sighed. "I don't know, Rhonda. News spreads like typhus around here."

"Plausible deniability," she said. "We aren't even going to take off our clothes." She pulled off her boots and lay down on her side on top of the sleeping bag. "Please?"

It had worked so well before, I guess she thought she'd try it again. I sat down on the edge of the mattress and took off my own boots. Watched her lying there with the moonlight on her face.

"I heard what happened to Zane," she said.

"Already?"

"Well, the sheriff called Samuel and Eleanor, and Eleanor called Trudy, and then Sam called Jim. So . . ."

"The grapevine," I said.

"Exactly. Zane's all right?"

"What did the grapevine tell you?"

"That they kept him in the hospital. For observation, they said."

"Then you know as much as I do." I pushed a stray curl back from her forehead.

She smiled. "Do you have someone at home? You do, don't you? Guys like you, they always do."

"She's on sabbatical in South America. Building a school for underprivileged kids."

"Very noble." She rolled onto her back. "We have that in common. We both have someone, and we're both alone."

"We made choices," I said, watching the rise and fall of her breasts as she breathed. "And now we live with them."

I didn't tell her that Elisha and I had made no long-term commitments or that increasing references to someone named Roderigo had crept into her infrequent texts and e-mails. It seemed wiser to keep as many barriers as possible between myself and Rhonda Lister.

"You lied to me today," Rhonda said. "You said you were looking to see what the Walking Horse thing was all about."

"That wasn't a lie," I said.

"You didn't say you were investigating that fire at the Underwoods'."

"Sin of omission."

"What's it like, investigating crimes?" She gave me an appraising look. "Did you ever kill anyone?"

"When I had to. It's not something I'm proud of."

"You live a dangerous life." She patted the mattress beside her. "Join me? I promise not to bite."

"It's not biting I'm afraid of."

She smiled. "Are you afraid of me?"

I eased onto my back beside her. "Terrified."

"Liar." She rolled onto her side again, slid a finger between two buttons of my shirt. I sucked in a breath, and a pain shot through my side. My groin throbbed. She toyed a button open and slipped her hand inside.

I said, "In fact, you might just be the most dangerous person at this show."

She propped herself on one elbow, left her other palm on my chest. My skin, beneath her hand, grew warm, then hot. "Why, Mr. McKean, that's the nicest thing anyone's ever said to me."

I lifted my arm, and she slid closer, her breasts against the side of my chest, her knee over my thigh. The pain in my ribs was a dull throb, the stirring at my groin a pleasant ache.

She said, "You think one of us started that fire?"

"I'm not ruling anything out yet."

"Have you decided which one?"

"Not yet. Could be a Trehorne. Could be Mace Ewing. Or even Trudy. She doesn't like Carlin much."

"Can you blame her? She and Zane planned to get married from the time they were kids. Then, three months before the wedding, Zane met Carlin."

"Just like that? He meets Carlin, and bang, he dumps Trudy?"

"I hear there was a lot of it's-not-you-it's-me stuff but basically, yes." Her fingers made a lazy circle on my chest. "Trudy's started hanging out with Mace, but people say she's still pining for Zane." She laughed softly. "Of course, they say it behind her back."

"You think she's capable of setting that barn fire?"

"I think anybody's capable of anything," she said. "If you dig deep enough."

"What about you? I'm told you like fire."

She didn't bother to ask who'd told me. Instead she was quiet for a long moment, then said, "I promised you a story."

"About your father."

She blew out a long, slow breath and said, "I told you he was a stock car driver. He was good, really good. I never once saw him not qualify. He was even starting to beat out the Winston Cup guys. And fearless. It was like he knew he was charmed on the racetrack. Until one day he wasn't."

"I'm sorry."

It had happened on a curve, where he'd been clipped by another driver and spun into the path of a third. The car flipped three times, she said, then crashed into the wall and burst into flames. He was dead, thank God, before the fire reached him.

"He thought he was going to live forever," she said. "And he didn't even live to see thirty. My mother went through his insurance money like it was water and then married a dot-com millionaire."

"So your dad never met Jim."

She smiled. "Oh, he would have hated Jim. 'Baby girl,' he'd say, 'why are you settling for a man twice your age?'"

"Why *are* you settling for a man twice your age?"

"I'm settling for a million-dollar mansion, two Caribbean cruises a year, designer jewelry, and all the spending money I want. Does that sound cold? My mother used to say it's just as easy to fall in love with a rich man as a poor one." She gave a self-conscious laugh and touched the diamond at her throat. "Funny, I was always a daddy's girl, but I guess I'm my mother's daughter."

"And the thing for fire?"

"I didn't set that fire at the Underwoods'." Her hand slipped down, her finger circling my navel. She nuzzled my chest, gave my nipple a playful nip.

"Rhonda—" I said.

"Ssshhh." She nestled into the curve of my arm. "Don't ruin it."

She yawned.

It was still hot and humid, but the air had cooled with sunset, and an occasional breeze wafted across the back of the truck. I lay on my back with Rhonda Lister in my arms and watched the stars, smelling diesel fuel and horses and the lemon scent of her shampoo. Her body relaxed against me, and her breathing grew even. For a long time, I thought about nothing except how good it felt to have her there. Then the case crept back into my mind, and I wondered how Carlin and Zane would take the news that Samuel Trehorne had hired me to spy on them. I wondered how or if the string of murders Eli thought he'd uncovered was connected to the fire at the Underwood barn. And then I was back where I'd started, wondering if Jim Lister's interpretation of "a certain amount of freedom" was compatible with his wife's.

Not that it mattered. A line was a line, and this was one I didn't intend to cross. All the same, I lay awake a long time, breathing as deeply as I could stand and savoring the lingering scent of Rhonda Lister's perfume.

22.

Friday morning

At first, I slept fitfully in the truck bed. My cracked ribs made it hard to get comfortable, and I snapped awake every time a leaf skittered across the metal skin of the Silverado. It was a few hours before dawn when I gave in and took one of the pain pills Dr. Genaro had prescribed, taking it from my shirt pocket and swallowing it dry so as not to wake Rhonda. When sleep finally came, I dreamed of bloody hooves and figures in black. I dreamed my arms and legs were bound and that a great weight pressed against my face and chest. I couldn't move, couldn't speak, couldn't breathe. I woke up drenched in sweat.

My temples throbbed. My arms were empty.

Rhonda Lister was gone.

My watch said six A.M. when I pushed into a sitting position, teeth clamped tight against the fire that shot through my side. I closed my eyes, willed myself into that meditative state where you can detach yourself from pain, then forced myself to take a long, deep breath.

It felt like being gutted with a serrated knife. So much for meditation.

I did it a few more times just to prove I could, then gave myself a break and returned to normal breathing.

I left the air mattress and sleeping bag where they lay and slid out of the truck bed, then unlocked the door to the living quarters, and slipped inside to look up Eli's story in the *Sextant* and get the frozen gel packs Doc had given me. Khanh stirred, and I held my breath until she rolled over and went back to sleep. After a quick and fruitless search of the *Sextant's* site, I grabbed the gel pads and crept back outside. Took a text from Billy—*All Quiet on the Western Front*—and sent one back—*Good work. Carry On, My Wayward Son.*

A few embers still glowed in the fire pit. I stirred them gently with the poker and revived the fire with some tinder and a chunk of walnut wood. When the alarm on my cell phone dinged, I put the gel packs back in the freezer and fed and watered the horses, taking it slow and easy, dropping the hay into the corral one flake at a time and mixing Tex's mash with slow, measured strokes. Bending hurt, and I took care to do it as little as I could manage.

The horses seemed to realize something was amiss. Tex gave my hand a gentle nuzzle, and Crockett lipped my ear. I drank in the sweet, hay-and-leather smell of them and rubbed the broad flat spot between their eyes. I rubbed them down with my hands, first Tex and then Crockett, feeling the heat of their skin, following the contours of their muscles as they pressed against my palms. I was standing in the corral scratching Crockett's withers when Khanh came out, bleary-eyed, and said, "How you sleep?"

"Like the dead, once I took Doc Genaro's miracle pill."

Khanh frowned, made a gesture to ward off evil spirits. "Never say that, sleep like dead. Bring bad luck."

"I slept fine," I said.

"Rice inside," she said. "Coffee too. Vietnamese kind and also American. Black like you like."

I shot her a grateful look and went inside for sustenance and revival. The hot shower loosened me up and soothed my aching muscles. The coffee—black, American—sent a jolt of energy through me. I forewent the rice.

We drank more coffee by the fire. Then I laid a cooking rack across the pit and scrambled eggs and bacon in an iron skillet. Khanh brought out two plates and more coffee. I plopped a spoonful of eggs onto her plate and said, "You know, you said you'd never seen a horse show. Well, now you've seen one. Been here long enough to bore yourself to tears. Might be a good time to go back home and work from the office."

She gave me a narrow look, waved off a proffered strip of bacon. "Good time for us, or good time for you?"

"I have to stay. You know that. I haven't found whoever set fire to the Underwoods' barn."

She sat down and set her plate on her knees. "You stay, I stay too."

"I'm not sure I can protect you, Khanh."

"I not sure you can protect *you*."

"What am I going to tell Tuyet and Phen if I get you shot?"

"What I going tell them if I leave you and you get you self shot?"

"They've known me, what? Three months? I think they'll get over it."

"Maybe get over. But no more apartment. No more medicine for mother. No more counselor for Tuyet. Anyway we used to you now. Be sad, you die."

There was no arguing with that. I told her she was stubborn and hardheaded, and she said she thought it must run in the family. I couldn't argue with that either, so I fell back on the oldest, least effective argument in the book. "I write the paychecks, and I say you go."

"Free country," she shot back. "I stay."

❦

We might have gone on like that forever, except that the door to the *Lost in Space* camper creaked open, and Eli Barrington spilled out of it. He was barefoot and bleary-eyed, moving stiffly in a baggy T-shirt and a pair of jeans with a worn spot over one knee. He'd abandoned the contacts for a pair of Clark Kent glasses, which made his eyes less bloodshot than they'd been the day before.

He put his fists to the small of his back and stretched. Gave us a small smile. "If I ever do this again, I'm getting a new mattress. This one has lumps on its lumps."

I offered him coffee, and Khanh went to fetch it. Black, American.

"God," he said. "Why does morning have to come so early?"

"It's almost seven. Time to rise and shine."

"Sadist."

"Well, you've got the rising part," I said. "Need a little work on the shine."

He dragged over a chair of his own and set it by the fire, but he didn't sit in it, just stood behind it with his hands resting on its back. It was already almost too hot for the fire, but for now we simply pushed our chairs farther away from the circle of stones that enclosed it. Close enough to watch the flames, far enough away not to be enveloped by the heat. Khanh brought out the coffee, and Eli took a cup in grateful hands. Closed his eyes and took a sip. I let him take another drink, then said, "Someone tried to kill Zane Underwood last night."

His eyebrows lifted. "Seriously? Why? How?"

"*Why* is anybody's guess. *How* was a pillow over the face."

"Awful. But you said someone tried. What stopped them? Not Zane."

"No, not Zane. The guy got interrupted."

"Lucky."

Khanh smiled. "Lucky boss man come along."

Eli gave me a speculative look. Something glinted behind his glasses. "Boss man, huh? So what we have here is a genuine, bona fide hero."

I said, "Let's not go overboard here."

"No, seriously. You saved someone's life. That's, like, enormous."

Khanh said, "Oh, he save people all the time. Catch so many bad guy, jails almost too full."

"Well, I didn't catch this one," I said.

"You catch soon, I know." She stood up and jabbed a finger toward my chest. "You talk. I go get you ice."

Eli watched her go. "Your number one fan, huh?"

"You know how it is. Family."

He took a sip of coffee, held it in his mouth like a sommelier with an expensive wine.

I said, "I went to the *Sextant's* site, looked for your article about the show. The only articles with your byline are sports and lifestyle stories from about six months ago."

His fingers tightened on the cup. "You were checking up on me?"

"I wasn't checking up on you. You said you were writing an article. I thought I might read it."

"They didn't think a fistfight at a horse show was newsworthy. And this isn't even a major show. Not like the Celebration in Shelbyville."

"But you're here."

He shrugged again. "I guess I disagree with them. But they'll have to change their tune now, won't they?"

"You might try sounding a little less eager, considering a man almost died last night."

"Forgive me if I don't shed any tears over Zane Underwood. Considering—" He cut himself off.

I said, "Considering his father may have killed your grandfather? Zane probably has more in common with your granddad than he did with Dalt."

"Even so. Sins of the fathers and all that stuff." He shot a quick glance in my direction, then lowered his eyes like a pup caught with a forbidden shoe. "I'm sorry. That was tasteless. Of course, what happened to my grandfather wasn't Zane's fault. How long have you known?"

"Since last night. Why didn't you tell me Thomas Cole was your grandfather?"

He looked down at his cup, a wash of pink creeping up his neck. "I didn't think you'd take me seriously if you knew."

I thought about that for a moment, then said, "Why so long since your last byline?"

He made a face. With a flip of his wrist, he splashed his coffee onto the fire, which steamed and hissed in protest. "What is this, an interrogation? You want to know why I'm not on their website? Because I'm not important enough." He didn't bother to hide the ache in his voice. "They let me write filler these days, strictly freelance, strictly print, buried in among the ads."

"That can't pay much."

"I do okay."

"You have a bee in your bonnet about Tom Cole. Maybe it's the conflict of interest that bothers them."

"I'm covering the show. That's not a conflict of interest. My grandfather's story, I'm doing on my own time. And why shouldn't I? They're not paying me to be here."

I said, "Is that why you became a reporter? To emulate him?"

He looked down at his cup as if he wished he still had something left to throw onto the fire. Or as if he wished there were something stronger in it. "No," he said. "To vindicate him."

"Start at the beginning," I said. "Why are you so sure he was murdered?"

"I told you. He wouldn't have done what they said. He wasn't a drunk."

"People who aren't drunks sometimes *get* drunk."

"Not him. Not like that, so drunk he'd pass out with his face in a creek."

I said, "I asked the sheriff about Sylvia Whitehead. He said there were no bruises on her shoulders."

"Of course he'd say that." He stood up, paced the length of the fire pit and back again. "You think I'm tilting at windmills now?"

"The pot asks the kettle if it's black?"

That brought a smile. "Maybe so. But I want to know. You think I'm out of line?"

"I think some of the cases you picked out were probably accidents or suicides. The sheriff said being an activist doesn't make you immortal. Much as I hate to agree with him, it's true."

"My grandfather was no accident." He paused behind his chair, gripped the back of it until his knuckles whitened. "Of course Hap tells you there were no bruises on Sylvia Whitehead. What else was he going to say? But her daughter says there were, and why would she lie? And look at Dan Bitmore. An experienced hunter, out with other experienced hunters. You think that gun just happened to go off when Dan just happened to be in front of it?"

"It does sound suspicious. But not ironclad. Tell me about Tom Cole. Why was he so gung-ho against soring?"

"He always loved animals. Crusaded against cockfights, dog fights, you name it. When he heard about what they were doing to the horses, he jumped on it. He knew his stuff, did the research, found the sources. And he knew how to write so ordinary Joes and Janes could understand. There was a massive groundswell of opposition. It looked like it might blow the Walking Horse world apart."

"And that's what he wanted?"

Eli shrugged. "He was on a mission. He was going to burn the whole metaphorical field and watch the snakes come crawling out."

I'd read about his crusade online. Graphic descriptions of horses in pain and photos from shadowy sources made his stories like kindling for the coming conflagration. The Walking Horse Mafia, as Carlin had jokingly called their latest incarnation, warned him to stay out of their affairs. When he didn't, they started a campaign to ruin his reputation.

"They pulled out all the stops," Eli said. "Prostitutes came out of the walls saying they'd serviced him. Random drunks would swear they'd watched him drink himself under the table. Even some of his sources switched sides. Said he'd bribed, coerced, or just plain misquoted them. But he stuck to his guns, and because of the kind of guy he was, his editors believed him, and his wife—my grandmother—stood by him."

"And he wouldn't stop."

"He wouldn't stop, and he wouldn't go away." He laughed, a small sad sound. "Funny, if he'd been less of a paragon, he might still be alive."

On a windy Tuesday night in April, Tommy took a call from someone he described only as a source. He told his wife he was going out to meet a man who had an inside track on who was soring and who was taking bribes to look the other way.

"I'll be back by nine," he said. He put on his jacket, gave his wife a kiss, and left the house with his notepad in one pocket and his tape recorder in the other.

At ten o'clock, she started to worry. By eleven, she was frantic. At midnight, she dialed 911 and was told he'd probably lost track of time and to call the next day if he wasn't home by supper.

But they found him before that. Early the next morning, a guy heading to Blackwater Creek to fish found Tommy's car parked by the road and Tommy lying facedown in the water. His tape recorder was still in his pocket, the tape inside it blank.

Lori Mae Tillman, a woman who lived in the next county, came forward and said he'd spent an hour at her place, then headed for home, still drinking heavily.

"That woman lied," Eli said. "They must have paid her off. And we'll never know for sure, because she's dead now. Diabetes."

"You checked."

"Damn right I did. And whatever they paid her, I hope she choked on it."

I gave him a sharp look. His emotions were as raw as if Thomas Cole had been his father, someone he had known and loved and lost. But Cole was almost twenty years dead when Eli was born.

"What did the autopsy show?" I asked. "Young guy, died alone, there would have been one, right?"

"He drowned," Eli said. "That much of what they said was true. But his blood alcohol was way too low to have been drinking like the Tillman woman said."

"That should have raised red flags."

He shrugged. "I think it did, but anyone who ever cared about that case is either dead or retired. It'll never be solved, not while Trehorne and his friends stick to their guns."

Khanh came out with the frozen gel pad, and I pressed it gently to my side. A lance of pain shot through at the pressure, then ebbed beneath the coolness of the gel. She sat down on the trailer steps. I said to Eli, "Let's say you're right, that Tommy was murdered by whoever he went out to meet. This mysterious source. What makes you think it was Trehorne?"

"People who cross Sam Trehorne and his crowd tend to end up dead. Dead or broke or burned out. The number of barn fires in this county's almost double what it is statewide— way more than other rural counties—and I've done interviews with seven people who will say the Trehornes drove them out of business. I know that's not enough to make a case, but that's why I'm looking for other cases like Tommy's."

"You want to prove a pattern."

He bobbed his head. "That's right. A pattern. And when I can prove it, I'm going to bring the whole damn lot of them down."

23.

He thanked us for the coffee and went back to his camper. As he walked away, I turned to Khanh. "I need to grab some Tylenol and take a shower. Why don't you go over to the Underwoods' booth and see if Sue and Maggie need anything? If they're there, and if they don't already know, tell them what happened."

She nodded, started clearing away the remains of our meal. "Okay. I clean up here first, then go to booth."

I braced myself for the pain and kicked some sand into the fire pit to douse the flame. "Don't take any chances. You see anything off, you come and get me, you hear? Don't try anything heroic."

She threw a grin over her shoulder. "Yes, boss man. This family, only one hero."

⌘

I'd just washed down two Tylenols when my cell phone beeped and a text from Khanh popped in: *Trouble here. You come now.*

My pulse quickened. *Calm down,* I thought. *She's in a safe place. Safe enough to text.*

Sprinting was out of the question, so I broke into a gentle jog. It felt like being gored by a rhinoceros, but by the time I reached the edge of the campground, the pain had subsided some. Strangely, running felt better than sitting or lying down. I picked up the pace, ran past a woman longeing a colt in the warm-up ring and a few early bird vendors rolling up the plastic tarps that covered the entrances to their booths. Somewhere behind the arena, a tractor growled to life.

Khanh's text scrolled through my brain: *Trouble here.*

You come now.

Come now.

Come now.

I found Khanh standing in front of the TASA booth, her hand over her mouth. Relief that she was safe and whole washed over me. Then I noticed the booth—or what was left of it.

Torn pamphlets and flyers had been scattered across the ground and trampled. Someone had spray-painted *Horse fuckers, Get Out* and *Go home, PETA freaks* on the walls in neon red, then streaked the paint across the front of the "Walk On—Naturally" T-shirts. The tarp that had covered the front entrance overnight had been ripped away.

"You okay?" I said.

She nodded. Pointed to the front counter and made an arcing motion with her hand.

I didn't draw the Glock. Khanh had looked inside the booth, and she had texted me from here instead of running for cover. That she'd gestured me forward meant there was no one in that booth who was a threat to me. Still, I approached it cautiously and listened first. There was nothing, just a low, insect hum. I peered over the counter.

The torn tarp had been flung on the floor, then littered with more papers and pamphlets. The coolers were upended, empty soda cans scattered around. Cola and ginger ale pooled in the folds of the tarp, and flies and sweat bees buzzed around the puddles.

There was a bulge in the tarp that gave my stomach the same familiar leap I'd felt at the Underwood barn.

I didn't bother going around to the side door. Instead, too focused on the bulge to fully register the pain in my side, I climbed over the counter. A few flies swarmed up as I dropped onto the floor. They buzzed around me for an agitated moment, then settled back onto the plastic.

"What you see?" Khanh asked. "This bad, right? This very bad?"

I didn't answer her, just bent to lift one corner of the tarp.

Slowly I peeled back the plastic, saw more pamphlets and a broken ballpoint pen bleeding dark blue ink onto the floor. A smell rolled out, the smell of voided bowels and bladder, and I saw a leather cowboy boot in violet and indigo, painted like a Ukrainian Easter egg.

Maggie James.

24.

For a moment, I knelt beside her, remembering the plain woman with the dazzling smile, and a sudden rage flickered beneath my breastbone. She'd been kind and cheerful and harmless, and someone had snuffed her out with less thought than if she'd been a mosquito.

I touched her calf just above the boot she'd loved. The skin was already cool to the touch. I wanted to pull back the plastic to see how she'd died, but this was a crime scene now, so instead I stepped around the tarp to the side door and, for the second time in two days, punched in 911.

It took less than fifteen minutes for the sheriff to pull up beside the booth. Behind him were a couple of deputies in county vehicles, an ambulance, and a brawny woman in an unmarked Impala. While the deputies taped off the area, the woman strode into the booth, pulling her hair into a quick bun as she went, then snapping on a pair of latex gloves.

The sheriff sauntered to where Khanh and I stood watching the proceedings. He didn't look happy to see me.

He ran me through the story twice, then said, "You just attract trouble, don't you, boy?"

"Seems to me like I find trouble that's already there."

"Could be." He scratched his chin. "You do know the person who finds the body is the first one we look at."

I raised my eyebrows and looked at Khanh. "You think this little one-armed woman is your killer?"

The corners of his mouth twitched upward. "Somehow I think she's stronger than she looks."

"She is, at that."

The hint of a smile faded, and he rubbed his face with his hands. "I liked Maggie," he said. "Everybody did. Not a reason in the world for anybody to kill her."

"TASA," I said.

"That's all Carlin. Maggie's got a big heart, and it's easy to lead her around by it. Carlin sells her a load of bull about the poor abused horses, of course Maggie's gonna want to help." He shook his head. "I bet there's not a person in this county hasn't had a sickness or death in the family, but Maggie showed up on their doorstep with an apple pie or a tuna casserole."

"The vandalism," I said. "She must have seen who did it."

"Nobody would kill a woman to get out of a vandalism rap."

He had to know that wasn't true. There were people who would kill for fifty cents, or because they didn't like the look on a stranger's face, or just for kicks. There were people who would do it just because they could.

I said, "He covered her up. That wouldn't have delayed finding the body, so he did it for another reason."

He gave a dry laugh. "You saying this piece of scum felt some remorse?"

"Remorse or maybe guilt. He felt something, anyway. Either he didn't want to look at her, or he didn't want her to look at him, or he felt bad about killing her and didn't want to leave her exposed. I don't think killing her was part of his plan."

"That's a lot of or's."

"Nature of the business, Sheriff. Mind if I take a look?"

He hitched up his pants. Seemed to consider it. "Don't touch anything, and don't get in my medical examiner's way." He nodded toward the woman with the bun. "That's her there. You can call her Dr. Walsh. And I guess you might as well call me Hap."

I left Khanh with the sheriff and stepped into the booth's side entrance, where I stopped to watch the crime scene being processed. The tarp had been pulled back. While one of the deputies photographed the scene, Walsh plucked a hair from Maggie's blouse and tucked it into an envelope.

Maggie lay on her back, hands crossed over her chest. Her corneas had begun to cloud, and the blood had begun to settle, giving her face a waxy pallor and staining the back of her neck, arms, and legs a purplish color. A livid bruise circled her neck. I leaned forward for a closer look. Saw blossoms of petechiae in the whites of her eyes.

Walsh looked up. "Excuse me? Who the hell are you, and what are you doing in my crime scene?"

"Sorry." I stepped back. "Jared McKean. I worked homicide in Metro Nashville for a while."

"Past tense." She gave me a stern look. "And another jurisdiction. I don't have time for rubberneckers."

"I can appreciate that. I'm on the private ticket now. This seems to be related to an arson I'm looking into." I nodded toward the sheriff. "Hap said I could take a look if I stayed out of your way."

"And are you out of my way?"

"I hope so, ma'am. You're pretty terrifying."

That brought a laugh. "Good. I guess you can stay. Just don't go getting too comfortable."

❧

I stayed until they loaded Maggie's body into the ambulance. By then a crowd had gathered, shuffling their feet and murmuring, pressing against the yellow crime scene tape. Mace Ewing stood near the back of the crowd, his arm around Trudy, who looked shaken. No sign of Sam Trehorne, or his family, who lived close enough to sleep at home. Sue Blankenship stood off to one side, hugging herself as if a word might break her. Khanh saw where I was looking and went to put her arm around the older woman.

At the other end of the crowd, Eli stood tapping notes into his phone. I stepped over the tape, and he came over to me, smiling. "Guess it's going to be hard for anyone to say there's nothing going on now, huh?"

I frowned. "What's that? Gallows humor?"

His smile dissolved. "I know, I know. I'm sorry. I meant no disrespect. It's just that I can't think about it too much. That poor woman, what she must have gone through. I have to think about it as a story or I'll drive myself insane."

"I can see that," I conceded. Cops are known for gallows humor too. "Whatever it takes to get you through."

❦

When the ambulance had gone and the crowd dispersed, Khanh said, "What now?"

"Depends," I said, watching the deputies start to bag the evidence. They looked competent enough, but I wished Sheriff Hap had called in the TBI with their expert technicians. "How are you feeling?"

"Sad," she said. "Sad for Maggie, sorry for all this hurt. But life very hard. Every day, something sad, something good." She gave me a small smile. "About time for something good."

I pulled my keys out of my pocket and dangled them in front of her. "You want to drive the truck?"

"With trailer or no trailer?"

"No trailer."

Her eyes sparked, and the smile grew. "Yes. Where I'm driving to?"

"We passed a county courthouse back at the town square. Can you go and see if you can get access to the public files for these twelve cases?"

We walked back to the trailer, where I handed her the list with the names and dates I'd gotten from Eli, not counting Thomas Cole, whose file would be in Davidson County. While she packed her laptop, I climbed into the truck and pushed the front seat forward as far as it would go.

"Don't give them all the names unless you have to," I said. "If you're lucky, they'll let you in the archives without a fuss. If you have to tell them something, say your father served in Vietnam, you're looking for his relatives. If you have to give a name you're looking for, start with the oldest one. Sylvia Whitehead."

"Lady who drowned in bathtub."

"Right. The older the case, the less likely it is to raise a flag."

She nodded.

"If you can make copies, do it. You can use our office credit card. If not, take notes. The officers who worked the case, the medical examiner who signed off on it. I don't think it will be dangerous, but if you don't want to do it—"

"I want to do it," she said.

"If the person you're talking to seems the least bit suspicious, abort the mission and get out of there."

"Abort, get out. Got it," she said.

"And text me every hour. If I don't hear from you, I'll assume you ran into trouble and come get you."

"Every hour. Got it," she said, and reached for the keys.

I held them up above my head, too high for her to reach. "And wear your seat belt. No seat belt, no driving."

"Text every hour, abort if trouble, wear seat belt. *Got it.*"

25.

I'd planned to tell the Underwoods about my deal with Trehorne, but between Zane's hospitalization and Maggie's death, that plan had been derailed. While I waited to hear from Billy that Zane had been released, I sent a text to my son—*happy face, kiss, thumbs up, Love, Daddy*—and then used my 4G LTE connection to spend an hour on the Internet, trying to piece together Eli's thirteen cases.

Tommy Cole and Sylvia Whitehead had died before the Internet explosion, but thanks to the push to put public records online, it took less than five minutes to find both their obituaries. I wrote down the names under "survived by," then tracked down a few archived news articles that didn't add anything to what Eli had said.

Daniel Bitmore should have been easy. He'd died in a time where news is digitally enshrined, where great-grandmothers Tweet about quilting and log on to Facebook to share kitten videos. But Bitmore had been a hunter, an outdoorsman, not one to tie himself to his computer. His Facebook page, rarely updated, had a photo of a buck he'd shot, a meme about beer someone had shared on his wall, and a few pictures of his children. The page languished, a single post on the anniversary of his death from Mace Ewing, the man who had shot him: *I miss you, Buddy.*

The rest of the deaths stretched from the late seventies into the twenty-first century, all plausible accidents or suicides, but all, as near as I could tell, vague enough in detail to raise questions in the mind of someone who was looking to ask them.

Eli had been right to focus on Whitehead, Cole, and Bitmore. If they could be confirmed, it would give weight to the rest. And while some were, no doubt, exactly what they seemed, there was a chance there was more beneath the surface.

When I thought I'd found all I could online, I put in a call to Frank Campanella. Before I'd joined the private sector, Frank and I had partnered on Nashville's Murder Squad. He was all but a father to me, and a few years from retirement, but the old fire was still in him. At least it had been until his wife, Patrice, was diagnosed with cancer. Now it blazed and receded by turns, depending on her most recent prognosis.

"Hey, Mac," he said, before I could identify myself. "Angling for another cruise?" He chuckled at his own joke.

When I'd last seen him a few weeks ago, we'd spent an afternoon on his fishing boat, trolling for trout and sampling craft beers. We'd made a pact not to discuss police work or politics and failed to keep it, then come home sunburned and a little buzzed, bearing dinner from McDonald's.

"Not this time," I said. "How's Patrice?"

"Hanging in there. She had chemo yesterday, and the day after that is always rough. She's sleeping now."

"Give her my love, will you?"

"She sends you hers," he said. "When can I tell her you'll be coming by?"

"Next week sometime. Right now I'm at a horse show in a little place called Hidden Hollow."

"Business or pleasure?"

"Business. I'm working a case."

"Thus the call," he said.

"Thus the call."

He was silent for a beat. Then, "Am I going to be sorry I heard from you?"

"I don't think so. Not on account of anything I'm about to say."

"Hang on." I heard him shift the phone, heard the rustle of paper and his footsteps on the hardwood. A drawer opened and closed, and I guessed he was finding a pen. "Okay. What do you need?"

I ran him through it, from the arson to Eli's conspiracy theory to Maggie James's murder. When I'd finished, he said, "And you think the same person who started your barn fire committed these murders?"

"I think it's possible. Several of the major players are in their late fifties, early sixties. That would put them in their late teens, early twenties, when Sylvia Whitehead and Tom Cole died."

"Forty years," he said. "The guys who worked those cases are—"

"I know. Dead or retired. And I get it if you don't have the time to run them down."

"I have time, Cowboy. I'll make time. But no promises. A lot of water's run under that bridge."

"I know. I just want to get your take on the guys who looked into Cole's case. See if their hands were tied or if you get the sense they're covering something. I've got Khanh working on the records here, but Tom Cole's are in your neck of the woods."

"I'll do what I can. Get back to you later."

"Save my seat on the boat."

I hung up and found a text from Khanh. Short and sweet, it just said, *IN. OK.*

I took this to mean she'd gained access to the public records archive and no one had tried to kill her. A good sign. Relieved, I put away the laptop and went to the arena. A sign taped to the front doors invited everyone to a memorial service for Maggie at dawn on Sunday. No mention of how she'd died or that someone might have killed her, just a candid photo of a smiling Maggie someone had probably taken on a cell phone.

Inside, the crowd was thin, whether because of the time of day or because of the murder, I wasn't sure. The former, I guessed. News traveled fast among the in-group, but it would take some time before the details reached the general public. I wandered to the concession stand for an order of nachos and a Pepsi and was waiting for my food when a text from Billy came through. *All okay. On our way there. Have beer waiting.*

I went back and bought us each a bottle, then watched Doc do inspections until the next text came from Khanh: *Still OK.* Doc was quick and competent, sparing a few moments to stroke each horse gently when he started and again between each step of the inspection. It didn't seem to be for show.

He was using a portable thermal imaging machine, which looked like a camera but was connected to a TV/VCR setup that showed a color image of the thermal pattern created by the horse's circulatory system. Abnormally hot or cold spots could both be indicators of soring.

If the image showed a problem, another machine allowed him to test for the presence of caustic agents, like kerosene, or numbing agents, like lidocaine, which were used to mask pain long enough for the horse to get through inspection.

There were many facets to the art of pain.

He passed three horses, disqualified one. Mace Ewing, eyes blacked and nose splinted, brought his little red mare through, followed by Trudy Valentine with Sultan. As they chatted in line, Trudy touched a hand to the bun at the back of her head, gave the net that covered it a gentle tug. Grooming. He was a young thug and she a woman who dropped *ergo* into casual conversation, but she was definitely interested.

I watched them flirt for a few minutes, then tossed my empty containers and went back to the TASA booth, where the last of the deputies was removing the crime scene tape. It was early to release the area, but then, it was a very small crime scene. Beyond the tarp and the TASA promotional materials, there hadn't been much to it.

Sue stood off to one side, one arm crossed tight around her chest, the other hand holding a cigarette.

She sniffled, took a long drag from the cigarette, and wiped her eyes.

"You hanging in there?" I said.

She bobbed her head, a quick nod. "I just can't believe she's gone. She was the kindest person I ever knew. Never met a stranger. Why would someone do this?"

"Some people are scum," I said. "I know that's not much comfort."

"Not very PC," she said, with a sad laugh. "We're supposed to feel sorry for the poor little killer, who probably had a bad home life, or who had a great life except for some traumatic experience, or who has a wire loose somewhere in his head. Oh, excuse me, they'd have some high-falutin' way of saying that."

I forced a smile. "An aberration in the primordial ooze of his psychopathic brain."

She sucked in a lungful of smoke, held it, then slowly blew it out. "Maggie could talk the ear off a deaf man," she said. "I don't know how many times I rolled my eyes at her, told her she didn't have to tell us every thought she had. You didn't have to give that girl a penny for her thoughts. She'd give you every one she had for free."

"She did know how to carry on a conversation."

She said, "I'd give anything to take those eye rolls back."

"I didn't know her well," I said, "but she didn't seem the type to take offense."

"No," she said. "She was a kind soul. A truly bright spirit. And so damn chipper you'd just about want to strangle her sometimes. But I sure am gonna miss her chatter."

"Lotta people will," I said.

"I hated those damn boots," she said, and burst into tears.

26.

There was little comfort I could give her. I'd liked Maggie, but I hadn't known her well. Vows of vengeance, or even justice, would neither bring her back nor give her spirit peace. I was convinced that, however dark her end, Maggie James had gone well into whatever afterlife there was. All the same, a vision of her cheerful ghost chattering into her killer's ear until he wanted to tear out his own eardrums made me smile.

There were still a few classes before Carlin was supposed to show. I hoped she'd make it, figured if yesterday's judging was any indication, it didn't much matter. Since I had time, I took the long way around, through the preparation area, and found Trudy and Doc chatting near the inspection corner, where two other judges were checking out horses. Doc had a Styrofoam soda cup in one hand and a barbecue sandwich in the other. Trudy, dressed in black slacks and a black blazer nipped in at the waist, held the reins of a chestnut mare with a flaxen mane.

Across the room, Eli watched them with a hard, flat gaze, then headed in their direction like a homing missile. They looked up when they saw him coming, closing up like flower petals at sunset.

I changed course and wandered over to join the party.

Eli acknowledged my arrival with a nod. Then with an affable grin, he said, "Hey, Doc. Killed anybody lately?"

Doc's fingers tightened on his soda cup. "For Christ's sake, Barrington."

Eli said, "It's a legitimate question."

"It's a slanderous question."

"Depends on how you answer it."

Trudy said, "No, it doesn't. It's like, '*Have you stopped beating your wife yet?*' There's no good answer."

Eli shrugged. "Maybe there shouldn't be. How about it, Doc? For the record."

"For the record?" Doc stalked to a nearby trash bin and tossed his soda and what was left of his sandwich into it, sending up a buzz of flies and sweat bees. "Go screw yourself."

Eli's easy smile belied the hardness in his eyes. "You'd have been better served with '*No Comment.*'"

Trudy shooed at him as if he were one of the flies. "Move along, little boy. The adults are talking."

"You mean plotting." Eli smirked.

"That's right," Doc said. "We're part of a vast conspiracy. It started on the grassy knoll, and who knows where it might end?"

He tipped an invisible hat to Trudy and looked pointedly at his watch. "I have work to do. Y'all have a nice chat."

"Enjoy it while you can," Eli said. "I learned some interesting things from Mace down at Jake's Place yesterday. You can tell Junior his junkyard dog has turned."

"Tell him yourself," Doc said over his shoulder. "I'm not your carrier pigeon."

As Doc stalked back to the inspection area and stepped over the barrier tape, Eli flexed his fists. "I hate that smug bastard."

I said, "I thought you media guys were supposed to be objective."

"The writing is supposed to be objective. *We* can be however we like. Besides sometimes a little agitation is a good thing. Like stirring up the embers of a dying fire." With a mocking smile toward Trudy, he touched the brim of his Stetson. "Ma'am."

"Don't *ma'am* me," she said. "You know damn well Mace hasn't turned on Junior."

"Just messing with the good doctor," he said. "No harm, no foul." He touched his hat again and sauntered toward the exit.

"Idiot," she muttered to his retreating back. She looked back at me. "I take it he's been filling your head with ideas."

"Ideas are a bad thing?"

Her lips twitched, a quirk of annoyance. "Spend enough time listening to crackpots, you're just going to confuse yourself."

"Is he a crackpot?"

"So cracked, there's almost no pot left."

"So if he said your friend Mace Ewing is a murderer—"

"You leave Mace out of this." She drew up to her full height, tipped back her head to look me in the eye. "Just because he beat you up—"

"He didn't beat me up."

"Mace is no more a murderer than I am."

I gave her a moment to think about that, then said, "Which could just as well mean that you are as that he's not."

Her nostrils flared, and she went the kind of still that usually comes before an explosion. Then she drew in a slow breath and reined it in. "If you knew how close he and Dan were, you wouldn't even think a thing like that."

"But I don't know. So I gotta think, he's an experienced hunter. How could he have let it happen?"

She looked away, fiddled with the mare's bridle. "It was an accident. Just the kind of stupid thing you couldn't possibly plan for."

"You telling me that undercover video Dan made didn't cause a rift between them?"

"I'm telling you there's no way Mace would have shot Dan on purpose." She slid her hands down to the saddle, gave the girth a tug. "Did Mace feel angry and betrayed? Of course he did. We all did. But that's a far cry from killing him."

"Why would you feel betrayed? If you don't sore, why wouldn't you be happy to expose the ones who do?"

She glanced up, rolled her eyes. "Because we're all tarred with the same brush. One of us goes down, nobody says there's one bad apple. They want to crucify us all."

"So what should he have done?"

"I don't know. Kept his damn mouth shut. Talked to the board so we . . . so they . . . could deal with it in-house. You want change, you make it from the inside. You don't throw out a net that's going to catch all your friends in it, whether they're guilty or not."

"You guys had a grievance. You, Mace, all of you."

"We had a grievance. That doesn't mean we wanted him dead." She gave an angry laugh. "At least, it doesn't mean we *made* him dead."

"Two different things," I agreed.

She turned away and stroked the mare's neck, her hand sliding beneath the corn silk mane. "You say that. But why do I feel like your heart's not in it?"

ళౡ

I got back inside just as Carlin's first class was about to begin. Gerardo stood just outside the gate, talking distractedly with

Eli, gaze flicking toward the preparation area. Relief flooded his face as Carlin rode up, slightly out of breath, and he turned to give the girth a final tug. As she rode into the ring and the steward closed the gate, Gerardo settled beside it, arms folded on the top rail, gaze riveted on the ring, the reporter forgotten.

Eli's cheeks pinked. He glanced around as if to see if anyone had witnessed his dismissal, then gathered himself when he saw me. "Got a few questions for you about last night."

I answered them while he scribbled in his pad. Then he excused himself and I went to stand beside Gerardo. Anxious energy rolled off him like steam.

"How's Zane?" I asked.

He looked at me with tired eyes. "Resting. Your friend Billy is bringing him when he feels stronger."

I nodded. Between the seizure and last night's attack, Zane must have felt like an old dishrag. "And Carlin? How's she holding up?"

His gaze swept the ring until he found her. "How do you think? Señor Zane is still a cripple. The stable is still burned, two horses are still dead, and still there is no insurance money."

"I'm recommending they pay."

He laughed without humor. "I thought you spent all your time punching gringos like Mace Ewing over things that will never change."

"They'll never change if nobody does anything about them."

At the far end of the arena, Carlin emerged from a cluster of riders. Gerardo followed her with his gaze. "Señor Zane tried to do something about them, and look what happened to him."

I laid my forearms on the rail. "Are you talking about last night, or are you telling me his accident was no accident?"

"I'm telling you bad things happen to people who put their noses into other people's business. Accident or no accident, he put himself in harm's way. Now here you are, doing the same."

"Samuel Trehorne told me not to get on the wrong side of this."

He gave his head a rueful shake, the concern in his voice taking the sting from his words. "Sign the insurance papers before you take him on. Señor Trehorne is a bad man, but he is not a stupid one. A smarter man than you would listen to what he has to say."

27.

I took Billy his beer and popped the top off my own. We stepped outside to drink them while Zane dozed.

"No action last night?" I said.

"Deader 'n roadkill. I'm gonna start charging you double when the bad guys don't show. I almost punched the Coke machine just so I could say I got to hit something."

"Quiet is good, my friend," I said. "Quiet is the cherry on the banana split of life."

He laughed his rumbling laugh. "If you thought that, you'd be in a different line of work."

"I like quiet just fine," I said. "For other people."

I filled him in on the case to date. When I got to Maggie's murder, he sighed and said, "Shit. I hate collateral damage."

"I'll drink to that." We clicked our bottles together.

From inside, Zane called, "Bih-yee!"

"We're on," Billy said. "I'll help you get him up, then you can take him to the show while I catch me some shut-eye. All that standing around doing nothing takes a lot out of a guy."

⁓

Carlin rode in seven more classes. She placed only once, a single blue ribbon in a sea of undeserved losses. With the exception of that one class, it was as if she were invisible. Zane watched from the wheelchair-accessible section, the hair around his face lifting in the breeze made by a small plastic fan clamped to the arm of his chair. Even with the fan, sweat beaded on his forehead and upper lip. Every time she lost, his expression got grimmer.

I watched the classes from the railing, taking note of who cheered and who booed, and watching the emotions roil across Gerardo's face. Hope for my positive recommendation to the insurance company and gratitude that I'd saved Zane's life mingled with a heaping helping of pride and possessiveness. He clearly saw me as a contender for Carlin's affections, but whether he felt the threat was to Zane or to himself, I couldn't say.

We would have both been happier if I'd gone back up to sit in the bleachers, but that would have felt too much like letting him win. A better man than I was might not have cared.

I took four more texts from Khanh, then one that said, *I com bak now.* Forty minutes later, as Carlin finished her last class, I realized Khanh still hadn't returned.

I texted her, got no response. Punched in her number, and her phone went straight to voice mail.

I'd said, *If I don't hear from you, I'll come and get you.* What I hadn't thought about was how. A vision of me riding into town and tying Crockett to the cannon made me shake my head. By the time I got there, whatever trouble she was in would be long settled. I caught a glimpse of Rhonda Lister on the other side of the arena, hurried over, and said, "Hey, give a guy a ride?"

"Jim's showing in a little while. Will I be back in time to watch him?"

"I hope so. Khanh didn't check in. I need to make sure she's okay."

"Of course." She touched my forearm with her fingertips. "I'm parked out back."

∽

Rhonda Lister didn't drive a Ferrari. She drove a candy apple Porsche 911. I loved my Silverado, but my heart beat a little faster when I climbed into the Porsche's passenger seat. The leather still smelled new.

"Sweet ride, huh?" she said.

"You do know how to transport a man in style."

She laughed. "That I do, and I'm not just talking about the car. Where to?"

"She was at the courthouse."

"So we take the main strip."

The traffic guard waved us out, and we followed the plastic flags and red Sharpie arrows back to the main road. We passed a saddle shop and the cowboy bar, with its neon sign flashing *Jake's Place*. Five miles out of town, we took a sharp bend, the Porsche's tires skidding on the shoulder. My seat belt dug into my ribs, and I clamped my teeth against a yelp. Then, pain forgotten, I pointed across the road. "There. Over there."

The Silverado lay on its side, front tires blown out, hood twisted and accordioned, front grille wrapped around a white oak. I was out of the car, bile rising in my throat, before the wheels of the Porsche stopped rolling. I imagined my sister slumped over the steering wheel or thrown like a rag doll through the windshield. Imagined the airbag shattering her bones with 2,000 pounds of pressure. How could I have let her drive, knowing how small she was, how close she'd be to the steering wheel? How she never wore her seat belt?

Then I saw her, and suddenly I could breathe again.

She sat on the ground behind the pickup, her arm cradled between her breasts. A young guy in bicycle shorts and a bike helmet knelt beside her, holding a bloodstained towel to the side of her head. Behind them a racing bike stood propped on its kickstand.

I knelt in front of them, and Khanh burst into tears. "Sorry, very sorry I wreck you truck."

In the three months I'd known her, I'd seen her beaten, battered, and in fear for her life and the life of her child. I'd seen her cradling her bloodied hand after a man had hacked a finger from it.

I had never seen her cry.

I put my arm around her shoulders. "Screw the truck. Are you all right?"

The guy in the helmet said, "I was crossing over when she came around the corner. I know, it was stupid, crossing so close to the curve. But there's not a lot of traffic around here, and I thought it would be no big deal, you know? She came around the corner, and she didn't slow down, and I thought *shit, she's gonna run me over!* Then I saw her standing on the brakes." He gave a nervous laugh. "I tried to jump out of the way, but I knew I'd never make it. I thought I was a goner. But she put it in the ditch instead. If she hadn't done that . . ." He shook his head. "She saved my life."

And almost lost her own. The cut on her head looked superficial, but that was nothing more than luck.

Rhonda had climbed out of the car and pried open the Siverado's crumpled hood. "I got your problem," she said. She came around to the back of the truck, rubbing her palms on the sides of her jeans. "Brake lines are cut. Not all the way, just enough so when you hit the brakes hard, the hoses would blow."

The biker's mouth dropped open.

"Hoses?" I said. "Both of them?"

She nodded. "Tricky to get them both to go at the same time, and kind of a crapshoot since there'd be no way to know for sure how hard she'd hit the brakes. But it worked. There's something else too."

Khanh dried her eyes on her sleeve. "Like that not enough?"

"The airbag," Rhonda said. "It didn't deploy."

"That very bad, right?" Khanh said.

"No, it was lucky." She looked at me. "Whoever did this expected you to be driving. The airbag might have saved your life, and they didn't want to take that chance. But small as she is and as far forward as that seat was, it was a good thing it didn't go off. If it had deployed, it could have killed her."

I turned away to check the cut on Khanh's temple, not trusting myself to speak, not certain what to feel. Relief that Khanh's injuries were minor, gratitude for the twists of fate that had saved her, anger that someone had put her in danger, shame that I'd allowed it to happen. And yes, a pang, more than a pang, for my faithful Silverado.

Whoever had done this must have sabotaged the airbag and brake lines sometime after I'd taken the pain pill. After Rhonda had gone but while most of the camp still slept.

Unless Rhonda had done it herself. She had the knowledge and the opportunity.

I didn't want to think about that. Either way, it had been a risky move; no way to know when someone in the camp might stir.

Khanh wiped her eyes again and said, "Hey, boss man. I wearing seat belt, like you say."

I forced a grin. "Good girl."

She was favoring her arm, so I put my hands under her armpits and helped her to her feet, careful to bend from the knees and not the middle. My ribs complained, and I ignored them. We were starting to develop a dysfunctional relationship.

Khanh hobbled to the driver's door and stopped, perplexed. Rhonda had left it standing open, but with the truck on its side and her only arm injured, Khanh couldn't climb in.

Rhonda said, "What do you need?"

"Black case, long strap."

Rhonda boosted herself up and slithered into the cab headfirst. Moments later, she emerged, holding out a black leather case with a file folder stuck in the front pocket.

I took it and handed it to Khanh, who hooked the strap over her shoulder and said, "We look at this when we get back, okay?"

"Sure. But first, you need to get that head looked at."

"No, boss man. Just a flesh wound."

"And your arm? Is that a flesh wound too?"

"Probably sprain," she said. "You got bandage, right? You wrap."

28.

I bandaged Khanh's cut and wrapped her wrist and forearm, then texted Billy with an update. We transferred the guns and the most expensive equipment to Rhonda's trunk before calling the sheriff and Triple A. What Hap didn't know about wouldn't get confiscated. While we waited for him to arrive, I pulled the bobblehead Batman from the dashboard and zipped it into a camera bag.

The sheriff took our statements, gave me a modicum of grief for form's sake, and called in a deputy to photograph the hulk that had once been my truck and was now a crime scene. I left the keys with the deputy and asked him to tuck them under the floor mat for Triple A. They could haul it to the shop just as easily without me.

The guy in the helmet rode off on his bike, shaken but wiser, and Rhonda Lister drove Khanh and me back to the showground.

"I'm sorry," I said. "I think we might have made you miss your husband's class."

"No harm, no foul. He'll ride again tonight in the Big Lick classes."

"He going to have a problem with this?"

"I texted him while you were doctoring Khanh's arm. He knows it was for a good cause. But do you mind getting your stuff out of the trunk later? I can still catch his last few classes."

"Sure," I said.

"Thank you," Khanh said, though it looked like it pained her to say it.

Rhonda parked in the VIP lot behind the arena, so Khanh and I cut through the prep area and the arena on our way back to the campground. As we made our way around the bleachers, Samuel Trehorne came in carrying his daughter on one arm and pulling a rolling cooler with the other. The girl had her arms around his neck and her head on his shoulder, and her hoarse, angry wails said she was having a tantrum and wanted the world to know it.

A matronly woman with salt-and-pepper hair and a sour expression waddled behind them, lugging a purse as big as a suitcase and a tote bag full of inflatable seat cushions. Trehorne's wife, Rebecca.

Trehorne squeezed sideways into a VIP box and plopped his daughter into a folding chair.

Khanh wrinkled her nose. "You need to talk Mr. Trehorne?"

"I guess I'd better," I said. "You don't have to stay. You could go back to the trailer or go shopping, or whatever it is you do when you're not working. Of course you could actually do some work."

"I working now," she said, affronted.

"Yes, you are. I'm teasing you."

"Oh. You want me do something else now?"

"You almost died a little while ago," I said. "You think you might deserve to take a break?"

"Maybe need shower," she conceded. "But then okay to work."

"You could do that skip trace, if you wanted to," I said. "The one you told me about on Wednesday."

Her eyebrows shot up. "Me?"

"Why not? You know how to do it. If it's pretty straight-forward, you just use the databases I showed you. If you run into a dead end, I can try some other things later."

"You keep trade secret, huh?" She gave me a conspiratorial smile.

"If I didn't, pretty soon you wouldn't need me anymore."

"True. I very resourceful. Okay, I try. But first, I maybe call mother and Tuyet."

"Don't tell them about the wreck," I said. "They'll just worry."

"Got to tell," she said, then flashed me a mischievous grin. "But maybe wait and tell when we get back."

I walked her to the door and watched her leave, then sat down in the bleachers and watched Trehorne and his family from the corner of my eye. He helped his wife put cushions on the folding chairs, then opened the suitcase and gave Esmerelda a Disney princess bag. She pushed it away and pouted, and his wife took it and pulled out a coloring book and crayons. She offered them to the girl, who let out another wail and drummed her feet against her chair.

All kids have tantrums, but for the first time, I felt sorry for Trehorne.

He swept his gaze around the room. When he saw me, he gave me an embarrassed smile, said something to Rebecca, and headed in my direction looking grateful for the excuse to leave the tantrum to his wife.

He climbed up the few rows to sit beside me, the metal benches creaking beneath his weight. He looked around again. People were filing into the arena, but it was a slow trickle, and the room was far from full.

"Damn shame," he said. "Time was, this place would have been packed."

"Maybe they heard about the murder."

"Some of 'em, maybe. But a killing don't keep people home. Just makes 'em travel in packs. Could be the heat, I guess. But used to be, it could be pouring down buckets or so hot these benches would burn right through your jeans. They all came out to see these horses go."

I tried for a neutral tone. "Hard to see it go downhill."

"Not downhill. Dying. And there doesn't seem to be a damn thing I can do to stop it."

"You ever think of showing flat shod? There'd be a down-turn at first, but people would get over it once they got used to seeing the more natural gait."

He spat onto the floor. "Don't be an idiot." Then, "Your good friends over at TASA, they talk about their plans for that damn association of theirs?"

"Nope. Too busy saving Zane's life and mourning for Maggie and trying to put their booth back together."

"I heard they had some trouble. Reap what you sow, I say. But damn shame about Maggie." He put a foot on the bleacher beside me and leaned in close. "Last month they put out a newsletter. All the names of the breeders and trainers who've ever had violations. Nothing about how the tests are fallible. Nothing about how the judges are corrupt. You know how many people read that newsletter?"

I shook my head. No idea.

"Fifteen thousand." His fists curled and uncurled. "Fifteen thousand tree huggers who wouldn't know a Walking Horse if it stepped on 'em. But hell, they all have an opinion."

"You know what they say about opinions. They're like ass-holes. Everybody has one."

He laughed as if I'd partially redeemed myself, then said, "Just out of curiosity, what did young Zane remember yesterday?"

I said, "He said something about a guy named Owen Bodeen. Carlin said Bodeen disappeared after the accident, never even visited Zane in the hospital. Didn't anybody think that was strange?"

"It's a transient lifestyle," Trehorne said. "Grooms, trainers, stable hands . . . They come and go."

"Not Bodeen. He'd been with Zane's family a lot of years."

"That's so. But Zane was like a son to him. I don't think Owen could face what happened to him."

"Any idea where he might have gone?"

"None."

"You think Zane's family might?"

"No idea. You ask a lot of questions for a guy who's supposed to be giving me answers."

I shrugged. "It's what I do. Follow leads. Some mean something. Others don't. I don't know until I follow them."

He took his foot off the bleacher. "You do what you have to do, but don't forget whose check is burning a hole in your wallet." He pressed his fists into the small of his back and stretched. In his VIP box, Esmerelda had stopped wailing and settled into a series of loud, angry hiccups. "I've got to get back to my family."

"Looks like somebody's having a bad day."

"She's tired and bored. Nobody to play with. And she wanted a Happy Meal instead of the sandwiches her mother made us at home." He lifted his hands, palms up. *What can you do?* "You think about what I said. Carlin Underwood has a plan, maybe to accuse me of soring, maybe to plant undercover workers at my barn and manufacture evidence. Whatever it is, I want to know about it."

I gave him a mock salute, and his small eyes narrowed even smaller.

"Don't mess with me, boy," he said. "Or, as God is my witness, I will make you very, very sorry."

"Duly noted," I said, and watched him stalk down the aisle to console his sobbing child.

29.

When I got back to the trailer, Khanh was sitting at the table in the breakfast nook, tapping something into the laptop. The side of her face and the skin around the butterfly bandage on her forehead were starting to bruise. Her hair was damp from the shower, and the file folder lay on the table beside her. As I slid onto the bench across from her, she pushed it over to me. Copies of the reports.

I read them in silence. They were what you'd expect in a rural community. Crushed by a tractor, killed in a car wreck, neck broken in a fall from a haymow. Two suicides: one by gunshot, one by hanging.

I'd gotten most of that online. What I hadn't gotten were the names in the blanks for medical examiner and investigating officers. The name Trehorne came up often. When I had time, I'd run the rest through my family-tree databases, but I knew now what I'd find. A web of links by blood and marriage.

There wasn't much to read. The cases had been ruled accidents and suicides, then quickly closed. If there was a smoking gun other than small-town nepotism, I wouldn't find it in the official files.

I put the reports back into the folder and closed it. Khanh looked up. "You learn anything?"

I nodded. "Not about the deaths, but about the investigations. I can see why Eli latched onto a conspiracy theory."

"You think he wrong?"

"My guess is, yes and no. What happened to Maggie and Zane—and you—proves something's going on. But I doubt all these cases are related."

"You think some, maybe?"

"I think some, probably." I pushed the folder across the table. "You did good work today."

She looked up, smiling. "You, me, make good team. You do good work today too."

My cell phone chirped, announcing an incoming text. I looked at it and said, "Billy says they're over at the TASA booth trying to put things back together. Want to go give them a hand?"

"Sure. Maybe stop for donut." She turned off the computer and pushed herself off the bench. "Those donut very good. Have one yesterday while you go get ice. Maybe have one now. You want try one? I go get us some, meet you at booth."

"Sure, why not?"

She held out her hand like a child asking for her allowance.

"Seriously? I thought you were offering to buy."

"You rich American, I poor Vietnam relative. Also you boss man, write off on taxes."

I sighed and pulled a twenty out of my pocket. "Don't spend it all in one place."

∽

While Khanh went for the donuts, I took a couple of extra-strength Tylenols and walked to the booth. The sky was darkening, and the lights came up. The crowd milled, stocking up on festival food before the Big Lick classes began.

At the booth, Carlin and Billy were separating torn pamphlets from salvageable ones, while Zane sat at the counter painstakingly burnishing promotional buttons and dropping them into a box. He fumbled a button back onto the counter, picked it up with his thumb and four fingers like a carnival claw.

Gerardo stood in the middle of the wreckage looking like he didn't know whether to grab a broom or an AK-47. He bent to pick up one of the T-shirts and folded it awkwardly with his bandaged hands, watching the rest of us from the corner of his eye.

"You look like the wrong side of midnight," Carlin said to me. She tossed a handful of torn flyers into a plastic garbage can. "Billy told me about the accident. Is Khanh all right?"

"She's a little banged up, but she's okay. The truck, however, is done for."

Carlin made the sign of the cross, last rites for the Silverado. *Rest in peace, old buddy.* "I'm sorry about the truck, but I'm glad Khanh came through it in one piece."

"Speak of the devil," Billy said.

Khanh shuffled through the crowd, her bandaged arm hugging a plastic milk crate. Inside were a bag with a dozen donuts in it and a cardboard carrier with six cups of coffee. She made a show of offering me the change, which I made a show of telling her to keep. There wasn't much anyway.

"*Gracias*, sweet lady," said Gerardo, with a rare smile. Khanh blushed and took a sip of coffee.

The donuts were homemade, heavy with grease, grainy with sugar, and more delicious than they had any right to be. The coffee was bitter and burnt, but maybe I'd just gotten used to the taste of Khanh's sweet Vietnamese blend.

"We need to talk about last night," I said. "The attack on Zane. This isn't going to go away until we make it go away."

"I know," Carlin said. She pitched another handful of flyers, then went to the counter and took Zane's hand in hers. "I've been racking my brain ever since it happened, but I just can't figure it out. I get why someone might target me. I've made a lot of enemies. But why would anybody want to hurt Zane?"

Billy said, "Who knows why people do what they do? Maybe someone felt threatened. Maybe someone thinks they'll get a mention in the will."

Carlin snorted. "If they know us well enough to think that, they know they won't get anything but debt."

Billy picked up a torn pamphlet and ripped it to confetti, watching the pieces flutter into the can. "Maybe someone thought they were doing him a favor."

"Some favor," she said.

"We can't rule it out," I said. "But considering everything else that's happened, I don't think that's it. I think they're neutralizing a threat."

Carlin ran her fingers over the veins in the back of Zane's clawed hand. "He's no threat to anybody."

Zane looked down, pulled his hand away. No man wants to be considered 'not a threat.'

"There's more 'n one way to be a threat," Billy said.

She started to speak, closed her mouth again. You didn't have to be psychic to know what she'd almost said.

Billy said, "You blackmailing somebody, son? Got information that could put somebody behind bars?"

Zane shook his head. "NOTHING. I KNOW NOTHING."

"He knows soring," Carlin said. "Who does, who doesn't. But why try to kill Zane? Everybody in the industry knows all that."

"Could be," Billy said. "The question is, do they—whoever did this—do *they* know that?"

"No," I said, and looked at Zane. "The question is, what do you know that you don't know you know?"

Zane blinked.

Gerardo said, "How can he tell you, if he doesn't know he knows?"

I looked at Zane. "You saw Junior and Eli standing in the sun, and you remembered something."

Zane gave a slow nod. "BUT IT WASN'T ANYTHING IMPORTANT."

"Maybe," I said. "But maybe someone was afraid it might lead to something that was."

Zane cocked his head, then looked at Carlin and typed, "I WANT TO GO TO JAKE'S AND HAVE A BEER WITH MY FRIEND."

She shook her head. "Honey, you know he isn't here. Owen left after your accident."

"I WANT TO HAVE A BEER WITH MY FRIEND JARED."

She started to protest. There were a thousand reasons to say no. It had been a long day, he was tired, the alcohol could interact badly with his seizure meds. But Zane clenched his teeth and pressed *repeat* on the DynaVox until the robot voice wore her down.

She pressed her fingers to her temples. "Were you always so hardheaded?"

"YES."

That brought a smile. "I remember now. Fine. We'll take the van. It has the wheelchair lift."

"NO," Zane typed. "JUST ME AND MY FRIEND JARED."

194 A TASTE OF BLOOD AND ASHES

Hurt flashed in her eyes. Then she sighed. "I get it. Guy talk. At least take Gerardo with you." She gave me an apologetic smile. "No offense, but you're hurt."

"So is Gerardo."

"We hardly know you."

Billy shifted his weight. "You know he saved your husband's life, right?"

"Yes, but I'd—"

Repeat.

Repeat.

Repeat.

"Enough." She flipped the power button off. He glared at her and pushed it back on. His finger hovered over the *repeat* button.

She put her hand over his. "No, don't. I concede."

Billy said, "I'll look out for Khanh while you're gone."

"Not need babysitter," Khanh said, but she smiled. "Maybe could use bodyguard."

Gerardo sighed. "Fine. Let them go. But, *hombre*, if you let anything happen to him . . ."

"Yeah, yeah, you'll kill me. I've heard that from better men than you."

"I doubt it," he said with a grin, and went to pull the van around.

30.

It felt late, but it was only eight thirty. By the time we got to Jake's place, the bar was hopping. A bartender who probably doubled as a bouncer flexed his biceps as he tapped draft beer into a frosted mug. There was a steer's head over the bar and a live band playing up front, just a guy on guitar and another on bass and a girl on the drums. She had shaggy dark hair and pale skin, dramatic eyes, and lipstick the color of swamp moss. She could play the hell out of the drums.

The hostess looked fresh out of high school, a pale, freckled girl with red hair tied back with a red and white bandana. She wore tight jeans and a checkered shirt knotted at the midriff. Her gaze lingered on Zane's chair for half a beat too long, but she recovered, flashed him a dutiful smile, and said, "Two for the bar?"

I looked at Zane. "Do you remember where you sat before?"

He swept the room with his gaze. Landed on a booth in the back corner near the dartboard and the pool tables. A couple sat there on the same side of the table sharing a plate of deep-fried onion straws.

"THAT ONE."

I looked at the girl. "You heard the man."

"It's occupied."

I pulled out forty bucks and said, "Ask them to move to another table."

"Really?" She grinned, snatched the two twenties, and tucked them into her bra. "What's in it for them?"

"I was going to say forty bucks, but I didn't take the middle man into account."

"Business 101. You have to account for the middle man."

I peeled off another twenty. "One for you, two for them. There are two of them, and they're being inconvenienced."

"I'm being inconvenienced too," she said, but then she must have decided there might be a chance for greater rewards later. She sashayed over to the table and talked to the couple for a few minutes. They got up and moved, giggling, to another booth.

"Do you need the chair?" I asked.

He shook his head and pulled up his shirt to show me the supportive abdominal binder beneath. "I CAN SIT UP. MOSTLY."

I got Zane and his DynaVox onto the far bench and myself onto the other, facing him across the table. The wheelchair sat at the end like a guest of honor.

"What's your poison?" I asked him.

"SAM ADAMS."

"And what's mine?"

He gave me an appraising look, then said, "CORONA."

"My luck," I said, but I put in the order. While we waited, I said, "You wanted to talk to me. About Owen Bodeen?"

He nodded. "REMEMBERED WE CAME HERE THAT NIGHT."

"The night of the accident."

"HE SAID SOMETHING IMPORTANT."

I waited. When he didn't add anything else, I said, "What was it?"

"I DON'T KNOW. THOUGHT MAYBE HERE—" He stopped, gave his shoulders a little hunch.

"You thought maybe if you came here, you'd remember something. Worth a try."

He hung his head. "NOT WORKING I DON'T RE-MEMBER ANYTHING. USELESS."

"Don't think about it so hard. Let's just talk."

He looked unhappy, but he nodded.

"Tell me about Owen. He worked for your family?"

It took him a long time to type. Patience, I reminded myself, and wondered how long it had been since he'd had a real conversation with anyone but Carlin and maybe Gerardo.

I waited, and finally, the machine said, "MY DAD'S AGE. I LIKED TO HELP HIM WHEN I WAS A KID. HE ALWAYS HAD TIME FOR ME."

I nodded. My father had died when I was four. I understood that yearning for a man to look up to. But Zane's had been alive when he was growing up. A troubled relationship long before his parents had disowned him. "Your family sored their horses?"

"CALLED IT FIXING THEM. I THOUGHT THAT WAS THE RIGHT WAY TO TRAIN A HORSE."

"Then you met Carlin."

"SHE WAS SO BEAUTIFUL." He smiled at the memory. "I'D TAKE HER PLACES. MOVIES. RESTAURANTS. WOODS. REALIZED I DIDN'T WANT TO TAKE HER TO THE FARM. I DIDN'T WANT HER TO SEE WHAT WE WERE DOING AND THAT'S HOW I KNEW IT WAS WRONG. BECAUSE I DIDN'T WANT HER TO KNOW."

"She and your family didn't get along."

"SHE WAS EVERYTHING THEY HATED."

"And Owen?"

"HE WAS DISAPPOINTED BUT HE UNDERSTOOD. I THINK HE GOT WHERE THE SORING BOTHERED HIM AFTER A WHILE."

"But he didn't quit."

"WHERE WAS HE GOING TO GO, A MAN HIS AGE AND WITH A DISABILITY?"

I lifted an eyebrow. "What kind of disability?"

"HURT HIS BACK IN A FALL FROM A BULL. HE DID THE RODEO CIRCUIT WHEN HE WAS YOUNG. HE WAS A CHAMPION."

"You say he spent time with you. What did you do?"

"WHEN I WAS A KID? TALKED, FISHED, WHIT-TLED, RODE HORSES. HE TAUGHT ME HOW TO TRAIN A HORSE."

"How to sore a horse."

"AND MORE. IT'S COMPLICATED. HE LOVED THEM."

"And he hurt them."

"YES, BOTH. HE DIDN'T LIKE HURTING THEM. PEOPLE DO WHAT THEY KNOW HOW TO DO."

"And when you came here that night, you sat over there, where you are, and he sat over here, where I am."

He nodded.

"You drank Sam Adams, and he had a Corona. Did you eat?"

"NACHOS. THE WORKS."

"What was the band playing?"

He thought a minute. "'FRIENDS IN LOW PLACES.'"

I got up and put in an order for nachos and a request with the band. Came back and slid into my seat. "Anything else?"

"PRETTY GIRL ON THE MECHANICAL BULL." He grinned as if appreciating the memory.

"I can't help with that one. Who else was here?"

"EVERYBODY. JUNIOR. HE SAT THERE."

He nodded toward the next table. Close enough to hear something, maybe. Or maybe not.

"Was he by himself?"

He thought about it. Shook his head.

"Who was with him?"

He squeezed his eyes shut. Shook his head again. "DON'T REMEMBER."

I led him through the conversation with Owen Bodeen, getting the broad outlines and circling back to fill in the gaps he'd forgotten. There were a lot of them.

I said, "Why do you think he left?"

He spread his hands and looked down at his broken body. "THIS."

It was the act of a coward, leaving so abruptly, not even stopping at the hospital to say good-bye. But then, so was soring horses out of fear of unemployment. I felt a sudden dislike for the man.

"DAMN." Zane slapped the DynaVox. "HE SAID HE SAID HE SAID HE SAID."

"You're close. Just give it a minute."

The door banged open, and the sheriff swaggered in. He scanned the room, then sauntered over to our booth. He nodded to me, then said to Zane, "Haven't seen you out and about for a while."

"HAVEN'T BEEN OUT IN A WHILE."

"Heck of a few days you and your little lady are having. Just wondered if, now that you're remembering things, you've come up with anything that might shed light on the investigation."

Zane's face was all innocence. "THERE'S AN INVESTI-GATION?"

Hap flushed. "Of course there's a damn investigation. You know what we think so far?"

"NO. ENLIGHTEN ME."

"The way we see it, Carlin isn't likely to have put the remains in the stables. We don't have a cause of death yet, but keeping bones as trophies isn't the sort of thing women usually do."

"Makes sense so far," I said. "But why are you thinking trophies?"

"What other reason to keep human remains in your own barn long enough for them to skeletonize?"

"Trophy-taking implies serial killer. But there's only one body that we know of."

"That we know of," he said. He turned back to Zane. "With Carlin out of it, that leaves us with you and Mr. Gonzales. Can't tell when the victim died because of the fire, so we can't rule you out. You might have killed the vic before your accident and not been able to get back there to dispose of the bones. Or you might have kept them on purpose, reliving your kill."

"RIDICULOUS."

"Is it?" He cocked his head, looked at Zane. "Grant you, I've known you a long time, and I wouldn't think you were the type. But what do we really know about your Mr. Gonzales? All we know is there were human bones in a barn he had access to."

"That's the theory you're pursuing?" I said. "That either Zane or Gerardo is a serial killer?"

"More likely a budding one. Could be there's just been the one so far, and either Zane got hurt before he could kill again, or Gonzales is in a cooling-off period." As theories went, it was unsupported but not completely unreasonable. He said to Zane, "For what it's worth, my money's on Gonzales. Though that doesn't explain why somebody else tried to kill you last night. Anything you remember that could shed some light on that would be appreciated."

"I DON'T REMEMBER ANYTHING," Zane said.

"Your memory's coming back. You must remember something."

"NO, NOTHING."

Hap looked Zane over slowly, like there was a bad taste in his mouth, and said, "If that's the way you want to play it."

"THAT'S THE WAY I WANT TO PLAY IT."

"Then don't bitch to me when the guy gets away with it."

We watched him walk away.

"Nice guy," I said.

"SOMETIMES YES," Zane typed. "SOMETIMES NO."

And then, the way a song you've been trying to remember will pop into your head when you finally stop thinking about it, it came to him.

"I REMEMBER."

He turned off the sound on the DynaVox and tapped something into it. It took him a long time, and when he was finished, he sat back and watched me turn the screen so I could read it. I stared at the letters he'd typed as if I could look past the words and absorb the story behind them.

Things were preying on his mind, Owen had said. He'd just been diagnosed with cancer, a bad one, pancreatic. Things hadn't gotten as bad as they would, but he knew his clock was ticking, and he hoped to leave this life a better man than he had been. He'd done things he wasn't proud of, soring among them. But the thing that bothered him the most was not something he'd done, but something he had failed to do. He'd failed to save a man's life, then kept his silence.

For forty years, he'd kept that secret, but now, with the Grim Reaper tapping at his shoulder, he needed to come clean. Forty years ago, he said, he'd seen Dalt Underwood, Samuel Trehorne, and Doc Willoughby kill Thomas Cole, erase the tape in his recorder, and leave a bottle of whiskey in his hand.

"Well," I said. "Now we know what someone thought was important enough to kill for."

31.

We left our beers half-finished and went back to the van. I sent Zane up on the lift and strapped him in, my ribs protesting as I secured his chair with fasteners on the floor and the wall. He seemed subdued, but it was hard to say whether that was because of the memory he'd recovered or the stresses of the past few days.

"Feel like taking a side trip?" I said.

"SIDE TRIP WHERE?"

"I want to take a look around your barn again."

"YOU THINK HAP MISSED SOMETHING?"

"We'll see, I guess. If you're up for it."

"I'M UP FOR IT."

I climbed into the driver's seat with a grunt of pain. Shot Khanh a quick text and put the phone back in my pocket. "What did you think of the sheriff's theory?"

"THAT I'M A SERIAL KILLER? NOT MUCH."

"And Gerardo? Is he capable of that?"

The DynaVox was silent.

"Zane?"

"I DON'T THINK SO."

"But you aren't sure. Carlin wouldn't tell me his story yesterday, but maybe it's time somebody did. What do you know about him?"

In the rearview mirror, I saw him bend over his keyboard. "I KNOW HE'S IN LOVE WITH MY WIFE."

It wasn't a surprise, but hearing it made it seem more real. "How does she feel about that? About him?"

"HOW DO YOU THINK SHE FEELS? HE'S HANDSOME. HEALTHY. WHOLE."

"It's pretty clear she loves you."

"I KNOW SHE DOES, BUT IT'S NOT THE SAME." His hand hovered over the board. "I'M NOT THE SAME."

There were a dozen platitudes I might have quoted. *You'll get through this. Love overcomes all. You are more than your scars.* They were all trite and superficial, and none of them would have helped.

I said, "Have you talked to her about it?"

"NO. I DON'T WANT TO KNOW." He was quiet for a moment, then said, "I WISH I DIDN'T KNOW."

"You think they're having an affair? My line of work, I know a lot about these things, and I'm pretty sure they're not."

"NOT YET." He took a long breath, then typed, "FOR A LONG TIME AFTER THE ACCIDENT, I WANTED TO DIE. I STILL THINK ABOUT IT A LOT. PLAN HOW I COULD DO IT. IT WOULD SAVE EVERYONE A LOT OF TROUBLE. CLEAR THE WAY FOR THEM TO BE TOGETHER. I THOUGHT IT WAS THE BEST THING. MAYBE I STILL DO. BUT THEN LAST NIGHT. WHEN I FELT THAT PILLOW OVER MY FACE. I FOUGHT SO HARD TO LIVE. WHY DIDN'T I JUST LET HIM KILL ME?"

"Maybe you aren't done yet."

He thumped the arm of his chair. "LOOKS TO ME LIKE I'M DONE."

I said, "I watched that video of you training that colt in front of the crowd. You had something. It wasn't just the way you moved or the way you talked. They were hanging on your every word."

"I WAS A GOOD-LOOKING GUY WITH A GOOD SMILE," he said. "PEOPLE LIKE THAT."

"It was more than that. It was style, charisma, confidence. That thing nobody can define. It's who you are, which means you still have it. You just have to find it again."

"MAYBE, MAYBE NOT," he said. "BUT YOU WANTED TO KNOW ABOUT GERARDO. HE'S FROM MEXICO. A SMALL VILLAGE. LOTS OF TROUBLE WITH THE CARTELS."

I nodded. So far it was a familiar story.

"SOME OF THE VILLAGERS FOUGHT THEM. LIKE FREEDOM FIGHTERS. GUERRILLA FIGHTERS. GERARDO WAS ONE OF THOSE."

While Zane typed, I took the main road out of Hidden Hollow, then followed a ten-mile stretch of winding roads that led to the Underwood farm. The story unfolded in the metallic voice of the DynaVox.

"HE WAS ENGAGED TO A WOMAN IN THE VILLAGE. ROSA WAS HER NAME. BUT THE LEADER OF THE CARTEL WANTED HER, AND WHAT HE WANTED HE TOOK. GERARDO SWORE HE'D GET HER BACK. IT TOOK HIM FOUR YEARS, TRAINING HARD, GETTING BETTER AND BETTER AT COMBAT, FINDING GUNS AND MEN. IN THE END, HE CUT THROUGH THEM LIKE THEY WERE BUTTER AND TOOK HER, LEFT THE LEADER OF THE CARTEL CHOKING TO DEATH ON HIS OWN BLOOD."

"Which made him a fugitive."

"THE CARTEL PASSED TO THE LEADER'S SON. HE PUT A BOUNTY ON GERARDO'S HEAD. ROSA'S TOO."

"So they came here."

"AND FOUND WORK WITH SAMUEL TREHORNE. GERARDO WORKED IN THE STABLES. SHE WORKED IN THE KITCHEN."

There'd been no woman but Carlin at the Underwood farm. I said, "I take it things went bad."

"SHE DIED IN CHILDBIRTH. THEY WERE ILLE-GAL, SO THEY HAD NO INSURANCE, NOT MUCH MONEY. TREHORNE AND HIS WIFE CONVINCED HIM THEY COULD GIVE THE CHILD A BETTER LIFE. A LITTLE GIRL."

"Esmerelda."

"YES."

"Why'd he leave there to work for you?"

"IT HURT TOO MUCH TO STAY. EVERYTHING REMINDED HIM OF ROSA. BUT HE WANTED TO STAY CLOSE BECAUSE OF ESMERELDA. AND—."

"And?"

"TREHORNE WAS SORING BACK THEN. GERARDO HATED IT. BUT WHAT COULD HE DO? HE WAS AN ILLEGAL IMMIGRANT AND THEY HAD HIS DAUGHTER."

"Does she know he's her father?"

"I DOUBT IT."

I tried to imagine watching Paulie grow up, having no say in his upbringing, missing his first words and his first steps, him never knowing he was mine. I couldn't have stood it.

Then the sign that marked the Underwoods' driveway loomed up, and I turned the van onto the gravel drive and pulled it to a stop. I turned the headlights toward the charred ruins of the barn, found a flashlight in the glove compartment. "Wait here," I said.

For the first time since I'd met him, he laughed. "WHERE WOULD I GO? AND HOW WOULD I GET THERE?"

Sweeping the flashlight beam in front of me, I crunched across the gravel, crossed the circle of parched grass, and stepped into the rubble that had once been the stables. I climbed over a fallen beam, careful of my injured ribs, and found the place where I'd discovered the fragments of bone.

I knelt in the ashes and began to dig with my hands. Trehorne's people had done a better job this time, and I found no more teeth or bones. Sifting through the ashes, I found splintered wood, melted metal bits, and finally, a misshapen metal oval.

In the glove box of the Silverado, I'd had latex gloves and plastic baggies. Since the van was lacking in forensic investigation supplies, I held the tarnished oval by the edges and blew the soot off, then looked at it in the pale beam of the flashlight. It was a silver filigree belt buckle. The engraved letters read: *1969 Bull Riding Champion.*

Owen Bodeen.

I felt a pang of guilt for misjudging him, then a crushing sadness that was less for the dead man than for the one who'd loved him like a father.

I trudged back to the van and punched on the overhead light. Held the buckle up for Zane to see.

An animal moan came from his throat.

"Owen?" I said.

He nodded, then turned his head away, shoulders shaking with silent sobs.

32.

The courthouse was dark when we passed through Hidden Hollow. The flagpole was bare, the cannon a black glint in the moonlight. We passed the place where Khanh had wrecked the Silverado. In the headlight beams, the damage the grille had done to the tree was a pale wound against the bark. I gave myself a moment to grieve, then turned my thoughts back to the case, this new development.

We passed the steakhouse, which was closed, and then the bar. The parking lot at Jake's was still packed, and tinny music leaked from the doors and windows. The band must be on break.

I turned into the main gate of the showground and wound back through the trucks and trailers. Rolled to a stop beside the Underwoods' trailer, where Carlin and Gerardo were waiting for us by the fire pit. He had a beer in his hand, and when we pulled up, he put it down and came to operate the lift.

"I guess you don't have to kill me," I said, trying to unfasten the chair from its moorings without bending in the middle.

Looking at Zane's tear-streaked face, Gerardo said, "That remains to be seen. What happened to him?"

I took the buckle from my shirt pocket, still holding it by the edges, and showed him the embossed letters. Carlin came and looked over his shoulder.

"Oh no," she said. And then to Zane, "Oh, baby, I'm so sorry."

I put it back into my pocket. Thought of calling the sheriff again but decided it could wait. It was late, and I was tired and sore, and if his people had been better, he would have had the buckle already.

While Gerardo wrangled Zane's chair out of the van, I motioned Carlin aside. I brought her up to speed about Zane's memory and the trip to the barn. Then I said, "There's something else. It's not my business, but you probably ought to know."

She gave a wary nod. "Go on."

"He knows there's something between you and Gerardo."

A wash of pink crept up her neck. "There's nothing going on with me and Gerardo."

"Just because you haven't acted on it doesn't mean there's nothing going on. And don't look at me like that. I'm just the messenger."

She closed her eyes and laced her fingers behind her head, as if she could unhear what I'd said. "I love Zane," she said. "I really do."

"I know you do," I said. "You need to talk this out with him. Figure out what you want."

"It doesn't matter what I want." She brought her hands down to the nape of her neck, rubbing out the tension. "I'm his wife. I took a vow, for better or worse. This thing with Gerardo . . . We're trying to do the right thing. Maybe it's wrong to do the right thing for the wrong reasons. I don't know. But I don't know what else to do. I can't leave Zane, not now, not like this."

"Just talk to him," I said.

"Last night when you called to tell me you'd saved him, you know what I thought? I thought things would have been easier if you hadn't. I hate myself for thinking that. I wish I could unthink it, but I can't. Am I supposed to tell him that?"

"That's not for me to decide," I said. "It would hurt him, for sure. But I don't think he'd be surprised. I'm pretty sure he thought it too."

I left her with her problems and walked back through the maze of trailers. The night smelled of grilled meat with undertones of sawdust and pine. Most of the trailers were dark, but I could see the glow of an occasional campfire. I heard a low grumble, turned to see Mace Ewing staring at me. He was standing by a campfire, a bottle of Jack Daniel's in one hand. The trailer behind him was about the size of mine. A magnetic sign on the side gave a phone number, website, and the simple message *Horses Broke and Trained.*

He swayed on his feet, blinked at me with glassy eyes. The bruising around them was shiny and purple, the splint on his nose a metallic glint. "What're you looking at?"

"You tell me. A guilty conscience?"

"Asshole." His words were already slurred. "You don't know anything about me."

I'd misstepped with the smartass comment. It had felt good to say it, but it wouldn't get me what I needed. It had only served to make him more defensive.

"Where's your bandana?" I said, and watched his face for a reaction.

"My what?"

"Harley Davidson, got skulls all over it."

He swayed on his feet, thinking about it. "Around, I guess. Don't matter. They're a dime a dozen."

I decided to let it go for now. "I owe you an apology for yesterday. The thing with your mare."

He took a swig of Jack. There wasn't much left.

I said, "I shouldn't have barged in. I should have come and talked to you about it."

"You should have minded your own business." He waved the bottle in my general direction. "I'm a good trainer."

"So I hear."

"Been trainin' since I was fourteen. Never sored, neither. Never have, never will."

Trudy had told me as much. His pride in that fact made me feel just a hair better about him. Unless, of course, he'd been the one who'd attacked Zane.

"I've done a little training myself," I said. "Maybe we could compare notes sometime."

"Don't need to compare notes. I got all the notes I need."

"What if I bought her from you? The mare."

"Not for sale."

"Not for sale, or not for sale to me?"

"Take your pick. Then take yourself out of my sight." He tipped back the bottle, found it empty. "Shit."

He looked at it as if it had betrayed him.

"I hear you're a big outdoorsman," I said. "Fishing, hunting, horseback riding."

"All of the above." He swayed again, then stumbled forward and caught himself inches from the fire. "I know what you're doing there."

"What am I doing?"

"You want me to tell you what a hotshot hunter I am, how I bagged my first deer when I was eleven. Bet you never shot a deer in your whole life."

"Can't say I have."

"Pansy. My grandmother's tougher 'n you."

"Your grandmother is a deer hunter?"

"Damn straight she is. But you leave Grandma out of this." He staggered to a red and white Igloo cooler and rooted around inside. Handed a beer to me and took another for himself.

Southern hospitality. He wanted to kick my ass, but damned if he could drink a beer without offering me one.

He took a long swig, wiped his mouth with his wrist.

I said, "How full was that bottle of Jack when you started?"

"Full enough," he said. "What's it to you?"

"Just wondering if I should worry about alcohol poisoning."

He laughed. "Don't you worry about me. I got the constitution of a bull buffalo."

"I talked to Trudy earlier," I said.

"You stay away from her." He emphasized each word with a little jab of the bottle. "She's a good woman."

"Her honor's safe with me."

"Yeah, you're a real gentleman, sniffing around Rhonda Lister."

"Let's leave Rhonda out of this. She took me to see Doc, gave me a ride when I needed one. That's all."

He smirked. "I bet she gave you a ride."

"Trudy said you were a decent guy. You're making that hard to believe."

"You looking to be my new best friend? I'm not a good guy to be friends with." He knocked back the beer, went back for another. "You want one?"

"I'm good."

He fumbled the lid back onto the cooler, then sank down beside it, scratching at the pop top. He stared at it as if it were engaged in an act of calculated resistance. "Fuck."

A tear rolled down his cheek and caught in the stubble on his jaw.

I eased onto the ground beside him, leaned my back against the cooler. My side ached, but it was bearable. "You passed happy drunk a long time ago."

He growled, a primal sound. "What do you know about it?"

I said, "A blind man could see something's eating you up. Your friend Dan?"

A sob tore from his throat. "You aren't my friend," he said. "You want me to say I killed him."

"You did kill him," I said.

"I did," he said softly. His gaze was unfocused with alcohol and memory. "Yes, indeed I did."

The need to talk rolled off of him like steam. You could look at him and tell he was burning up with it. I looked away from him, watching the flames in the fire pit leap and dance, and said, "How did it happen?"

A silence stretched between us. Stretched and filled with all the words he wanted to say but was afraid to, and when it had taken in all it could, it burst open like a rain cloud.

It had poured for three days before the hunting trip, but the morning they met, the rain had slackened to a drizzle. There were five of them, best friends and fathers and cousins, all guys who'd been hunting and fishing together since Mace was a kid. At thirty-two, Mace was the youngest of the group. Dan, twenty years older, was the oldest, but they'd formed a bond over the years, whispering in deer blinds, frying catfish over campfires, drinking beers and talking about NASCAR while the fire crackled and the wind rustled the leaves and blew sweet cedar smoke into their eyes.

There was tension between them now, though, because while Mace sympathized with Dan's antisoring stance, Dan had brought bad publicity down on all of them, and Mace's bottom line had suffered as much as anyone's. Junior Trehorne had been vocal about it, and tempers had flared and then subsided to a simmer.

The day of the accident, they'd set up their campsite, then hiked up toward Eagle Creek, Mace in the lead with his Remington .30/06, Dan with his lighter Sako Finnlight following behind. They planned to split up later, two to a blind and Junior alone in a tree stand. Mace and Dan were a team, and for the first time in years, Mace wasn't happy about it.

He was halfway across the creek, placing his feet carefully on the slippery rocks, when Junior, third in line, muttered something that made Dan turn around. "What did you say?"

Junior smirked. "I said, if I were Mace, I wouldn't turn my back on you like that. Might find a knife in it."

Dan's fist tightened on his rifle. "I did the right thing, turning that guy in. Hotshot trainer, raking in the bucks by hurting horses. Guys like that, they give us all a bad name."

"No, guys like you give us a bad name. Why didn't you just come to us, let us take care of it from the inside?"

"Because," Dan said quietly, "you wouldn't have. Don't tell me you didn't all know what he was doing."

Junior said, "Our profits dropped 50 percent last month. Two different reporters came sniffing around our farm. How about you, Mace? I know you've lost business."

Mace didn't answer. It was true, he had lost business, and God knew it wasn't fair, because he didn't sore. No one cared about that though. When they saw he did the Big Lick, they just tarred him with the same brush.

"What do you want from me?" Dan said. "It hurt my business too."

Mace spun around midstream. *That was your choice, not ours,* he started to say, but then his foot slid sideways off the rock, and he was falling, falling, his finger tightening on the trigger of the Remington.

The rifle barked and bucked in his hand.

Dan staggered sideways, a red bloom staining the front of his shirt. His mouth dropped open, and he slumped into the water in slow motion, a look of surprise and betrayal on his face.

❧

Mace's voice trailed off. "I play that moment over and over in my mind. Why was my finger on the trigger? Did I swing the barrel toward him as I went down?" His cheeks were wet, but he didn't bother to wipe the tears. "Do you want me to tell you I wanted him dead? That I had some crazy impulse when I started to fall and realized he was standing right in front of me? That for just a moment, just that wrong moment, I hated him?"

"Did you?" I said.

He leaned back against the cooler, his arms outstretched like Christ on the cross. The unopened beer can rolled from his open palm. "I'd tell you if I could," he said. "I really would. Because I wish to God I knew."

33.

Billy was waiting by the fire when I got back. He'd laid out my air mattress and sleeping bag and given the horses their evening meal. I thanked him and said, "How's Khanh?"

"Wrung out. She wanted to wait up for you, but I promised to wake her up if you got yourself killed, and she finally went on to bed. You want a beer?"

"I think I had enough."

I brought him up to speed, and he said, "How come all the good stuff happens when I'm somewhere else?"

"It's your imposing demeanor. Scares all the bad guys into good behavior."

"Right."

"How are you on sleep?"

"I'm good. You want me to keep an eye on the Underwoods?"

Knowing what I did about Gerardo, I thought they were probably safe enough tonight. "Nah. Take a break. You want to grab a room at one of those bed-and-breakfasts and meet me back here sometime tomorrow?"

He grunted. "Rest and relaxation in a beautiful pastoral setting. What are you tryin' to do? Kill me?"

∽

Saturday Morning

Khanh must have been exhausted, because she was still asleep when I woke up the next morning. I took two more Tylenols and did my requisite deep breathing, found it marginally more comfortable than being ripped open by shrapnel. I'd just finished feeding and watering the horses when a soft footfall scraped the ground behind me, and Rhonda Lister said, "I thought I'd come by and see if you needed some help."

She'd clipped her hair back on the sides and let the curls fall down her back. Her tight jeans had sequins on the pockets, and her powder-blue shirt was knotted beneath her breasts. She looked young and wholesome, like a woman on a cereal box.

I said, "I'm just about done here, but I'm about to take the boys for a walk. They could use the exercise. Want to come along?"

"Sure. I could use some too." She patted her stomach, moved in close enough for me to smell her perfume, some rich blend of spices and exotic flowers that fogged my brain and weakened my knees.

She looked just fine to me, but I didn't say so. Instead I got two halters and two lead ropes from the tack compartment, gave her Crockett's red ensemble and kept Tex's turquoise. It was early, but the sun was already bright, the sky a brilliant blue.

"I stopped by last night," she said. "You must have been out late."

"I took Zane down to Jake's. We had a couple beers."

"That was nice of you," she said. "I think his world has gotten very small in the last year."

"It wasn't altruism," I said. "We were talking about the case."

"Did you learn anything new?"

I told her about Zane's revelation and Owen's belt buckle. Watched her face for a reaction and thought I saw a flash of alarm quickly supplanted by a mix of sympathy and mild surprise. I wasn't worried that she'd spread the news. Hap or the Underwoods were just as likely to beat her to it. And maybe that was a good thing. Let whoever was behind the arson feel the net closing in.

"Poor Zane," she said. "And poor Owen. Do you think Junior killed him to protect his father?"

"Junior or someone he told about it."

"It doesn't change much, does it? It could still be almost anybody."

She was wrong, though I didn't say so. It changed everything. Because what were the odds that, on the very night he'd learned about Tom Cole's murder, on the very night the man who'd told him had been killed, Zane would end up bleeding on a stall floor with a broken back and a fractured skull?

The horses plodded at our sides as we wound between the trailers and out onto a grassy field behind the showground. It had been recently mowed but not raked, little mounds of clippings brown and drying in the sun.

She ran a hand down Crockett's neck. "Can I ride him?"

Maybe she was giving me a gracious out, maybe the open field had simply brought the thought to mind. *Go with the flow,* I thought, and said, "Depends. How good are you?"

"Good enough."

"Go ahead then."

She laughed, twisted a hank of mane around her fist, and in one fluid move, swung onto Crockett's back. Settling into the curve of his spine, she wrapped her legs around his sides.

I said, "You're a ringer. I thought you said you weren't a horseman."

"I said I'd rather drive a Ferrari. That doesn't mean I don't know how to ride. I learned right after Jim and I got married. Your horse, he neck reins?"

"If you want him to. But leg pressure's all he needs."

She urged him forward, then pushed him into a running walk and circled him around the field. His gait was smooth, his front legs arcing up and over like a water wheel. Her curls bounced softly between her shoulder blades.

I watched them circle once, twice, take a lazy serpentine. Then she pulled him to a stop in front of me, sitting deep with her hip bones and tugging gently on the lead rope. Her cheeks were flushed, her smile broad as she leaned forward and brought her far leg over his hips to dismount.

She landed lightly on the balls of her feet. Laughed again. "He's lovely."

"Better than a Ferrari?"

"I wouldn't go that far. Give me the smell of gasoline over the smell of horses any day."

"You're a madwoman," I said. "Not that I'd turn down a Ferrari, if somebody's handing them out."

We walked back toward the campground, a lightness between us that I knew couldn't last. I let the horses loose in the corral, and when I'd hooked the panel back in place, I realized Rhonda was kneeling by the fire pit, stirring up the flames. Another chunk of firewood and a small pile of twigs lay on the ground beside her knees. The air grew sweet with the smell of burning walnut.

She glanced up as I came to join her. Turned back to the fire as I sank into one of the director's chairs. She gave the wood another prod and watched the flames leap and the embers swirl. Her expression was rapt, almost covetous.

I watched her stare into the flames and finally said, "Tell me about the fire."

She blinked as if reeling herself back from a faraway place. The fire crackled and danced and she tore her gaze away from it and clasped her hands in her lap. "What about it?"

"You tell me."

She licked her lips and looked away. After a long moment, she said, "You know how you said you were looking to buy a horse? And I called you a liar?"

"And I told you—"

She held up a hand. "I lied to you too."

Not what I'd expected. "Oh? What did you lie about?"

She gave the firewood a fierce jab. "We talked about my father. I don't know why I told you about it. Maybe because you asked. Most people don't."

The weight in her voice said she was leading to some deep and private place, a place she'd kept locked down tight for a long time. An anxious flutter settled in my stomach, a fear of saying the wrong thing, of being trusted and found wanting. "And?"

"I told you he was dead before the flames reached him."

"That wasn't true?"

Her hands fisted on her thighs. "I watched all his races, every one I could talk my mother into taking me to. I was in the stands that day. The car spun around and around, and parts were flying, and gas was spewing, and then it crashed into the wall and . . . I don't know. I guess the impact, something sparked."

"And it went up."

"It went up." She fed a smaller stick into the fire, watched the bark glow red, then gray to ash. "It went up like a torch."

She was aware of people screaming. She could see their mouths move, like characters in a silent movie, but all she could hear were the squeal of tires and the clash of metal. Her mother's fingers dug into her upper arm. Then there was a whoosh of flame, and a high thin wail she knew must be her father's.

The windows filled with flames. Space compressed, and the crowd fell away, then the track, then the car itself, until all she could see was the square of glass and the terrible, beautiful flicker of fire.

Her eyes had welled, but she'd held them open wide and unblinking. As if by watching hard enough, she could will the door to open and her father to stumble out. He would be bruised, maybe even burned, but okay.

Then she saw it. A hand, *his* hand emerging from the flames, fingers spread wide, pounding on the glass.

"They said he died on impact," she said. "That he didn't feel a thing. Why would they say that?"

"Probably to give you comfort."

"It didn't comfort me," she said. "It just made me not trust anything they said."

"And you're still carrying it, aren't you? You never left that night behind."

"What do you want me to say? That I can't get it out of my mind? Well, I can't. That I go to fire-walking retreats and keep a lighter in my purse? Well, I do. A fire is like a tiger in a cage. You can't deny the beauty or the power. You can't tame it, but you can use it. You can keep it under control."

"Can you?"

"I didn't set that fire at Zane and Carlin Underwood's. I know that's what you're asking, and the answer is still no."

"Is that what I was asking? It wasn't meant to be an accusation."

She pushed herself up, dusted her hands on her jeans. Gently, she placed a hand on either side of my face and said, "Oh you silly, beautiful man. Of course it was."

She pressed her lips gently to mine, flicked her tongue between my teeth, then walked away, leaving me with an ache in my groin and the taste of her mouth on my tongue.

34.

While I waited for Khanh to wake up, I got my laptop from the tack room and did a quick background check on Lori Mae Tillman, the woman who had claimed to be drinking with Tom Cole on the night he died. She was deceased, dead almost two years from causes the obituary listed simply as natural. She was survived by three children, the oldest one a daughter, Sharon. I looked up her married name and tapped her into my database. Two small children, bachelor's in accounting, reasonable credit, no police record.

It was early, but a quick look at her Facebook page showed she was online. The wonders of modern technology. I dialed her number, and the phone's default voice mail directed me to leave a brief message. I did, and she called me right back. She had a pleasant voice, warm and open, even when I told her who I was and what I needed.

"I'm investigating an arson out near Hidden Hollow," I said. "Something's come up that ties this case to a man your mother knew some forty years ago."

"Tommy Cole," she said at once. "She talked about it some, there at the end."

"What did she say?"

"She wasn't exactly in her right mind by then, mostly lucid, but not always. She was ashamed of what she'd done. Said that, by all accounts, he was a decent man and she'd tarnished his memory. She felt bad for his wife, thinking he was with another woman."

"She never tried to make it right?"

She hesitated. Then the words came out in a rush, as if she was afraid that if she stopped to take a breath, I'd hang up. "I don't want you to think badly of her. She was kind and funny, and she'd give you the shirt right off her back, but Daddy left when I was three, and she was a single mom with no marketable skills and not much education. She waited tables thirty-five years and barely made enough to put clothes on our backs and food in our stomachs. What those men paid her was enough to get us by and send us all to college."

"And if she went back on her word, they'd take it back?"

"I think she was afraid they would. Or worse."

"She never wondered why someone would pay that kind of money to discredit a dead man?"

"I don't think she wanted to think about it. It frightened her."

"Do you know who paid her?" Silence on the other end. I said, "Sharon, it's important."

"It was forty years ago. Why does it suddenly matter now?"

"I think you know why it matters. If Cole was with your mother, then he wasn't with the men who paid her. They were establishing an alibi."

I ran down the high points, and when I finished, she was quiet for a long time. I counted my breaths in and out, comparing levels of pain with varying breaths, trying not to fidget.

At last, she said, "She never told me who they were, just some men she met at the diner. Customers, you know. But she never threw anything away. We still haven't had time to go through all her things, just put them in the shed. There might be something there. A bankbook, a copy of the bank statement for that month. Something."

"I'll send someone by tomorrow. She can help you look." I didn't ask because I didn't want her to say no.

"We go to early service, but we won't be home from church till after ten."

"She'll be there at ten thirty," I said, then remembered that my truck was on its way to Silverado heaven and added, "She and her driver."

I hung up just as Khanh came out of the trailer, moving stiffly, a cup of coffee in her hand and another tucked between her forearm and her stomach. She handed me one of them.

"How do you feel?" I asked. The bruise on the side of her face looked swollen and had darkened to a purplish blue.

"Okay, but not so pretty. No more fashion model for me." She smiled. "You got pretty nice black eye too."

"You need to ice that," I said. "Make the swelling go down."

"Hot shower too," she said. "All my muscle sore. What we do today, boss man?"

I filled her in on what we'd learned last night and said, "I'm going to talk to Doc, see what he has to say. Then see if I can find the sheriff, give the buckle to him."

"Sheriff not be happy," she said.

"That I found it, or that I didn't give it to him last night?"

"Maybe both," she said. "Maybe he not wanting it found."

"Maybe," I said. "But I can only think of one reason for that."

She nodded. "Same reason he not like it when you find Owen Bodeen bone. He know who set that fire, and it somebody he know."

"Somebody he wants to protect." It made sense. The man was no fool, but the cursory investigation of the arson scene was too sloppy for a man who'd studied murder trophies and cooling-off periods. But was he protecting himself or someone else? Whichever it was, it was eating him alive.

"Let's see what Doc has to say," I said. "Then we'll worry about the sheriff. You want to come?"

She shook her head. "You go talk to Doc. I finish you skip trace."

॰॰॰

I found Doc in the inspection area, examining the pasterns of a pretty chestnut mare. I stood three feet away and put my hands in my pockets. "Doc, I need to talk to you."

The rider whose horse he'd been checking gave me a sour look. Seven more riders waited in line, and none of them looked happy either.

Doc didn't look up. "Kind of busy here."

"It's important."

He glanced up then. "Is Zane all right?"

"Far as I know."

He let out a breath. "I'll catch you when I finish here."

"It's about Owen Bodeen."

He stiffened, then ran his hands lightly down the horse's legs. "All right. Give me a minute." He straightened and set the thermography camera aside, then pressed his fists into the small of his back and made a quick apology to the riders in line. He looked back at me and jerked his head toward the clinic, a gesture I interpreted as an invitation to follow him.

He closed the door behind us and said, "I haven't seen Owen in more than a year. By all accounts, he left town the night of Zane's accident."

"Why do you think that was?"

"I couldn't say."

"Owen told Zane he'd seen you and Sam Trehorne kill a man."

"He . . . what?" His confusion looked genuine. "When?"

"Last year, the night before Zane's accident. He said he was with you when you did it. Thomas Cole, wasn't it? You knew him back in the day."

"I knew him. He was a good reporter, which meant he was an annoying man."

"Annoying enough to kill?"

"Nobody murdered Tommy Cole," he said. "And if you've looked into this thing at all, you know Samuel and I were at my house all evening. There were witnesses."

"Your wife and Trehorne's wife."

"Plus Dalt and Eleanor Underwood and the Listers."

"A cozy little group."

He sighed and spread his hands. "You got this idea from Zane, I guess. But you have to remember, brain trauma can play tricks on the memory, and those seizures only make it worse."

"I did get it from Zane. But I think the fact that someone tried to smother him with a pillow Thursday night gives some credence to his story."

He was quiet for a moment. "You have a point."

"And then there's Lori Mae Tillman. Someone paid her to say she was with Tom Cole that night."

He cocked his head, gave me an appraising look.

"I know she's dead," I said. "I guess you know it too. Must have been a relief to learn she'd passed away. But she carried that guilt a long time. That's the kind of thing that, when the end is getting close, people tend to want to shed."

"You're saying she lied about being with Tommy. And you're saying she told someone."

"That's exactly what I'm saying."

He said, "You're a thorough man. But what does it matter? Whether he was with her or with someone else, or drinking alone in his car, Tommy's death was a tragedy, not a murder."

"Then why would someone pay her to lie about it? And why was his blood alcohol level so low?"

He rocked back on his heels, not stepping away, but putting space between us. "I can't explain that. All I know is, Sam and I didn't murder anyone."

"Someone tried to kill Zane less than a day after he remembered being with Owen Bodeen. And Owen's bones were found in the ruins of the Underwoods' barn. Odds are, he was killed the night he vanished. The night he told Zane about Cole's murder."

Doc's face went pale beneath his tan. "What makes you think they're Owen's bones? There are a lot of transients in this business. Grooms. Stable hands. They come and go. One of them could have gone missing, and no one would be the wiser."

"Like Owen?" I asked.

"I wouldn't have called him a transient. He'd have been missed."

"But he wasn't. Because of Zane's accident. Think about it. Owen sees—or thinks he sees—you and Trehorne kill a man. Then someone takes advantage of the confusion around Zane's accident to make sure Owen doesn't talk to anybody else. Did you ever actually see him after Zane was hurt?"

His gaze slid up and to the right. "There was a lot of confusion. I can't say for sure if he was there or not. My sense of it is he wasn't. But his truck was missing, along with some of his clothes and other effects. We figured he must have just picked up and gone."

"Whoever killed him must have gotten rid of them. So, Doc, you need to make me understand what anyone but you and Samuel Trehorne would gain by killing Owen and by trying to kill Zane."

Doc held up a hand. "Slow down there, Sparky. If Sam and I were going to kill Owen Bodeen over a murder we didn't commit, we'd have done it forty years ago."

"Maybe," I said. "But all indications are he was solid then and had a recent change of heart. He'd been diagnosed with cancer, wanted to make things right."

"And you think he came to us with that, and we killed him? Now you're moving into tinfoil hat territory."

"I think he told Zane, and Junior overheard him. Are there any drugs that could make a normal horse go bat-shit crazy?"

His eyebrows lifted. "Some drug that might have made Rogue go nuts when Zane went into his stall?"

"Maybe. Is it possible?"

"You'd have to know when he'd be going in there. You'd have to know how much to give and when to give it so it was at its peak right when he went in. But then the horse would be showing aberrant behavior, which would have tipped Zane off."

"What about an electric buzzer? Something where you could control the timing from a distance?"

"It would still be iffy. You couldn't know how badly the horse would hurt him, or if it would hurt him at all. Zane was an athletic guy. He might have just gotten out of the way. But even if you could guarantee it, why go to all that trouble?"

"If I'd killed someone forty years ago," I said, "and someone who was with me started talking, I might want to shut him up. And then I'd shut up the guy he told."

He pushed away from the wall. "I might do that too. If I'd murdered someone forty years ago. But Tom Cole's death was not a murder. It was just a tragic accident. Now, are we finished here? That line back there's not getting any shorter."

35.

❈

There was a missed call from Frank on my cell phone. I called him back, and he answered on the first ring. "Quick update," he said. "The lead detective on the Tom Cole case said he'd always been pretty sure somebody held Cole underwater. Said it always bothered him he couldn't make a case."

"No physical evidence?"

"Not a shred. Might be different if it happened today. We could maybe pull prints from the body, but back then, tests were less sophisticated."

"But your guy is pretty sure?"

"Sure as you can be. But the guys he suspected were all solid. They and their wives. Nobody would give anything away. He says he calls one or another of them every now and then. They never budge."

"Must be frustrating."

"He says Cole's wife would call him once a year on the anniversary, send him a dozen roses from her garden. He thought it was her way of reminding him he'd let her down. Nice gesture, he said, but not so nice under the surface."

"If it was a conspiracy, it was a big one. Hard to keep that many people quiet."

"They were a brick wall. He said he never saw anything like it. None of them ever faltered. Not once."

"One of them might have, but he never got the chance." I told him about Owen Bodeen.

"Bodeen's name didn't come up. Could be the detectives never knew about him."

"He was a hired hand," I said. "I'm not even sure why they brought him along."

"Scapegoat," he suggested. "Someone to blame it on if things went wrong. Now about your fires . . ."

He sent a printout to my phone and my computer. The print was too tiny to read on my cell phone, so he gave me the high points.

No wonder the sheriff was worried.

༜

I found Hap drinking coffee in front of the donut booth. I handed him the buckle wrapped in a handkerchief. He unwrapped it carefully and squinted at it in the sun, his jowls trembling, a sheen of sweat on his forehead. It was a look I'd seen before, on young men hearing the clang of a prison door for the first time, on parents opening their front doors to men in dark suits, bad news on their faces.

Hap Trehorne was afraid.

He wrapped the buckle back up and put it in his shirt pocket. Said, "Where did you find this?"

"Last night at the Underwood barn."

"So why am I just now seeing it?"

I shrugged. "It was late. I was tired."

"You should have called me. I'd have come out to get it. But now . . . You broke the chain of evidence. You could have gotten this anywhere."

"Or I could have found it anywhere and put it in the ashes before I called you. Could have done that the day after the fire, in fact. Pretty lax, for a crime scene."

He sucked in an angry breath. "As far as we knew, it wasn't a crime scene that first night. Barns catch fire all the time. Especially soring barns. They're like meth labs. Lots of unstable chemicals."

"But the Underwoods weren't soring."

"So they say. But that's not what it looked like. No reason to look deeper. Not until you found those bones."

"Owen's bones."

"Likely. Not certain. We'll never be certain. Not enough there to do much with."

"Maybe, maybe not. Could be, if you called in the guys from the TBI, you might still get mitochondrial DNA from the teeth." I knew this because I knew a forensic dentist who'd identified a victim in exactly this way, more than a decade after the body had been burned and buried.

The muscles around Hap's eyes tightened. I guessed he didn't like the idea of bringing in outsiders. "Maybe," he said finally, "but it wouldn't do us any good. There's nothing to compare it to."

"No family?"

"Not that anybody knows."

I made a *que sera sera* gesture with one hand. "We may not be able to prove it, but I think we know. What we don't know is who put him there."

He gave me a measured look, then took a swig from his coffee cup and grabbed a donut from a grease-stained cardboard box open on the counter. "The simplest explanation is usually best," he said carefully. "Zane or Gonzales put him there."

"Considering when Owen went missing, Zane has a pretty ironclad alibi."

"You got me there." He looked annoyed at his own carelessness. "Gonzales, then. And whoever set the fire, assuming it *was* set, didn't know about it. Why you got to make things so complicated?" He shook the excess sugar off the donut, stuffed it into his mouth.

"I don't make 'em complicated. They just get that way. I hear you get a lot of fires around here. About double the state rate."

He chewed methodically, finally swallowed. "Is that so?"

"Seems like a lot of them belonged to your brother's enemies."

"Probably a lot of 'em belonged to his friends too. In this county, pretty much anybody with horses is connected to my brother one way or another. As for fires, this is horse country. Lots of barns. Lots of hay. These young guys get impatient, don't give it time to dry."

This was true enough. When hay is baled damp and stored before it's fully dried, microscopic organisms at the center of the bale start reproducing. Being brainless and without the distractions of Facebook and cable TV, they reproduce until they generate a mighty heat—enough to ignite the surrounding hay. Still, there was no reason for there to be more fires in Hap's little kingdom than in, say, nearby Bedford County.

"I grant you that," I said. "But with those kinds of statistics, I'd think your fire department would be a little quicker. Forty minutes to get to Zane and Carlin's farm? I could be almost to Nashville by then."

He brushed a dusting of sugar off his shirt. "They're volunteer. It's not like they just sit around at the fire department waiting for something to happen. These guys have jobs. Families. Sometimes it takes awhile to round 'em up."

I said, "It's a little too coincidental for my blood."

"Your blood will just have to get over it." He took another donut from the box and raised it in a toast. His voice was light, his smile forced. "To coincidence. Next time you have a breakthrough, you call me, you hear?"

I gave him a mock salute and walked back to the stables. At Trehorne's, Junior and Esmerelda stood in front of the lobby area, playing hopscotch on a grid scraped onto the concrete. She tossed the marker, hopped, and toppled.

"Nice try." He tousled her hair, looked up when he saw me.

I said, "Lobbying for brother of the year?"

"I deserve it too," he said. "Plus maybe hazard pay."

"Around our house, it's Beanie Babies. They multiply like coat hangers."

Esmerelda held out a stone. "You want to play? Junior, tell him we want him to play."

Junior sighed. "How about it? Care for a match?"

"Mighty generous of you," I said.

"I'm a generous guy."

"Really?" I lifted an eyebrow. "I heard you were pretty rough on Dan Bitmore before he died."

He hunched a shoulder. "Dan turned on his own. I didn't give him any grief he didn't deserve."

"Still. You don't feel bad about that now? Considering what happened?"

A muscle in his cheek pulsed. "I might feel bad if I'd 've shot him. I don't feel bad about calling bullshit when I hear it."

"Bullshit because he reported the soring?"

"Bullshit," Esmerelda sang. "Bullshit, bullshit, bullshit."

"Now look what you've done," he said to me. Then, to her, "Princess, go get your My Pretty Ponies and find Mama.

And don't say that word. Mama will skin me alive and wash your mouth out with soap."

She pouted until he put his hands on her shoulders and spun her around. Giggled as he gave her a nudge in the direction of the arena. She broke into a skip, and he watched with a protective eye until she passed out of sight.

"Dan Bitmore," I said. "Why exactly were you calling bullshit?"

"Because he was one of us, and he gave the other side ammunition he knew they'd use to hurt us, all of us, whether we sore or not. You're supposed to take care of your own. We Trehornes know that. Apparently Dan didn't."

"What about Zane? You hold a grudge against him too?"

He gave a bitter laugh. "He pretty much declared war on us when he jumped feet first into Carlin's anti-Big Lick camp. Just because he's crippled doesn't mean he ain't a traitor."

"Interesting word, considering the penalty for treason is death."

"Aw, man." He spat onto the ground beside his feet. "You can't pin that on me. I was out at Jake's bar with a couple dozen witnesses."

"Mace Ewing one of them?"

"I don't know where Mace was. I'm not his keeper."

"I was thinking more his handler. There's some evidence he was at Zane's trailer the night of the attack."

"And you think I'm the one who sent him there? Good luck proving that." He laughed again, and reached for a lead rope on the little display table. "I gotta go get Rogue ready to show."

"Sweet horse," I said. "I met him at your father's barn."

"Aw, he's a clown." He smiled at some secret joke. "But at least he ain't sore."

I watched Carlin ride her classes, while Zane looked on from his chair and Gerardo kept a watchful eye, adjusting a stirrup here, a bit there. Junior rode two classes in between, a competent rider, light hands, good seat. Trudy had said he could ride anything, but there was little artistry in it. Rogue did his job well. Once in the ring, he was all business.

While Junior rode, I walked over to Carlin. She was fiddling with Tesora's girth, her gaze turned away from the ring. Gerardo hovered nearby.

"I can't stand to watch him," Carlin said as I came to stand beside her. "I used to think he was the most beautiful horse I'd ever seen, and now I can't even stand to look at him."

"What was he like?" I said.

"He took his job seriously."

"And when he wasn't working?"

"He was a worrier. Any big change, he'd get those worry wrinkles around his eyes. He really wanted to please you. And once he got to know you, he was a sweetheart. He used to come and lay his head in my lap."

"You trusted him."

"I guess that's why it hurt so much. I wanted to put him down, but Sam Trehorne offered to buy him, and we needed the money, and . . . Well, it's not like Sam didn't know what he was getting."

"You think Sam Trehorne sores."

She shrugged, didn't answer.

"So you were punishing Rogue?"

"I didn't think of it that way." She reached up and smoothed Tesora's mane. "But maybe you're right. I shouldn't wish that on any animal, but maybe I did. Maybe I think he deserves whatever he gets."

"Would you have called Rogue a clown?"

"He was a thinker. A little reserved at first, but a lover once you got to know him. He was so serious. We used to call him Your Honor." She gave a sad little smile and gestured toward the ring. "They're calling me. I have to go."

She finished her classes, and as we left the arena, a group of brown-skinned children playing soccer kicked a ball across our path. A taller boy darted past and snatched it up, gave us a crooked grin before loping back to his teammates. The others laughed, and another boy called out something in Spanish.

Not far away, in the lobby of the empty Trehorne block, Esmerelda sat in a chair too large for her, kicking her feet and heaving aggrieved sighs. Even her Cartier watchband seemed to have lost its appeal.

"Hey, Kiddo," I said. "Why the long face?"

She brightened, then scooted off the chair and scampered over.

She dismissed Khanh and Gerardo after a quick glance, then stared at Zane until he gave her a crooked grin and said in his robotic voice, "BOO."

She gave him an uncertain smile. Looked at Carlin, then at Zane again, and slunk behind me as if suddenly realizing she was fraternizing with the enemy.

She tugged at my shirt. "Do you want to play Chutes and Ladders with me?"

I nodded toward the soccer game. "Why don't you ask those guys if you can play?"

"I can't play with them. It wouldn't be proper." She held up her watchband, shook it so the diamonds caught the light and splintered it. "They aren't like us."

Gerardo sucked in a quick hiss of breath.

I said, "I'm not like you either. How come you can play Chutes and Ladders with me?"

She gave me a bewildered look that said I didn't know much. "Aren't you buying a horse from my papa?"

"I don't know yet. The price is a little steep."

She looked uncertain, her classification system suddenly awry.

Gerardo said, "These children. They're people, just like you."

"Oh no." She screwed up her face and jangled her watch-band again. "They aren't like me. I'm a young lady, and they're just a bunch of wetbacks."

The innocence with which she said it was somehow worse than if she'd said it with hatred or contempt.

Gerardo looked like he'd been slapped. Carlin, on the other side of Tesora, reached across and squeezed his hand. Esmerelda looked from one face to another. She'd said something wrong, her expression said, but she wasn't sure exactly what it was.

"Oh, kiddo," I said. While the others stood back and watched, I took her little brown hand and walked her back to Trehorne's tricked-out lobby, picked her up, and sat her in the too-big chair. If she'd been mine, I would have known what I should say. I would have talked about how people are the same, no matter how much money they have or the color of the skin they were born with.

She wasn't my child, and it wasn't my place, but I told her those things anyway. She listened with her brows knit and her mouth in a skeptical "o," and when her mother called her name, she gave my hand a sympathetic pat and skipped away not having understood a word I'd said.

"*Madre de Dios*," Gerardo said as I walked back to rejoin the group. His voice broke. "Look what they've made of her."

36.

I thought the Trehornes had meant well. They'd bought their daughter nice things, tried to make her happy. And in the process, they'd neglected to teach her that the world was more than other people living in her universe. Like Junior, the Trehornes' crown prince, Esmerelda had been steeped in entitlement since the day she was born. I wondered how long it had taken Gerardo to realize the magnitude of his mistake.

I spent the rest of the day doing the thing PIs do most. While Khanh worked on the computer and Billy caught some shut-eye, I canvassed the showground, talking to everybody I could find who might have seen either Zane's attacker or Maggie's killer. I started at the TASA booth and circled outward, then did the same with the Underwood trailer. Two sets of concentric circles, neither of which turned up much. No one had seen Maggie the morning of her death. No one had seen the man in black running from Zane's trailer. Apparently, folks took "see no evil" literally around here.

There were some common themes—sympathy for Maggie, who seemed generally well-liked despite her alignment with the dark side, and a mix of guilt and anger toward Zane, who had betrayed his own but had, perhaps, paid his debt to the community in blood and suffering. Beneath it all was an undercurrent of resentment and anxiety. Fear was a palpable presence, and it had little to do with the killer in their midst and much to do with the dissolution of the industry that was their livelihood.

Three quarters of the way into the circle, an old man in faded jeans and a wife-beater T-shirt sat in front of a Sundowner gooseneck, rubbing leather oil into a western saddle that looked like it had been around since the Pony Express. His eyes were blue and watery, his chin and cheeks stubbled with white. His shirt was stained gray at the armpits, where a few wiry white hairs sprang free, and a blurred tattoo blued the skin of his upper arm: a mermaid, from the shape of her, wrinkled and out of focus, like a reflection in murky water.

"I'm—" I started.

"I know who you are." He gave the saddle a fierce rub.

"I'm just trying to piece things together," I said, then decided to shake things up a bit. "Figure out who might have murdered Maggie James and Owen Bodeen."

His eyebrows shot up. "Owen Bodeen? Murdered? Since when?"

"Probably the night he disappeared."

I filled him in, and he shook his head and said, "Maggie James and Owen Bodeen. Now there's a pair you wouldn't think to put in the same sentence." He tipped more oil onto a rag and rubbed it over the saddle horn until the tang of the oil filled the air and the leather gleamed.

"Why not?"

"Nothing in common. He ain't never been anything but a hard-drinking, hard-living stable hand. She's . . . she was . . . a nice, church-going lady. Not rich, but she didn't have to live on beans and rice."

"So you don't think they could have a common enemy?"

"Miss Maggie never had an enemy in her life."

"She was in with the anti-Big Lick group. That must have chipped some people off."

"No sir. Not anybody that knew her. She had a way about her. Even when she was yakkin' her damn fool head off about some stupid pie-in-the-sky cause, you knew she wasn't puttin' you down." He sighed and rubbed his rheumy eyes. "I reckon she was just in the wrong place at the wrong time."

"What about barn fires?" I said. "Braydon County has a lot more than the average, even when you take into account that this is horse country."

The old man swung his head in protest. "Oh, no. I might be dumber 'n a box of bricks, but I know better than to take on the Trehornes."

"Who said anything about Trehornes? I'm talking about barn fires."

"Then you're talking about Trehornes." He wiped sweat from his forehead with his wrist, smoothed back his damp hair with his palm, and dried his hand on his shirt. "But if you say I said so, I'll say you're a lying sack of skunk shit."

I raised an eyebrow. "How would they find out? No offense, but you don't seem the type to run with the Trehornes."

"Meaning I don't shit dollar bills? Naw, you're right. I used to do some work for 'em, though, back in the day. Saved up, bought my own barn. Small stuff, enough to get by. But I know my place, and I know better than to step on anybody's toes."

"You think they'd hurt you?"

He seemed to consider this. "I don't know. You hear rumors. Who can say how true they are?" He gave the saddle skirt a vigorous rub. "With them, it could go either way."

"About these fires . . ."

He said, "Why should I talk to you? You ain't a friend to us."

"People are dying."

"All the more reason to keep my trap shut. I've said all I'm gonna say about barn fires."

"Fine." I rocked back on my heels. "Maybe you could talk about Mace Ewing instead."

"Not much to say about Mace. He's been hangin' on Junior's coattails since they was knee high to a tater bug."

"So if Junior told him to put a pillow over Zane's face . . ."

"Well, Mace seems to have a mind of his own, so I don't rightly know. On the other hand, when a Trehorne says jump, best just ask how high and when can I come down." He shifted the saddle on his lap, poured more oil onto his cloth. "Junior ain't as hot-headed as his daddy used to be, got too much of his mama in him for that, but that don't mean he don't know how to take care of business."

"Can you think of anyone he might confide in? Someone who might talk to me about the fires?"

He ran his hand over the stubble on his jaw. "There's a woman he used to go with. Jane Barstow. Seemed pretty serious for a time, but they ain't been seein' each other for a while."

"Do you know where she lives?"

He draped the rag over the top of the oil bottle, then eased the saddle off his knees. It landed on its side, then slowly toppled upside down onto the grass at his feet, a thin line of dirt adhering to the oil on the tip of the saddle horn.

He blinked at it for a moment, then sighed and pushed out of his chair. "She's in the book. I think I might have one inside."

37.

Jane Barstow lived in a rundown, one-story brick house with a dog pen in the side yard. A Redbone Coonhound lay on its side, panting in the heat. It lifted its head and barked once as I pulled into the driveway, then watched, tail thumping up dust, as I parked beside an aging Pinto and got out of Billy's van, borrowed for the occasion.

It was late afternoon, but the heat and humidity still hung in the air like a damp sheet. I took a detour to the pen, saw a handful of kibble covered with flies and half a bowl of water inside. The dog wagged its tail and came over to the fence to lick my fingers. She looked healthy enough, and as I headed toward the house, she circled twice and lay back down.

The woman who answered my knock was in her mid-to-late twenties, heavyset, in tight white shorts and an oversized T-shirt with a grumpy-looking cat on the front. She peered through the screen door with a quizzical smile, then looked past me at Billy's van, with its custom paint job.

"Good Lord," she said. "What is that?"

"It's Van Gogh," I said. "*Starry Night.*"

"It's pretty," she admitted. "But why?"

"I borrowed it from a buddy who runs a shelter for veterans," I said. "It's supposed to remind them to hold on to their dreams. Or something like that."

"That what you're sellin'?" She gave me a mischievous smile. "Dreams?"

"Not selling anything. I'm hoping you might talk to me about Junior. You guys used to see each other, right?"

Her eyes hardened, but there was hurt in her voice. "If by *see each other*, you mean he'd stop by for fun and games but didn't think I was good enough to meet Mama and Papa, then yeah, we used to see each other. What's it to you?"

"I was told if he was going to confide in anybody, it was probably you. I don't suppose you'd let me come in, have a talk?"

She sighed. "Mister, you're about as cute as a bug's ear, and if I let you in here, I just might not let you out."

"I think I can handle myself," I said, and grinned.

"I hope so. Otherwise, what would be the point?" She unlatched the screen door but didn't open it. "You got some ID?"

I showed her my PI license, and she stepped aside to let me in. The house was cluttered but clean, half-finished afghans and crossword puzzles squirreled around the living room, a pile of laundry half-folded on the couch.

She scooped up the laundry and dumped it in a recliner across from the TV. "You can set on the couch. You want something to drink?"

"I'm fine, thanks."

She plopped onto the couch beside me and said, "Is Junior in trouble?"

"I won't sugarcoat it for you. He's been implicated in some barn fires."

"Oh." She looked down at her knees.

"Did he ever talk to you about that?"

"We talked about a lot of things. I mean, we got along really well, and I don't mean just things you do without your clothes on."

"But that wasn't enough for him?" I turned my body toward hers, just enough to seem more sympathetic.

"I don't know. Maybe it would have been if his family wasn't so stuck up. He said they'd never let him settle for someone like me." She looked at her hands. Picked at a nail. "He actually said *settle*."

"I'm guessing diplomacy is not his strong suit."

"Not that I ever saw." She gave a small, sad laugh. "You know, I used to wish I'd grown up rich. Now I thank God we didn't have a pot to piss in or a window to throw it out of."

"They say money is the root of all evil."

"Love of money," she corrected me. "But I guess it's easier to love it when you have some. Otherwise, you're just coveting, which is a whole other sin."

The logic made me smile. "So between his money and his family . . ."

"We were doomed." She gave a self-conscious laugh, acknowledging the melodrama. "Oh, we had some good times. Went to the fair. Cooked dinner together. Spent a couple weekends in the mountains. Course he told his folks it was a camping trip with the guys."

"He's thirty years old. You'd think he would have gotten past that."

"You don't know the Trehornes. They have a family slogan. It's, 'We take care of our own.'"

"I've heard that a few times."

"It's all they think about. Them against everybody else. Who's doing better than them? Who's a threat to their business? Who's good enough to hang out with them, and who's some little peasant girl who ought to be out selling matches on the street?"

"They're protective."

"Very. And they taught Junior from the time he was a little boy that Trehornes, they . . ." She cast about for the word. "When they see a threat, they . . . *neutralize* it. It bothered him sometimes, the things he had to do, but he had to do them, like his father had, and his grandfather, and his great-grandfather, all the way back to God knows when."

"And what were the things?"

She clasped her hands in her lap and looked away.

I said, "Are you afraid of him? Of what he might do if you told?"

"No, no. He wouldn't hurt a woman."

I thought of Maggie but didn't say anything.

She drew in a long breath and let it out slowly. "He trusted me. He's an asshole sometimes, but I really don't want to get him in trouble."

"Jane," I said softly, "people are getting hurt."

"And you think he's . . .?"

"Either he's doing it, or he's in the crosshairs. One or the other. This is your chance to help him."

After a moment, she said, "The fires." She crossed her arms and sank deeper into the cushions. I waited. She squirmed. Finally, she took another long breath and said, "The fires are a last resort. If someone's trying to drive them out of business or is so successful they're a threat, his father tries to negotiate. Like buy in or something. If that doesn't work, they try to drive them out of business. There's a whole long process of . . . they call it psychological warfare. But if none of that works, Junior has to burn something. Not a house or anything, nothing people would be in. Maybe a shed, if there's something really valuable in it. But mostly barns."

"Why doesn't he take the horses out first?"

She shot me a glance like I wasn't quite bright. "Because then it would be obvious somebody set the fire."

"But everybody knows he set it. Psychological warfare only works if the other person knows they're a target."

She shrugged. "Knowing isn't proving."

I scowled. "It's so Hap has plausible deniability. Does he know?"

"He might suspect," she said. "But I think he doesn't want to know, and Junior's good at setting fires that look like accidents. Even though everybody knows they're not. He hates it, but it's what he has to do to support the family."

I looked down at my hands, clenched into fists. "Why him? Why not his father?"

"He's too old to run away if something goes wrong. Besides it's like passing a torch. When his dad was young, he was the fire starter, and now it's Junior's job."

A dull throb started in my temples. "Why didn't you tell somebody?"

"Who would I tell? The sheriff? Besides . . ." She blinked back tears. "I love the stupid son of a bitch."

38.

Jim Lister was waiting for me when I got back to the trailer. He sat in my folding director's chair, nursing a beer, while Khanh squatted in front of the fire pit, prodding the firewood with the poker. She didn't look happy.

When he saw me, he set the beer down on the ground beneath his chair and said, "Walk with me."

I bristled at the command, but held my peace. If he wanted to play alpha male, let him. I glanced at Khanh, who gave the largest log a vicious poke and watched the embers swirl.

"I'll be back," I said.

She nodded, something unreadable in her eyes. "Probably I be here."

Lister put one hand on each arm of the chair and pushed himself up. As we passed out of Khanh's earshot, he said, "She doesn't like me much."

"Were you there long enough to make her dislike you?"

"She thinks I mean to threaten you. She's very protective."

"My own little pit bull."

"What happened to her?"

"She stepped on a land mine when she was a child."

"Tragic." His sincerity needed some work. Maybe that was what Khanh didn't like about him. "I donate to that cause, you know. Gave $20,000 last year to a charity that removes land mines from third-world countries."

"Did you tell her that? Maybe it would make her dislike you less."

"Dislike me less? Not like me more?" He bared his teeth in a humorless grin. They were too white and too perfect to be real. An image flashed into my mind, his toothless mouth on Rhonda's breast, and my stomach recoiled.

"Depends," I said. "Where did she get the idea you meant to threaten me?"

"I may have said something to the effect that my wife seems to have a certain fascination with you. That seems innocent enough, don't you think?"

"Tone is everything," I said. "Maybe she heard something in yours she didn't like."

We passed from the campground and through the vendor booths. Sunset streaked the sky with rose and gold, and the arena lights came on with a hum. As we neared the barns, the splash of the fountains underscored the cheers from the arena and the soft jangle of Mexican music from someone's radio.

Lister's barn was decorated in black velvet trimmed with gold thread and strands of pearls. In the center of his lobby was a glass-topped table, and on it was a gold chalice, and it too was filled with pearls.

"You're wondering if they're fake," he said. "They're not."

"Was I wondering that?"

"If you weren't, then you suffer from a serious lack of imagination." He chuckled, but it sounded forced. "I had you checked out. I know what you make. I know how much you owe. Your son had open heart surgery a few months ago."

Heat washed my cheeks. "My son's not part of this."

"You mistake my meaning. It's a simple statement of fact. You're a self-employed, divorced father with medical bills to pay, a man with a defective child and a modest income."

My teeth ground together. "There's nothing defective about Paul."

"An unfortunate choice of words. My apologies if I offended."

We walked around the corner and paused at the first stall, where a sorrel horse with a star on its forehead poked its head over the gate. Lister reached up to scratch its neck and said, "I'm merely pointing out that, youth and athleticism aside, you have little to offer a woman like Rhonda."

"She took me to the clinic and gave me a ride to find my sister. That's a far cry from what you're insinuating."

"Is it? She was seen leaving your campsite early this morning and the morning before."

"Seriously? You've been spying on her?"

"Little birds." He laughed. "But honestly, there's no need to spy when the gossip mill is so very finely honed. You deny she was there?"

"She was there. Nothing happened."

He raised an eyebrow. "You're incapable? What a shame."

"I'm plenty capable. But what kind of a jackass talks about his wife that way?"

He spread his hands, palms up. "I'm being realistic. When you marry a whore, you have to expect her to act like one."

My fists clenched. I forced them open. There was no honor in punching an old man.

He gave me an amused look. "I spoil my wife in a number of ways, Mr. McKean. Including the occasional shiny new boy toy. I'm just making sure you understand your place in the scheme of things. She wants what's in my wallet more than she wants what's between your legs."

"You cut a wide swath," I said. "According to you, I'm a bounder, she's a whore, and you're an old john who has to buy sex with his own wife."

His eyes slitted. "That mouth of yours will get you into trouble one day."

"Maybe so, but not from you. I checked you out too, old man. I know you paid half a million dollars for a horse you couldn't sell for a hundred thousand. You're bleeding money."

"If you know that, then you know I can afford it. I could buy and sell you a hundred times over."

"You could, if I were for sale."

He showed his perfect teeth, but the smile didn't reach his eyes. "Everyone's for sale."

Ignoring the pain in my side, I stretched up to scratch the sorrel's throat. "Tom Cole wasn't. Or if he was, you never found his price."

"Tom Cole. It's been a long time since I heard that name."

"I'm surprised. His grandson's been pretty vocal about looking into his case. And you were with Trehorne and the others the night Cole died. You saying they didn't tell you Zane remembered Owen Bodeen telling him Tom Cole was murdered?"

Lister rocked back on his heels. "If you're going to revisit the past, Mr. McKean, you'd best be sure you're prepared for what you might find."

"I'm prepared," I said. "Are you?"

He gave me a cold sneer. "You do whatever you need to do with my wife. A day from now, you'll be nothing but a pleasant memory, like a pair of shoes she bought on sale and will never wear again. But don't take me on, my friend. Not about Tom Cole or the horses or my livelihood. You do, and you'll be very, very sorry."

"Funny, your friend Sam Trehorne told me pretty much the same thing."

"Funny, I'm betting you didn't listen to him either."

39.

By the time I got back, Khanh had wrangled the grill into place over the fire pit. A pair of foil packets and two cobs of corn sizzled on top, and in the ashes I could see the shapes of two potatoes baking. On the platter beside her knee was a rib eye soaked in a marinade of garlic, butter, and Worcestershire sauce. When I stepped into the firelight, Khanh waved a two-pronged meat fork at me, skewered the steak, and plopped it onto the grill. The marinade dripped and sizzled, and the air filled with the aromas of garlic and seared meat.

Suddenly I was ravenous.

She said, "That skip trace lead to deadbeat dad. He living in Vegas."

"That was good work. If you liked it, I can give you more."

"You give me raise?"

"Getting greedy?" I said. "We'll split the fee. Got another job for you, if you want it. Billy will have to drive you." I told her about Lori Mae Tillman's daughter.

Her face lit up. "This PI work, right? I doing real PI work?"

"You've been doing real PI work all day. I think you're ready, don't you?"

"Yes. No. Wait. Something I not understanding. What happen to you work alone?"

There were a lot of things I might have said, sappy sentimental things that would have made her suspicious and me uncomfortable. I shrugged and said, "It's lost some of its appeal. What do you say? Partners?"

She nodded. "Partners."

We shook on it. Then she said, "You think we find something tomorrow?"

"I hope so, because otherwise all these guys have to do is stick to their story, and they'll keep right on getting away with it. It won't be anything as obvious as a canceled check—these guys are too smart for that—but maybe something she wrote, like a letter or diary."

"You think Owen Bodeen telling the truth?"

"He had no reason to lie. Not then, not to Zane."

"These man. They kill Owen Bodeen, put bones in fire?"

That was the million-dollar question. Owen had died a year ago. Had his bones been in the Underwood barn all along, or had the arsonist put them there? And if the latter, why?

"It's tied to Tom Cole somehow," I said. "Owen disappeared the night he told Zane about seeing Tommy murdered. That's too big to be a coincidence. Plus, Jim Lister warned me off about it."

She shook her head. "Lot of people at that party. All guilty, none guilty, some guilty others cover. Too many possibility. Make my head hurt. I going clean kitchen. You feed horse, figure out."

After I'd fed and watered the horses, I went inside and pulled up the *Sextant's* site on my computer. Eli had said he wrote for the print-only edition, but Maggie's death and the attack on Zane had made the online issue. I checked the byline and saw a name I didn't recognize.

On impulse, I dialed the paper's number. A woman's voice answered. "*Nashville Sextant*." she said.

"You keep late hours."

"Newspaper hours. Just putting tomorrow's edition to bed. What can I do for you?"

I told her who I was and what I wanted, and there was a long pause. "Eli Barringer? He's a stringer, not a regular contributor."

"Is that his choice, or yours?"

"I don't know if I should answer that," she said. "These are litigious days."

"I'm not out to make trouble for you. Or for him. Just trying to understand. The article that ran today about the horse show, shouldn't that have been Eli's?"

There was another pause. Then she said. "A news piece has to be unbiased."

"And Eli's wasn't."

"Let's just say he definitely has a dog in the hunt."

"He thinks his grandfather was murdered," I said, "and he's probably right."

"He may be right. But he's obsessed with it, which doesn't lend itself to fair and objective reportage. The truth is, I'm worried about him. He's there at the show?"

"He is."

"If half of what he says is true, he's dealing with some very dangerous people. And for the last few weeks, ever since his grandmother died, he's been fixated on exposing them."

"Like a mission."

"She's the one who raised him, and I think he feels he owes it to her memory."

I shifted the phone to the other ear. "When you say he's obsessed . . ."

"I think he'd let them kill him if he thought it would bring everything to light. I think he might consider that a noble death."

"Like his grandfather's."

"Exactly. He's a sweet boy, but I get the feeling he grew up in a very big shadow."

40.

The moon was high and Khanh was long in bed when Rhonda Lister came out of the shadows. The campground was quiet, illuminated by moon and firelight and the dim spill of light from the streetlamps near the arena. I was sitting on the air mattress half watching the flames, and when she stepped out of the darkness and I felt my heartbeat quicken, I knew I'd been waiting for her all along.

She stopped just inside the flickering circle of firelight, shook back her hair, and said. "I came to tuck you in."

"Rhonda—"

She held up a hand. "Don't. Don't be so damn noble. No one's sneaking around on anybody here."

"What happened to 'a reasonable amount of discretion?'"

"Who decides what's reasonable?" She came around the fire pit and knelt to kiss me lightly on the lips.

I slid my hand beneath her hair and cupped the back of her neck. Her mouth opened just a little, and we kissed again, her tongue tasting of peppermint.

"I'm not exactly at my best," I said. "The doctor said not to do anything too strenuous."

"Don't worry." She slid her palms across my chest, then gently pushed me down onto my back and tugged my shirt out of my waistband. "I'll do all the work. But first, I need to show you something."

She rocked back on her heels, unzipped her jeans, and slid her thumbs beneath the waistband of her panties. Peach, a hint of lace at the waist. Beneath them, just above the crease of her inner thigh, was a thick gauze rectangle held in place by surgical tape.

"What's this?" I said.

She peeled back the edge of the gauze to show a cluster of weeping burns. In the silence that stretched between us, she said, "Do you hate me?"

"I think the real question is, do you?"

"I don't know." She pressed the tape back into place, not meeting my gaze. "My therapist says I'm punishing myself. Because it was my fault."

I didn't have to ask what was her fault. I'd known her for three days, and the defining event in her life was already clear. She said, "He wasn't supposed to race that day, but it was my birthday, and I'd been begging for this necklace I'd seen in a catalog. A dragonfly. Real gold, with diamonds. He was racing so he could buy me that necklace."

I found my voice. "That doesn't make what happened to him your fault."

"I wish I could believe that." She smoothed the edges flat against her skin. "Sometimes I don't know if I want to scream or cry or burn the world. This helps." She dug a fingernail into the gauze over the wound and gasped.

I pulled her hand away, kissed the palm. "Don't. You know he wouldn't want you to."

"How do you know what he'd want? I burned him alive."

"You didn't."

"As good as. If I hadn't been so selfish—"

"If he hadn't raced, if somebody hadn't bumped him, if he hadn't lost control. You can kill yourself with ifs."

She unbuttoned her shirt and shrugged out of it, then reached behind and unhooked her bra. Her breasts were full and firm, and I pulled her down and tasted her, felt the nipple harden beneath my tongue.

She used one hand to shuck out of her jeans and panties. Unbuckled my belt with the other. I lifted my hips and she tugged down my jeans, raising her eyebrows at the extra weight of the Glock at the waistband. Then she lowered herself onto me, and I lost myself in her warmth. The pain in my side merged with the pleasure in my groin, and I closed my eyes and thrust upward until we cried out together and she shuddered against my chest.

I lay gasping beneath her for a moment, the pain in my ribs writhing like a live thing. When it finally subsided, I opened my eyes and saw a figure in the shadow of the trailer. He was tall and thin, his shoulders hunched forward in the same crabbed posture he'd used in the saddle.

"He's watching, isn't he?" she said, lifting her head. "He likes to watch."

There were tears on her cheeks, and I brushed them away with my thumbs, pulled her down for another kiss. "There's no one there," I said. "There's no one here but you and me."

∞

We slept. Sometime later, I felt her stir, and woke to find her looking at me.

"I'm sorry," she said. "I don't usually cry when I make love. I don't know what got into me."

"I could make something up," I said. "About how women cry when they're overcome with sexual euphoria."

She smiled. "There might be something to that." She trailed her fingers down my stomach. "Are you up for another round?"

I took her hand, moved it lower. "What do you think?"

"I want it to be just for you this time. Just for us."

I scanned the shadows, found them empty. Jim Lister was gone. I'd taken more from him than he'd given, but it was nothing he valued or appreciated, and while I should probably have felt guilty, I didn't.

Afterward she kissed me on the chin and said, "I have to get back."

"I'll walk you."

"I'll be fine."

"I'm sure Maggie would have said the same thing. I'm going with you."

She stopped me before we reached her trailer. Kissed me once more, long and lingering. I watched from the shadows as she made her way up the aluminum steps, blew me a kiss, and closed the door behind her. Through the warmth of the afterglow, the serpent in the garden whispered in my ear: *How far would this woman go to protect this life?*

41.

A line of gold edged the horizon when I left the Listers' trailer. The campground was still, and the morning smelled of grass and sawdust. I wondered if Maggie's killer was awake and if our paths might cross, if she had met him at a moment much like this and smiled her open smile before realizing the danger. I wondered if this gilt-edged sky was the last good thing she'd seen before she died.

I wound my way back through the campground and into the vendor area, passed the booth where Maggie had been killed, and paused to look behind the counter. Nothing seemed disturbed, but there were faint traces of graffiti from the day before. *Go home, horse fu*— . . .

The streetlights gave off a faint hum.

As I trudged up the concrete walkway to the arena, the sky lightened and the campground came to life. I heard a dog bark in the distance, and the cry of a baby, and then, as I pushed open the arena doors, a tinny recording of "Amazing Grace."

I slipped into a seat beside Sue Blankenship, who clutched a frayed tissue in one fist. Scattered around the bleachers were thirty or so faces I didn't recognize and almost a dozen I did.

Carlin and Zane sat near the front, Gerardo shifting uncomfortably in the row behind them. On the opposite side of the arena, a few rows behind the Trehornes, Mace and Trudy murmured to each other, hands clasped and heads close together. Mace looked bleary-eyed, and I wondered if he'd gone through another bottle of Jack the night before.

From the center of the arena, in the judges' pavilion, a microphone squealed. A man in a black suit rose from a folding chair, one finger marking his place in the Bible he held in one hand. Hap stood off to one side, looking tired and rumpled in his tan sheriff's uniform.

The man in the suit positioned himself in front of the mic and said, "Please stand and join me for a moment of silence for our sister, Maggie James, whose life was so cruelly cut short."

A tear rolled from the corner of Sue's eye and came to rest, quivering, at the tip of her nose. I watched it through the moment of silence, most of a lengthy prayer, and a speech by Hap about Maggie's role in the community. Then Sue dabbed at it with her tissue and walked down to the mic.

Hap sank into a folding chair and crossed his arms over his chest.

Sue said, "If Maggie were here, she'd have brought a big platter of fried chicken and a couple of buttermilk pies." Her voice, wavering at first, steadied as she spoke. "I asked her a million times for those recipes, and she'd always say, *Now Sue, if I told you that, I'd have to kill you. I'll leave them to you in my will.* I figured, being ten years older, I'd never see those recipes. I'd give anything to have been right."

A stream of Maggie's friends shared memories, and by the time they'd finished and the preacher gave the benediction, I felt like I'd known her myself—the pint-sized chatterbox who'd crocheted afghans for our boys in the service, covered one living room wall with a mosaic of colored glass, and raised a litter of orphaned 'possums.

As the small audience filed out, Hap came over and handed me a manila envelope.

"What's this?" I asked, sliding the flap open with my thumb. When I tipped the envelope, a sheaf of photos slid into my hand.

"Sylvia Whitehead," he said. "Just putting your mind at ease."

The woman who had drowned in her bathtub was stocky and plain. She lay on her back in the tub, her head and shoulders out of the water. Flipping through the stack of photos, I saw that Hap was right. There were no bruises on her shoulders.

I said, "Why are you showing me these?"

"Just poking a hole in Eli Barringer's crazy conspiracy theory," he said. "There's no smoking gun here, just an angry woman who drank too much and slipped under the water."

I slid the photos back into the envelope and said, "His theory doesn't sound that crazy to me."

"Then maybe the two of you can share a padded cell." He held up his hands and heaved an exasperated sigh. "This fairy tale of his is just plain wishful thinking."

"Maybe so," I said. "But that doesn't matter anymore. Maggie's death and the attack on Zane say something's going on, and the timing says it's tied to Tom Cole's murder."

His eyes flashed with sudden anger.

I pressed on. "Add Junior's history of starting fires, and you start to get a pretty ugly pattern."

"Go on," he said, too quietly.

A new scenario unfolded in my mind. What if I'd gotten it backward? Hap's role was to protect his family using—and sometimes misusing—the tools of the law. But what if it was

Hap who'd killed Owen Bodeen? What if the thing that was eating him alive was not guilt at looking the other way, but the weight of a man's murder?

I pressed on. "You've misdirected this investigation from the start, when your people 'missed' the fact that there were human bones in that barn in the first place. They missed Owen's belt buckle and failed to investigate a half a dozen barn fires in the past year alone. You have to really work at it to be this incompetent. And since I don't think you're incompetent, that means you're fucking up on purpose."

He reared back as if he'd been hit, then spun away, digging his nails into his palms.

"Tell me I'm wrong," I said.

He squeezed his eyes shut and rubbed his balding pate with his hands. "I wish I could," he said finally. "But I can't. I don't know what to do. It's all falling apart."

"Confession is good for the soul," I said.

It must have been pressing on him ever since he'd seen the bones in the ashes of the Underwoods' barn, because after a moment, he drew in a hitching breath and said, "Follow me."

We pushed out the arena doors, where the vendors were beginning to pack their wares. A glance toward the campground showed that more than half the competitors had gone. With only a few classes left, none of them Big Lick, there was little incentive for most of them to stay.

"This way," Hap said, and I followed him into the barn area, past Mace Ewing's stable and to Samuel Trehorne's. He stopped in front of Rogue's stall and stepped aside with a sweeping gesture.

I unlatched the stall gate and pushed it open. Rogue swung his head toward me and stamped a foot, worry lines above his eyes. "Easy, boy."

The stallion nickered, stretched his neck, and nudged me gently with his nose.

"It's okay, fella." I stood up and went to him, caught a faint whiff of kerosene. I rubbed the three sworls on his forehead. A complicated personality, if the old-timers were to be believed. A horse that would guard his heart until you proved yourself worthy.

I slid my hand down his neck and scratched his withers, feeling sick and drained. I knew now how he could have been scarred one day and not the next. The horse I'd seen at Trehorne's, the one with one forehead sworl, the one Junior had called a clown, was an ambassador, the animal potential clients saw when they stopped by the barn, beguiled by the sign that welcomed visitors 24/7. Meanwhile the real Rogue's legs were soaked with turpentine and mustard oil, the soles of his feet bruised or scraped raw.

Chest burning with a sudden rage, I glanced back at Hap and said, "Why are you showing me this?"

"Why do you think?"

"You want me to stop them."

"I don't know what I want," he said. "I just know this can't go on."

"Did Junior start that fire at the Underwoods'?"

He rubbed his face with his hands, a washing motion. "I don't know. I really don't."

The rumble of a truck engine and the crunch of tires on gravel turned his attention. The Trehornes' rig pulled up beside the stall, and Sam and Junior Trehorne climbed out.

Junior crossed his arms and watched me with suspicious eyes as Trehorne looked from Hap to me and growled, "What are you doing here?"

Hap held his brother's gaze. "Just talking about Zane's accident. How it might have happened."

Trehorne tossed Junior a halter and lead rope, and the younger man pushed past me and slipped the halter over Rogue's ears. Rogue tensed, deepening the worry lines around his eyes.

"You're not showing today?" I said.

Sam Trehorne said, "The important part is over. And there's a lot to do to get ready for Shelbyville." He opened the back gate of the trailer.

I must have moved to stop them, because Hap's hand closed on my shoulder, holding me back while we watched them load Rogue into the trailer.

42.

Khanh was sitting on the front steps of the trailer when I got back, chopsticks in her hand, a bowl of sticky rice with peanuts on her lap. A steaming cup of coffee sat in the grass beside her feet.

I passed her by and went to the corral, laid one hand on Tex's withers and another on Crockett's, breathed in the clean, sweet scent of them, and tried to purge the smell of kerosene.

"Something happen," Khanh said. It wasn't a question.

I told her what I'd learned about Rogue, glossing over Rhonda's late-night visit. When I finished, she gave me a knowing look. "You play with fire," she said. "Be careful, not get burn."

Before I could answer, Eli's Dodge pulled into the camp and puttered to a stop beside his camper. He stepped out carrying a McDonald's bag and a matching cup, raised the cup in greeting, and headed over when he saw us. He was wearing his contacts again, his eyelids red and weeping.

"God." He rubbed them with a thumb and forefinger. "I don't know how people get used to these things. Gran always said they were just vanity, and now I get why." He held up the bag and said, "McMuffins. I brought extra, if you want one."

Khanh shook her head, held up her bowl.

"Not hungry," I said.

"You look upset," he said. "See that? Those are my jour-nalistic powers of observation."

"I just got back from Maggie's service."

He shook his head and took a sip from his cup. "Terrible waste. I probably should have gone. I thought about it, but then I thought it would be too sad. Just thinking about it reminded me of Gran's funeral."

"Recent?"

"Couple of weeks. You know . . ." He rubbed absently at the stubble on his chin. "Maybe Maggie's killer was there. Don't they say a lot of killers go to their victims' funerals?"

"Sometimes the funeral, sometimes the cemetery, some-times both. One guy we busted visited his victim's grave every year on the anniversary of her murder."

"Romantic," he said dryly.

I gave him a quick recap of Maggie's memorial service, leaving out the part about Rogue.

I also didn't tell him what I'd learned from the woman at the *Sextant*. It would only have humiliated him. He had the right to try and earn his place there, and if he could do that and still vindicate his grandfather, more power to him.

He jotted down some notes and went back to his trailer to eat his McMuffins. I watched him go, then turned to Khanh. "I'm giving Billy forty bucks to take you out to lunch after you finish at Lori Mae's. By the time you're done, the show here will be over and you can come and pick me up."

She gave me a shrewd look. "You always try get rid of me, boss man."

"Just a precaution," I said. "It would be a shame to lose you just when I'm getting so fond of your coffee."

43.

I breathed a sigh of relief when Billy's Vincent van Gogh van pulled out of the campground, the top of my sister's dark head just visible over the back of the passenger seat. With Khanh safely away, I fed and watered the horses, then took two Tylenols and went inside to shower. My side was bruised from armpit to hip, a mottled mass of purple. I turned the water on as hot as I could stand and let it beat the knots out of my muscles, then dried myself and dressed in clean jeans and a sea-blue shirt my ex-wife had given me. She'd said the shirt complemented my eyes.

I tucked the Glock into its waistband holster and the Tomcat at my ankle and told myself I hadn't chosen the shirt with Rhonda in mind.

I stopped by the Underwoods' trailer and, when no one answered my knock, wound my way back to the arena. I passed Gerardo longeing Tesora in the warmup ring, saw Trudy waiting in the inspection line, then pushed inside where the morning classes were just beginning. The crowd was thin and seemed subdued, perhaps due to the early hour, perhaps out of respect for the dead.

I scanned the bleachers for Rhonda without success, then told myself the pang I felt wasn't disappointment.

Down near the ring, Zane sat in his accustomed place, head bowed, picking at the buttons of his shirt. Carlin sat beside him in a rhinestoned blouse, her show chaps turned up so they didn't drag the ground. She searched the crowd, brow furrowed, then waved when she saw me and headed over.

"It was a good service," she said. "I'm glad you came."

We'd come a long way since the day I'd picked my way through the ruins of their barn. But then, a lot had happened since then.

"I'm glad too," I said.

I must have looked distracted, because she said, "Did something happen?"

"Hap took me to see Rogue this morning. I hadn't really had a chance to see him since we've been here. I smelled kerosene."

A quick, sharp sorrow flashed across her face. Then her eyes hardened. "He's not my concern."

"I've been thinking about that," I said. "About what happened to Zane. I've been making it too complicated."

"What do you mean?"

"Think about it. We know Owen was killed, probably that night. What are the odds Rogue would go bat-shit crazy that same night?"

"It doesn't matter what the odds are. It happened."

"Unless it didn't."

I glanced out over the arena, where a group of teenage girls rode in a novice youth class. She followed my gaze, calm on the surface, her small fists clenched at her sides.

I said, "Rogue's not a vicious horse. I wondered from the first if someone might have used a drug or buzzer to make him attack, but Doc said it would be almost impossible. Too many variables, he said. So I let it go. But I wasn't asking the right question."

"Okay, I'll bite. What was the right question?"

"What's the easiest way to make it *look* like a horse has attacked someone?" I didn't wait for her to answer. "You hit them over the head with a bat or a shovel and beat them half to hell. Then you drag them into the horse's stall, splash some blood around. Maybe you even spook the horse then, get some actual hoof prints."

"Break his spine," she said softly. "Oh, God. My poor sweet boy." A dawning horror crept across her face. Maybe she was thinking about soring and the stories Zane had told her of the Trehornes, or maybe she was thinking of the research she'd done for the TASA booth. "I have to get him back."

She knew, she had to know, that Trehorne wouldn't give Rogue up without a fight. That if he considered an offer at all, it would be many times what Trehorne had given for him. Even with the insurance settlement, the Underwoods didn't have that kind of money. Zane's accident had cleaned them out.

But those were practical matters, and Rogue's fate was a matter of the heart.

Carlin looked at her watch. "My phone's on the charger, but I have fifteen minutes before I show. I'll make it a quick call."

"You're about to go on. It can wait until after your classes."

"It's been a year," she said. "I have to get him out of there."

"It's been a year. A few more hours aren't going to make a difference."

"I know, I know. I'm being silly, but they make a difference to me."

"The show's over. They won't do anything to him today." The defiant chin and the steel in her eyes said this was not negotiable. I held out my hand. "Give me your keys. I'll go get your phone for you."

"I'll go," she said. "You're still moving pretty slow."

"I could run," I said. "Running doesn't hurt as much as some other things."

That brought a laugh. "I don't want to know what other things, do I? No, you stay here with Zane. I'll be back in two shakes of a lamb's tail."

She hurried toward the exit, and as she pushed through the double doors, I saw her break into a trot. Zane, watching from the railing, raised his eyebrows, and I went down to explain the latest turn of events.

"ROGUE DIDN'T DO THIS TO ME?" he typed. "WHY CAN'T I REMEMBER?"

"Do you remember being trampled?"

"NO."

"Then why would you remember not being trampled any better?"

I watched his face as he reframed his understanding of his accident. Tears welled, ran down his face. The mechanical voice said, "ALL THIS TIME I'VE BEEN THINKING, WHAT KIND OF HORSEMAN GETS TRAMPLED BY HIS OWN HORSE? I THOUGHT I DID SOMETHING STUPID."

"Maybe you did," I said. "But if you did, it wasn't trusting Rogue."

He lifted his hand to type a response. Then the boom of a shotgun echoed from the campground.

❧

There was no mistaking the sound of the shotgun blast for anything else. I spun and ran for the Underwoods' trailer. My ribs complained as I raced up the bleachers, but the blast of the gun had sent a pulse of adrenaline through me, and I was only distantly aware of the pain. Zane's wheelchair hummed to life, but I didn't wait for him to catch up.

I don't know how long it took me to reach her. A crowd was forming, but I pushed my way through.

The door to the trailer hung open. In front of it, Carlin lay crumpled on the ground, her blouse drenched in blood, the grass beneath her glistening red. Her shirt was torn at the shoulder, and beneath it, red meat, white bone. I glanced inside the trailer and saw the shotgun mounted on the far wall, a heavy string wound from the trigger to the handle of the door.

I tore off my shirt and folded it. As I pressed it against the wound, someone shouted orders: *somebody get Doc, somebody call an ambulance.* I glimpsed Gerardo, pale beneath his dusky skin and in his eyes a terrible rage. Beside him, Eli touched his arm and whispered something to him.

Then Doc was there, kneeling beside me. He pressed two fingers to her throat and said, "She's alive. I don't know how or for how long, but she's alive."

The world compressed to nothing but the sound of Doc's voice and the warmth of Carlin's blood on my hands. My shirt was sodden with it, and still I pressed against the wound as if to somehow hold the life inside her. A siren wailed, first distant and then closer. Someone jostled me, and strong hands pulled me from her. *It's okay, we've got her now.* When I looked up again, Gerardo and Eli were gone.

44.

This last violence was one too many for the spectators and the show crowd alike. Doc and I knelt in the grass, blood on our hands and the sun on our shoulders, as engines roared to life and competitors led their horses to their trailers. Zane sat nearby, sobbing silently, while Trudy knelt beside his chair and held his hand. Behind him, Eleanor stroked his hair, something that might have been triumph in her eyes. The interloper fallen, Eleanor had swooped in to reclaim her son.

Could she have engineered the shotgun blast? I thought it through and dismissed the idea. Maggie's death and Owen's took this way beyond a mother's desire to eliminate a hated daughter-in-law.

No, this was something more.

I looked at Doc and said, "When is it going to be enough?"

He wiped sweat from his forehead, and his hand left a streak of blood like war paint. "You think I did this? I helped save her life, for God's sake."

"It's tied to you. To whatever you and your friends did to Tom Cole and to whatever scheme you're into with Sam Trehorne."

He leaned back on his heels and closed his eyes. "Tom Cole," he said softly. "What happened to Tom Cole, that was an accident. We were kids, just out of high school. We only meant to scare him."

"What went wrong?"

He shook his head, and as he spoke, I saw it with him, smelled creek water and whiskey as they tipped the bottle to Cole's lips, then pushed him under water. I heard Jim Lister's voice, soft and cunning, smooth as the voice of reason: *Dunk him again, boys, he hasn't learned his lesson yet.*

"Jim wasn't a kid," I said. "He knew what you were doing."

"I don't know what happened," Doc said, as if he hadn't heard. "I don't know if he had a heart attack or if we just held him under too long or one too many times. Only the last time we pulled him up, he was limp as a dishrag. He wasn't breathing. I tried CPR, but nothing worked. I didn't really know what I was doing, just what I remembered from one class we had in high school. We panicked."

"Then Jim told you what to do."

"He said if we just held fast, nobody could prove we'd been there. And he was right. We staged the scene, covered our tracks. Jim hired a woman to say Tommy had been with her, drinking. And we did what he said. We held fast."

"Until Owen."

He lowered his head. "Until Owen. But I swear to God I didn't know they'd . . . that he'd been killed. Not until you told me."

"Let's get back to Tommy. You and Sam were the ones who held him under?"

"Me and Sam. But mostly me. I don't know what got into me." His voice was full of wonder, and he looked down at his hands as if they belonged to a stranger. "I was scared to death, and I guess it just swept me away."

"You had to know you couldn't let him live, not after you'd half drowned him."

"It wasn't like that."

"No?"

"No. I never thought that. Never once." He opened his eyes. They were wet, but his voice was steady. "I went to school, became an EMT, served in the war. I saved lives, trying to make up for it."

"But you can't make up for a thing like that. So you came home."

"I came home." He blew out a long breath and blinked hard. "I started my vet practice. Then one day Sam came to me and said I had to help him save his farm, or he and the others would say I wasn't with them that night after all. That they'd lied to protect me."

"He blackmailed you."

"If you want to call it that. I could have said no, taken whatever came." He tipped his head back, and the tears trickled down his temples and into his ears. "You try to balance it out, to do more good than bad. I helped make the industry better. Cited a lot of trainers, stopped a lot of folks from soring."

"But not Sam Trehorne. Not Jim Lister or Dalt Underwood or Eleanor."

"No." His voice was soft. "Not them."

"Doc," I said. "You say Tom Cole's death was an accident, and I believe you. You say you want to do good, and I believe that too. But these killings now, they aren't accidents."

"No. No, they're not."

"Then the question is, what are you going to do about them?"

He pushed to his feet, grass and dirt clinging to the blood on his palms. He looked resigned but also lighter, as if his confession had freed him from some heavy weight. "I'm going to clean up and go check on Carlin. Then I'm going to go home and hug my family. And after that . . . well, I guess we'll see."

I heard something in his voice that made me pause. "This is your chance to be a stand-up guy," I said. "I'm going to be awfully disappointed if you go home and eat a bullet instead."

He looked back over his shoulder and shot me a small, sad smile. "Life is full of disappointments. But shouldn't you ask yourself the same question? What are you going to do about it?"

"I'm going to wash my hands," I said. "And then I'm going to talk to Junior."

He nodded, and I could tell he saw it too. Junior was a fire setter. It was Junior who'd threatened Carlin, Junior who'd heard Owen's claim of seeing Tom Cole's murder. Sam Trehorne might have pointed the weapon, but if that were so, all indications were that Junior was the weapon he'd pointed.

The drone of Zane's wheelchair made me look up. Trudy stood behind him, a hand on the back of his chair. I said to her, "You'll take him to the medical center?"

She nodded. "Mace can drive the van, and I'll follow in the car." I opened my mouth to protest, but she held up a hand. "Whatever bad blood's between the two of you, he isn't the bad guy here. He couldn't have rigged that shotgun; he was at the stables."

"STOP," Zane typed. "LISTEN TO ME. I REMEMBERED."

"Remembered . . ."

"WHO WAS SITTING NEXT TO JUNIOR THAT NIGHT AT THE BAR."

"Go on."

It seemed to take him a long time to type the rest of it. "IT WAS THAT REPORTER. IT WAS ELI BARRINGER."

45.

It made sense then, why seeing Eli with Junior that first day had jogged his memory. He hadn't mistaken Eli for Owen. He was recognizing something he'd seen.

It might change nothing. Eli might not have heard Owen's confession, or not acted on it if he had. On the other hand, it might change everything.

I stopped at my trailer to wash the blood from my hands and grab a clean shirt, then walked over to Eli's camper. His Dodge was gone. I felt a pang of regret as I popped the camper door with my pocketknife and stepped inside. Despite his quirks, I liked Eli, liked his passion and his sincerity, and I hoped I would owe him an apology when all of this was over.

The quarters were cramped, a half bath and a single room with a cot, a counter with a microwave, and a table with an open laptop on it and an ergonomic chair pushed underneath. On the floor beside the bed was a pile of crumpled clothes. Black shirt, black jeans, black mask. Like the mask Zane's hands had scrabbled at the night of the attack.

Spread across the table were old newspaper clippings—Tom Cole's columns and the articles about his death, obituaries for Eli's mother, who'd died of a drug overdose when Eli was a toddler, and his grandmother, who'd died of a heart attack a few weeks before the Hidden Hollow horse show. On top, on a lined tablet, was a cryptic note: *M.E. at Jake's. Gerardo—cartel? Motivation?*

In a folder beside the bed were a foreclosure notice on his grandmother's house, an article praising her prize-winning roses, and a stack of Eli's own articles and musings. A quick skim showed a modicum of talent but a singular focus. Many were unpublishable rants about Tom Cole's murder and the failure of the system to bring his killers to justice. Some were snapshots of Eli's life, his shyness with girls, his grandmother's rigid rules, the hours spent helping her in her rose garden. I skimmed through his dreams, his resentments, his hopes of making her proud. And the one night—the night of Owen's death—when he'd finally earned her approval.

The stack was thick and had writings from as far back as junior high, when, in a barely legible scrawl, he'd written an essay about the grandfather who was both a martyr and a hero. The grandfather he'd been told from the time he was born he could never live up to.

Eli's grandmother had blamed all of her troubles, from her financial woes to her daughter's rebellion and eventual overdose, on her husband's murder. In the same way Sam Trehorne had molded Junior, in her bitterness she'd shaped her grandson into a weapon of retribution.

And an effective weapon he was, because, unlike Junior, he seemed so unlike one.

I turned on his computer. Eli was a writer, not a computer geek, and the user name and password came up autofilled. I clicked on his browser history. Job listings for journalists and other freelance writers, a parts store for old Dodge trucks. I scrolled down the list until I found what I was looking for.

A search for shotgun booby traps.

I ran the players through my mind. Doc and Zane were in a crowd of witnesses. Dalt Underwood was dead, along with Owen Bodeen. That left Jim Lister and the Trehornes. I dialed Sam Trehorne's number on the way out the door, got no answer, and cursed myself for not getting Rhonda's number. The Listers' trailer wasn't far, but the closer I got, the farther away it seemed.

I let out a relieved breath when I found her healthy and whole, packing their tack. She paused, hefting a saddle, and looked up with a smile that was almost shy. I forced a smile back and said, "Where's Jim?"

"Probably at the arena, glad-handing the judges. Why?"

"I need you to find him. Stay close to a crowd, don't let anybody get you alone, especially Eli."

"You're scaring me."

"I hope I'm overreacting. But humor me anyway."

She nodded. "I can do that."

"And I need to borrow your car."

She pulled out her keys. "You still have to get your things out of the trunk anyway. Can I drive you somewhere?"

"Not this time."

She handed me the keys. Touched her fingers first to her lips, then to mine. "Be careful."

"I'm always careful."

"That's why you have a black eye and a couple of cracked ribs."

"Imagine what would happen if I were reckless."

Hugging the curves in Rhonda's Porsche, I prayed I'd be in time.

It was coming on noon when I reached the Trehorne house. Two cars were in the driveway, and Junior's truck was parked in front of the barn alongside Trehorne's trailer. The front door of the house was standing open, and a slight breeze tapped the screen door open and shut, open and shut.

I drew the Glock and climbed out of the car, my stomach tightening.

A cobblestone walkway led from the circular drive to the front door. I eased up it, pistol drawn, and listened at the open door. Somewhere inside, a woman sobbed. The air smelled faintly of blood and gunpowder. I stepped into the living room, past a pair of high-priced, free-form sculptures and a mantel lined with antique knickknacks, and saw Sam Trehorne sprawled on a carpet the color of cream. The puddle of blood beneath his head was already going tacky in the heat. When I came in, he moaned and tried to push himself up, then thrashed against the plastic zip-ties on his wrists and ankles.

I bent to check the wound. It had bled a lot, as head wounds do, but it was shallow. He was groggy, but I thought he'd be all right.

Beside him, his wife slumped in a chair. Like her husband, her feet and hands were bound. When she saw me, she looked up, eyes wild. "It's Gerardo. He has Esmerelda. Please." Her voice broke. "Please don't let him hurt her."

"He isn't going to hurt her." I glanced toward the stairwell, then the doorway to the kitchen. "Where did he go?"

"Out the back." Her voice hitched. "Junior went after him. Please, cut me loose. I need to go after her."

"You're safer here," I said, moving toward the back door. I couldn't babysit her, and God knew what would happen if she tried to recover the child. "I'll be back."

"You'll bring her back?" Her chin quivered. "Please. Bring them both back."

༄

There was no cover in the no-man's-land between the house and the barn, so I went out the front and drove the Porsche, staying low behind the wheel. I parked it so it would block my approach to the barn, stopping long enough to put in a call to Sheriff Hap. "There's trouble at your brother's place," I said. "You better get out here quick."

"What's going on?" A note of panic in his voice.

"It's not as bad as it could be," I said. "But bring backup. I'm not sure what I'm getting into out here."

I hung up before he could ask for more, then climbed out of the car, Glock at the ready. I popped the trunk and took out two more 9-millimeter magazines, both loaded with hollow points.

The barn was much as it had been when I was there before. The false Rogue and, presumably, a false Galahad stood in their stalls, munching hay and soaking in cool air from their electric fans. Halfway down the aisle, I saw a trail of blood drops. The trail became a pool of blood, then drag marks leading to the end of the aisle and around the corner.

I listened at the corner, then peered around, leading with the barrel of the Glock. The blood trail ended at the far wall, where Junior sat propped against a stall door, eyes closed, hands pressed tight against his belly. Dark blood seeped through his fingers. On the ground beside him was a Colt .45.

His eyelids fluttered open as I rounded the corner. "Hurts," he said. A line of blood trickled from the corner of his mouth.

I knelt beside him. "Your uncle's on his way. Gerardo did this to you?"

He grimaced. "Tried to stop him. Too fast. Gone up to the other barn."

"What other barn?"

"Out back a ways. Where we fix the horses." He coughed. "I never hurt Maggie. I never would."

"Okay," I said.

He grabbed my shirt with a bloody hand. "Do you think we're going to hell for what we done to them horses?"

I looked him in the eye, a hardness in me that I hardly recognized. "Yes."

Fear flickered in his eyes. He took a final, bubbling breath. His hand fell away, and he was still.

The small cruelty sent a rush of satisfaction through me, followed by a wash of shame. It had diminished me, as cruelty always does. I reached up and closed his eyes, then headed for the secret barn.

46.

Behind the barn, I followed tire tracks to a thick line of brush and brambles. Behind them was a pasture gate. It swung open, and the brush swung with it, attached to the rails with slender, nearly invisible wires.

I suspected Hap already knew about the hidden gate, but I dutifully texted its location and closed it behind me. The track led through the forest. There was no wind, and the air hung damp and heavy, humming with June bugs.

I followed the edge of the woods, keeping clear of the main track, until the barn came into view. It was old and weathered, the paint faded to gray. Eli's Dodge was parked beside it, and somewhere inside, horses snorted and blew. I heard a moan, an animal sound I'd never heard from a horse before and hoped never to hear again.

I raised the Glock and moved toward the door. It creaked a little when I opened it, but the small noise was lost in the sounds of the horses. The smells of kerosene and diesel fuel were strong, and I fought to keep from coughing.

The barn windows were boarded over, and the only light came from a pair of dim incandescent bulbs hanging from the ceiling. In the shadows of their stalls, the horses shifted.

As I passed Rogue, he gave an anxious nicker and pressed his muzzle through the bars.

In the stall beside him, a copper-colored mare with a flaxen mane lay on her side, flanks heaving, her lower legs twitching and wrapped tightly in plastic. It was the same mare I'd seen being inspected while Jim Lister stood in line behind her. I remembered how still she'd stood, and my stomach rolled. She must have been stewarded—hurt and then punished until she'd learned that the only way to escape from pain was not to react to it. A rage I hadn't known I was capable of burned in my throat.

My hand was on the latch when reason reminded me that there was a man with a shotgun nearby. I stepped away from the mare's stall and gave Rogue's muzzle a gentle rub through the bars. Then with an aching heart, I left them there.

I forced my attention back to the layout of the barn. There were stalls on either side of me and an opening to my left, like the bar of an "H." Based on the size of the building, it probably led to another aisle of stalls. The doors at the opposite end of the barn were half open, and sunlight spilled through onto the concrete of the aisle.

I checked each stall as I passed to make sure Eli wasn't hiding in one. Then I moved cautiously down the connecting walkway. It was lined with stall rakes, Dura Forks, and two yellow plastic wheelbarrows propped against one wall.

The aisle to the right was empty. I eased around the corner and saw Eli backing away to the left, his eyes wide and his mouth half open in a silent protest.

"Stop right there and raise your hands," I said, Glock trained on the center of his chest.

"No, no, no, you've got this all wrong." He held his empty hands out, palms toward me.

"What have I got wrong?"

"What happened down at the house, I didn't do that. They were already dead when I got here."

I raised an eyebrow. "Best laid plans," I said. "The Trehornes aren't dead."

"Aren't—" He frowned. "Of course they are. They have to be."

"Why? Because you planned it that way? Wound up your weapon and pointed him at the Trehornes? I saw the search history on your computer."

"How did you—? You broke into my camper, didn't you? Yeah, I did a search. *After* what happened to Carlin. I wanted to see how somebody could have rigged a thing like that."

"I wondered why I kept seeing you with Gerardo. You've been grooming him all weekend, laying the groundwork so when you set the trap for Carlin, he'd think the Trehornes were behind it. You thought he'd do your dirty work. But he's not as cold-blooded as you thought he was."

"You're jumping to all the wrong conclusions."

"What are you doing here then?"

"I figured this was where Gerardo would come. You don't have to be a rocket scientist to figure out the Trehornes were behind that shotgun blast."

I laughed. "You followed a killing machine to his target's house? Why not call the sheriff instead?"

He snorted. "Call a dirty cop who's going to whitewash what his family did and try to pin all this on me? I don't think so. Look, I swear to God, I'm just here to get a story."

A flicker of his eyes warned me. Too late, I heard the scuff of a footstep behind me, and something cold and hard touched the hollow at the base of my skull. A familiar voice said, "Give my friend the gun, Señor. Two fingers, *por favor*. No funny business."

"He's not your friend," I said.

"Neither are you."

I flipped the pistol and held it up by two fingers. Eli stepped forward and plucked it from my hand. He turned it over carefully and pointed it at my head, holding it sideways like a TV gangbanger.

I forced myself to ignore him and said over my shoulder to Gerardo, "You're good. Very stealthy. Must've been all that time you spent sneaking around in the jungle."

"Probably. I'm going to take a step back now, Señor. You turn around slowly with your hands up."

I did.

He held the shotgun in one hand, relaxed but pointing at my chest. In the other arm, he was carrying Esmerelda. Her arms were clasped around his neck, but her cheeks were wet, and her eyes were huge with fear. Her utter silence was more troubling than her tantrum at the showground.

Keeping the shotgun level with my chest, Gerardo slid her to the floor. "Run into the stall, *Chiquita*. Close your eyes and cover your ears until I come for you. Some things are not meant for little ones."

She clapped her hands to her ears and scampered into the nearest stall. I heard her whimper and the sawdust shift beneath her feet and her back thump against the wall. I looked at Gerardo and said, "You're just taking her from her parents?"

His lips thinned. "They're not her parents."

"They're the only ones she knows. Maybe you could ease her into it?"

"She will forget them in time."

"I don't think so. And she won't forget Junior. He was trying to protect her."

"He left me no choice." He shifted his grip so that he held the shotgun in two hands. "She will come to understand that sometimes difficult things must be done."

"Difficult things like killing Maggie James?"

Before I registered the anger in his eyes, he had flipped the shotgun around and rammed the stock into my ribs.

I heard a crack, and pain shot through my chest and dropped me to my hands and knees. I couldn't move. I couldn't think. I couldn't breathe. A thought crept in around the edges of the pain. This man was the kind of quick you had to be to take on a cartel and survive.

Baiting him might not have been the smartest thing I'd ever done.

"Junior killed Maggie," he said.

"No." My voice sounded thin, and I drew in a shallow breath. It felt like being filleted. "He knew he was dying. No reason to lie. And that was the one thing he . . ." I took another breath. It was like sucking water through a straw with a hole in it. "That was the one thing he wanted me to be sure of."

His gaze shifted to Eli and then back to me, a flicker of doubt in his eyes. "Junior killed Maggie, and then he killed Carlin."

I shook my head. "Carlin's alive . . . She was still . . . breathing when the . . . paramedics came."

A flicker of hope flashed in his eyes.

This time I got out a whole sentence before I ran out of air. "She's hurt bad, but it wasn't Junior who did it. He was . . . afraid he'd go to hell for soring horses . . . If he'd murdered Maggie and . . . booby-trapped Carlin, I'm pretty sure . . . they'd have been on his mind."

Eli jabbed the gun in my direction. "Shut up. You're just trying to confuse him."

I looked at Gerardo. "Zane remembered who he saw with Junior . . . the night of his accident . . . It was Eli."

Eli said, "I talked to Junior, sure. I'm a reporter, hell, I talk to a lot of people. I went to the men's room to take a piss and when I came back, he was pretty upset about something. I didn't know then, but now I guess he must have heard what Owen said about Doc and old man Trehorne."

"That's the second time you've . . . mentioned that," I said. I was getting the hang of this talking thing. Incomprehensibly, it was easier than breathing. "But I never told you about it."

"Sure you did."

"No, I . . . really didn't."

"Then I heard it from somewhere else. What difference does it make where I heard it?"

"You heard it from Owen. And you killed him for it, for his part in it. And then you hurt Zane and . . . made it look like Rogue had done it."

"Why? Why would I do that?"

"Sins of the fathers, you said. Or maybe . . . he saw something. Saw you kill Owen. Your gran was . . . proud of that, wasn't she?"

His fists clenched. "You . . . you shut up about my grandmother."

"You buried Owen in the . . . rose garden. But then your gran died and the house was . . . in foreclosure. You had to move . . . Owen's remains. So you set the fire, made it look like a soring barn. Put the bones there. You got the idea because Trehornes . . . set fires. You ruin Dalt's son, or you . . . frame the Trehornes. Either way, a win."

He shoved the Glock against my temple, his hands shaking so badly I was afraid he might fire the gun by accident. I closed my eyes, my heart machine-gunning in my chest.

Gerardo swung the shotgun toward Eli. "Put it down," he said.

Eli blinked, slowly drawing the gun away. "Hey. Hey, you don't believe this guy?"

I pushed myself into a sitting position, ground my teeth against a wave of pain, and propped my back against a stall. Gerardo watched from the corner of his eye. I said to him, "He's right when he says he . . . talked to everybody. He talked to . . . Mace, and Mace knew Junior . . . all his life. Bet he knew about your . . . history."

"No, no." Eli licked his lips, looking around as if for some escape. "I swear to God he's crazy."

"Mace told you about . . . Gerardo," I said to Eli. "And that gave . . . you an idea. You planted that bandana to make it look . . . like Junior sent Mace after Zane."

"He did. It was Junior. He—"

"You wanted it to look like Junior. So Gerardo would go after him and his father. Once you learned about . . . Gerardo's past, he was your . . . secret weapon. You knew he'd do anything to . . . protect Zane and Carlin. Just wind him up and—"

"No, no, no."

"You vandalized the booth . . . wanted it to seem like Junior's work. Only Maggie saw you. You couldn't explain it away. So you killed her." Slowly I pulled my knees up, and another burst of pain pulsed through my side. I moved my right hand closer to my boot.

Eli gave Gerardo a pleading look. "Maggie was a sweet lady. I wouldn't do a thing like that."

Gerardo growled, low in his throat. "The shotgun?"

Eli moaned, the truth in his eyes. "It was Junior! It was all Junior!"

Softly and without emotion, Gerardo said, "I do not believe you."

"He's wrong!" Eli screamed. Sweat beaded his hairline. "He's got everything wrong!"

He jerked the gun up, but a moment's hesitation, as it wavered between Gerardo and me, gave me time to tug up the leg of my jeans and slide the Tomcat out.

"I'm not wrong," I said, and shot him.

Gerardo's shotgun boomed. My ears rang, and a thought ran through my head—that I was dead and that the blast was the last sound I would ever hear.

Then Eli crumpled, and I saw the red bloom spreading on his chest and the smaller blossom that my Tomcat had made. Gerardo lowered the gun and turned away.

I leaned back and closed my eyes, and the Tomcat fell from my hand. Somewhere in the distance, I heard a siren. Then my mind swam into darkness.

47.

On a golden day in November, I drove out to the Underwoods' farm. Carlin came out of the house and gave me a one-armed hug. She nodded toward the pasture, where Rogue was grazing. The silver stallion, Galahad, was nowhere to be seen. Inside the barn, I assumed, or in another pasture.

She nodded toward Rogue. "He looks beautiful, doesn't he?"

"He does. And so do you. How's the shoulder?"

"Not bad." She rolled it gingerly. "Still going to physical therapy, but it's coming back, a little at a time. How about you?"

"Better than I deserve." My ribs and the lung punctured when the blow from Gerardo's shotgun had snapped the bone were mostly healed, and I had been pronounced "almost as good as new."

"Thank you for the check," she said. I'd given them Sam Trehorne's check, which had rested so uncomfortably in my wallet. They had better uses for it than I did. "And for your report to the insurance company."

"Just doing my job."

"A little more than that, I think. Come in. Zane wants to see you. And we have beer."

"Well, if there's beer . . ."

Inside, Zane's new attendant, a muscular young man in scrubs, brought us three beers in sweating bottles, then retired to his room.

Zane typed, "HOW IS DOC?"

I'd been out a few times to see Doc at the men's prison. He looked good for a man pushing sixty in a prison jumpsuit, but then he was a survivor. He'd pled guilty and gotten five years for obstruction of justice and manslaughter, but he'd be out in three. Nobody does the full ride.

I passed on Doc's regards, and Zane said, "I KNOW WHAT HE DID WAS WRONG, BUT HE SAVED CAR-LIN'S LIFE. HE WAS MY FRIEND."

A good man living in the shadow of one evil act. I knew he'd carry that weight forever.

We talked about the TBI's investigation into corruption in Braydon County, the subsequent purge of Trehornes from government offices, and the pending trials—Jim Lister's and Samuel Trehorne's among them. Hap had been spared prosecution. Stress and grief had stopped his heart not long after the investigations began.

"I don't know how to feel about that," Carlin said. "He was no friend to us, but he was in a hard place. I feel sorry for him."

I felt sorry for him too, caught between the Trehorne code of honor and what he knew was right. In retrospect, I even felt bad for Junior, who, from childhood, had been forged into his family's enforcer, and for Eli, who had exposed his grandfather's killers and gotten, instead of the noble death he'd imagined, fifteen minutes of infamy and a neglected grave.

"How's Eleanor?" I asked.

"Cranky," Carlin said. "Bitter and lonely and impossible."

"BUT THINGS ARE LOOKING UP."

Carlin rolled her eyes. "If you can call it that. I took her a casserole yesterday morning, and she actually thanked me for it."

"BABY STEPS," Zane said.

We chatted for a few more minutes. Then Carlin walked me to my truck. "You know who else I feel sorry for?" she asked.

"No, who?"

"Rebecca Trehorne. I mean, my God, her husband's going to end up in prison, her son is dead, and her daughter's gone. She lost everything."

"I think Gerardo will come around," I said. "Give her some kind of hope."

"He already has." She reached into her pocket and pulled out a folded envelope. The postmark was a city in Mexico. "Look at this."

Inside the envelope was a postcard. No message, no signature, just two wild dolphins arcing out of a blue-green sea. And a picture of two horses, one black, one white, drawn in a child's hand and labeled: TO MOMMY I LOVE YOU.

She took them back and put them into the envelope. "Clearly I'm supposed to deliver the picture. But the card is just for me." She slid the envelope into her pocket and said, "I know he did some bad things, but I miss him."

"How does Zane feel about it?"

Her smile was sad. "Let's just say his feelings are more complicated."

⁓

That afternoon, I met Rhonda Lister at a Hillsboro-West End park affectionately dubbed Dragon Park by locals.

She pulled up in the Porsche and got out wearing tight black jeans and a pale blue cashmere sweater with pearls. Her hair, pulled back on the sides with a pair of enameled combs, shone in the sunlight.

The sapphire ring flashed in the light. She saw me looking and held up her hand. "For better or worse," she said. "Jim's aged a hundred years since the investigations started, and I'd be a fool to leave him now that he's likely to die in prison."

"Which part is that?" I said. "The better or the worse?"

She flashed me a mischievous smile. "You figure it out."

We shared an awkward hug and a peck on the lips. Then I held her out at arm's length and said, "You look gorgeous."

"So do you." She reached into the passenger seat of her car and retrieved two cups of coffee from a Starbuck's carrier. "I brought you the magical elixir."

"Bless you, my child."

We scuffed our feet through crisp, curled leaves, then settled side by side onto the mosaic dragon that gave the park its nickname.

"Cheers," she said, raising her coffee cup. "To sticking it out."

I lifted mine. "To making it work."

"I was surprised to hear from you," she said.

"I'm sorry it took so long."

She smiled again. It was a good smile. "Well, there was that little matter of a punctured lung. How are your boys? Tex and Crockett, I mean."

"Fat and feisty." I reached inside my jacket for a manila folder and handed it to her.

"What's this?"

"Something I checked on when I got out of the hospital. I don't know if you want it. Maybe you'd prefer to let things lie. But I really think you should look."

She opened it warily, crossed her legs, and balanced the folder on her lap. "My father's autopsy report. How did you get this?"

"It's what I do. I find things."

She snapped it shut. "I don't know if I can look. Are there photos?"

"I left the photos in the car. These are just words."

"Maybe you could just tell me what it says."

I didn't need to look at the file. I'd studied it enough to know what it said. "His injuries were extensive. The sudden deceleration of the car caused severe fractures to his spine and to the base of his skull. Either one would have killed him instantly."

"Instantly." She ran her palm over the outside of the folder. "But . . . I saw . . ."

"Rhonda, you couldn't have seen what you thought you saw. It's not possible."

She shook her head, trying to imagine it, then opened the folder and started to read. I waited quietly, watching the dry leaves do a slow dance across the grass.

After a long time, she closed the folder and hugged it to her chest. "I don't understand. I just imagined what I saw?"

I put an arm around her, and she laid her head on my shoulder. "You planted a false memory. Maybe you wanted so badly to see him get out that you saw what you wanted to see; you saw him moving, which gave you hope that he was alive and would climb out at any minute. Maybe the smoke and the flames just played tricks on your eyes. Maybe your brain saw a shape it thought it recognized and filled in the blanks. Our brains fill in the gaps all the time. It's one reason eyewitness testimony is so unreliable."

"What I did to myself all these years." She shook her head. "I don't even know how to process this."

We finished our coffee in silence, and I walked her back to her car. She held out the folder, and I pushed it back at her. "You keep it. You might need to read it again sometime."

She took it with a rueful smile. "My therapist will have a field day."

I opened the car door for her, and as she got into the Porsche, she turned back to me and kissed me gently on the mouth. "Thank you."

I watched her drive away, then walked back to the park, where three Asian women, one young and beautiful, one old and frail, one scarred and missing most of an arm, took turns pushing a blond boy with Down syndrome on the merry-go-round. They looked up and smiled as I came nearer. My son patted the empty space beside him, and I hopped onboard. I lay beside him, head to head, and together we watched the sky spin.

Acknowledgments

I'd like to thank Mike Hicks for his unfailing support, my mother, Ruthanne Terrell, and my brother, David Terrell, as well as the best in-laws a person could hope for: Thelma Hicks, Nikki-Nelson Hicks, Brian Hicks, Mike and Rene Osborne, and nieces and nephews Todd, Michelle, Brenna, and Daniel.

Thanks to super-agent Jill Marr for her hard work and loyalty on my behalf, to Lon Kirschner for a stunning cover, to Marty and Judy Shepard for their extraordinary faith and patience, to Chris Knopf for his gentle guidance, and to Barbara Anderson for her keen eye.

Thanks to Clay and Jacqueline Stafford for their friendship and support, and to the rest of the Killer Nashville family.

Thanks to my friends and instructors at World Champion Productions, the Hiking Buds, all my friends from Mystery Writers of America and Sisters in Crime, my fellow Permanent Press writers, my friends from Measurement Incorporated, and the Quill & Dagger Writers' Group: Chester Campbell, Kay Elam, Richard Emerson, Nina Fortmeyer, Nikki Nelson-Hicks, and Nancy Sartor. I love you all and will always be grateful for your support and for all I've learned from you.

Thanks to Dan Royse for brainstorming some sticky plot points; Timothy Hallinan for his syntactic expertise; Keith Dane for his insights into the Walking Horse industry; David Carpenter for answering my questions about insurance companies; Tim Farrell for his insights into hunting and hunting safety; Lisa Wysocky, Dana Chapman, and the owners and boarders at Butterbean Hill Stables for their expert advice on horses and showing; and to Kay Tyler, Lonnie Graves, Phyllis Gobbell, and Michelle Almandinger for being terrific "first readers."

Their counsel was sound, and any mistakes are mine alone.